Could she put her life in his hands?

"Sam, I know it was you who gave Jacquie her high school ring."

Sam looked up and met her gaze. "Listen, Ali, I told you before—that has nothing to do with this case."

"Are you sure, Sam?" Ali challenged, her own doubts sending a rush of adrenaline racing through her. "There's more to this case than you've told me. You're involved, aren't you, Sam? I know you are. Somehow. I'm just not sure *how*. But there's more than professional interest in your investigation of Jacquie's murder."

His eyes shot up to meet hers. Anger, mixed with something Ali could only hope was confusion, flashed in them. "What are you suggesting, Ali?"

She didn't answer.

"If there's something you know that you're not telling me—"

"I think there's something you're not telling *me*, Sam."

ABOUT THE AUTHOR

"Even as a kid, I was fascinated with the idea of psychic phenomena," writes author Morgan Hayes. "I read everything I could get my hands on. I guess it was only natural that when I turned my hand to writing, I'd give one of my characters psychic abilities."

Morgan loves to receive comments from her readers. Send correspondence to:

Morgan Hayes
c/o Harlequin Superromance
Harlequin Enterprises
225 Duncan Mill Road
Don Mills, Ont. M3B 3K9

Morgan Hayes

Premonitions

Harlequin Books

TORONTO • NEW YORK • LONDON
AMSTERDAM • PARIS • SYDNEY • HAMBURG
STOCKHOLM • ATHENS • TOKYO • MILAN
MADRID • WARSAW • BUDAPEST • AUCKLAND

To David, for absolutely everything

And to my editor, Brenda Chin,
for her steadfast support from the word "go"

ISBN 0-373-70632-4

PREMONITIONS

Copyright © 1995 by Illona Haus.

Premonitions

PROLOGUE

SHE HAD TO REACH Duncan—before it was too late.

She had to clear her mind. It was the only way. She had to get beyond the panic and focus on the vision, or she would never find him.

The traffic light still glared red through the rain. She clutched the steering wheel with an intensity as fierce as the vision hurtling toward her from a black and endless tunnel. A jagged pain sliced through her head.

The street vanished. She was there with him....

A decayed apartment building, the dull glimmer of a single light bulb, the odor of cooking—grease and onions. She can see Duncan climbing the stairs. He stops on the second floor, pauses and looks at the note in his hand.

Gerard and Thirty-sixth. Number 216.

A television blares. Someone shouts and a baby wails upstairs. Duncan's found the apartment. Panic rises in her throat, tasting of bile. This isn't right. He shouldn't be here without backup.

He knocks.

No answer, and he knocks again before unclipping his holster. "Detective Carvello, NYPD. Open the door."

The fear is strong now, wrenching up from inside her like a scream. If only she could call out to him, warn him—

The connection snapped. Reality surged through her as the street shimmered into focus. The driver behind her leaned on his horn. The light was green.

Gerard and Thirty-sixth. She knew where he was now, only minutes away. She jammed the car into gear, sped through the intersection, then barreled down one dimly lit street after another. Beyond the thrashing wipers, the street signs slid past into the darkness. Thirty-second Street. Thirty-third.

Without warning, the vision racked her again. She managed to pull over to the curb, seconds before a sharp pain cut through her head. She pressed her fingers to her forehead, struggling to see through the painful haze, desperate to hold her link with Duncan.

A flash of lightning, and she was with him again....

Duncan is in the apartment now. He's smiling, talking to another man in a suit.

"What's this all about, Wayne?" he asks. "Was that you who called the station?"

The man nods.

"What is this place, anyway?" He scans the murky room. A lamp reveals a tattered sofa and a stained coffee table.

"Just someplace to talk."

Duncan walks to the floor-to-ceiling window and looks out. Across the empty street a neon sign blinks, muted by the sheets of rain—Ruby's Bar. Parked at the curb is Duncan's pickup, steam rises from the hood.

"Look, Wayne, I don't know what's going on here. You place an anonymous call at the end of my shift, tell me you've got information on the Farthing murder, and then drag me clear across the city. Couldn't we have talked at the precinct?''

"Let's just say this is personal, Carvello. I've got a proposition for you. Have a seat."

Duncan remains at the window. "No, thanks. Why don't you just cut to the chase? Is this about Farthing or not?"

"You might say so. Let's just say it's a one-time offer."

"Go on." Suspicion creeps into Duncan's voice. He watchs a car pass below.

"Could mean an early retirement, if you're interested."

Duncan says nothing. Wayne's hand glides under his jacket.

"And if I'm not?" He turns, but it is too late. The other man's gun is already drawn and Duncan lifts his hands. "Easy now, Wayne. I don't know what the deal is, but we can talk, all right?"

"Hand over your piece first, Carvello. Slowly."

Duncan unholsters his revolver and slides it across the floor. "Okay now? So talk. Is this still about Farthing?"

"Yeah, it's about Farthing. Bastard had it coming to him. The man didn't pay his bills, if you get my drift. But you already know that, don't you, Carvello? You were onto me weeks ago. If it'd been up to your partner, the investigation would never have gotten this far. But you just had to keep digging and digging." He waves his gun wildly.

"You know we weren't getting anywhere with the Farthing case. You asked me about it last week."

Lightning flashes nearby. Duncan takes a deep breath, then slowly exhales. "Listen, Wayne, Gary's on his way here. Why don't you just put the gun away? We can talk later."

"Before or after you turn me in, Carvello? You think I'm stupid? I didn't ask you here to listen to a confession. You're either with me or you're not. There's big bucks in this, if you play your cards right. Lots of guys out there are just dying to give away their money, if you know how to play the game. Farthing was only one. You've got a badge, Carvello. May as well use it."

"And you'll show me how, right?" The sarcasm in Duncan's voice taunts Wayne, and he raises his gun.

She can feel the tension thick in the room. Her pulse quickens.

"Don't say I never gave you a chance, Carvello."

Everything shifts into slow motion. Duncan's hands come up, protective, useless. Lightning flashes behind him. A crack of thunder, louder this time. And then the roar of the gun.

She can only watch, a scream exploding in her throat.

Duncan's face twists with shock and pain. His eyes roll as the impact of the bullet hurls him back through the window. A burst of shattering glass glitters like a thousand daggers around him as he falls.

Her scream, real and piercing, brought her back. She gasped for air, the throb in her head forgotten as a new pain consumed her—Duncan's pain. Frantically she tore away from the curb. Vacant storefronts and abandoned buildings rushed past in a blur. Another sickening wave of pain surged through her. Duncan was near. She could feel him.

And then she saw his pickup, parked beside the neon sign. There were people now, drawing in a cautious circle around the dark huddle on the pavement.

Breaking abruptly in the middle of the street, she leapt from the car and raced to where she knew Duncan lay. Torrents of rain washed over her, drenching her clothes, soaking her hair, mingling with her tears. The other people said nothing, or if they did, she didn't hear them. For her, there was only Duncan.

Even as she stared down at him writhing in a pool of blood that no amount of rain could wash away, even as she saw the gaping wound in his chest, she clung to a small shred of hope. His hand reached out for her.

Broken glass stabbed through her jeans as she took his hand and knelt beside him. A small cry escaped her throat when she touched him. Her hand trembled as she wiped away the blood from his pain-stricken face. She lifted his head, cradling it in her lap as she whispered his name.

"Hold on, Duncan. You've got to hold on." Her hand found his again, and she bit back another cry when she saw the blood staining his gold wedding band. "The ambulance is on its way. Just hang on. Please."

He squeezed her hand, and his voice was a ragged whisper. "I'm sorry, Ali. I really . . . I don't think I'm going to make it. . . ."

"Don't say that, Duncan! Don't!" Her voice shook as she caressed his face.

"I shouldn't have . . ."

"It doesn't matter. Just be still."

He licked the rain from his lips as his body shuddered for air. "Wayne. It was . . ."

"I know, I know. I saw it all, Duncan. I was with you. Please, just lie still."

His eyes closed and she heard her own stifled whimper. "Damn it, Duncan! Don't do this to me!" Again she felt his hand squeeze hers, more weakly this time, and his eyes opened slowly. "You promised me this wouldn't happen, Duncan. Remember? You promised."

His lips twitched as if to smile. "I know, Al. Shouldn't make promises I . . . can't keep."

"You can't leave me, Duncan. You can't. Just hang on! The ambulance will be here any second. Promise me you'll hang on!"

Then there was Gary. He'd come out of nowhere and knelt beside her. "God, Duncan, what the hell have you gotten yourself into?" She could see her own shock reflected in his eyes. "Hang on, partner, hang on. Ali, stay with him."

And then he left her side. She heard him splashing back to his car, heard him on the radio. " . . . better get here fast. . . ."

Duncan took a rasping breath. A moan escaped his lips, and he gripped her hand harder.

"Ali?" he whispered.

She rocked him in her arms, brushing his wet hair back with shaking fingers.

"I . . . I love you, Ali."

She felt his breath on her skin, the smooth warmth of his cheek against hers. Her lips touched his ear. "Please, Duncan, I love you. Please don't leave me."

But even as she heard the distant wail of the siren, she knew she was losing him. His life was slipping away with the rain.

"Duncan," she whimpered. "Please, Duncan..."

The sirens grew closer. Louder and louder. A shrill pulse piercing through the wet blanket of night. Perhaps the ambulance would reach them in time. Perhaps it wouldn't be too late.

Ali called out Duncan's name one last time, called out into the darkness. One final, breathless cry.

CHAPTER ONE

"I THINK you'd better let me lead on this one, Sammy."

Detective Sam Tremaine pulled his gaze away from the two-story brick house and looked over at his partner on the passenger side of the old Buick Skylark's bench seat.

"And why's that?"

"Look, I know you don't agree with Harrington's decision. So I think it'd be better if I talked to the woman. Wouldn't want you ruining our only chance with that skepticism of yours."

Matthew Dobson had been unusually impatient all day. From the moment Chief Ed Harrington had suggested that the two detectives call on Alessandra Van Horn, Matt had been champing at the bit. And considering Sam's reservations, Matt was probably the best man to take charge of the situation.

It wasn't often that Sam disputed Ed Harrington's suggestions. For as long as Sam had known him, the chief had proved to be a clear-thinking and prudent administrator of the Danby Police Department. But the chief's latest maneuver on the Munroe case was not something Sam could really agree with.

Psychics.

He gazed across the quiet street again, his eyes following the walkway that led to the front door of the Nolans' house.

Well, he couldn't really blame the chief for grasping at straws. There hadn't been any fresh leads in the Munroe investigation for almost four weeks now—no leads and nothing conclusive enough to warrant the arrest of their only suspect, Peter Munroe. Still, that hardly justified turning to some oddball psychic for advice. But Harrington had been determined to acquire the aid of Alessandra Van Horn.

From the moment Harrington had heard about Van Horn's track record from one of the junior detectives and then discovered, through Matt's contact at the *Herald* that she was actually in town house-sitting for her sister and brother-in-law, Vicki and Richard Nolan, he'd been resolute in his decision to use the woman. The psychic was their last hope, he'd told Sam that morning over a mug of cold, burned coffee—their last chance of uncovering anything that might even resemble a lead in Jacqueline Munroe's murder.

As Sam had driven to the Nolan house, he wondered how much of Harrington's argument was really the chief's. If Sam's hunch was right, Victor Ballantyne, the victim's father, was the man behind this sudden shift in their investigative procedures.

Harrington was too rational, too careful. Certainly not a person who, overnight, developed a belief in clairvoyants and psychic detection. But Victor Ballantyne had been exerting pressure from the very start of the investigation, and because he was one of Danby's senior city councillors, his voice held significant weight with the chief of police. It was understandable, then, that with no immediate answers in sight, Harrington had been persuaded to consult Alessandra Van Horn.

Sam turned off the ignition. He raked his fingers through his hair and stared at the pristine house across the dead-end street.

It didn't feel right—consulting some psychic about Jacquie's murder. No matter how acclaimed Van Horn's reputation, it wasn't enough to convince Sam. They were wasting their time.

Of course, there would be no talking Matt out of this. Sam's partner sat quietly beside him in the faded brown Skylark that the Danby Police Department refused to replace. They'd been driving this car together for more than three years now, and it had seen its share of rough rides. Then again, so had their partnership. And after those three years, Sam would have sworn he knew his partner better than anyone.

Perhaps what surprised Sam the most this morning wasn't so much that Matt supported this psychic thing, but that he was actually enthusiastic about it.

"So, are we going in or are we just gonna sit here all afternoon?" Matt's voice was tinged with the same impatience that lurked in his eyes.

Sam drummed his fingers on the steering wheel. "You're really into this thing?"

Matt paused as if weighing his partner's beliefs against his own. "What, the psychic? Yeah, I guess I am. It's a shot in the dark, but at least it's something. I don't know about you, Sammy, but I'm getting damned tired of trying to dig up stuff on Peter Munroe and coming up empty." He nodded to the house. "Who knows? Maybe this woman can give us what we need on Munroe and we can put the man away once and for all. It's worth a try, isn't it?"

Matt waited a moment and then, realizing that his partner was still unconvinced, removed his hand from the door handle. "Man, I really don't get you. Of all the guys on the force, Sam, I would've thought you'd be the one willing to try anything to get Jacqueline's murderer. After all, you and Jacquie—"

"Don't start, Matt, okay? There's nothing personal in this case for me, you know that."

But Sam knew Matt saw through the facade of indifference he'd attempted to put on from the moment he'd walked into that bedroom five weeks ago, from the moment his eyes had looked down into Jacquie's lifeless stare.

"Look, I told you before," Sam explained, "I've read about these psychic-assisted cases, and they're nothing but sensationalism. People will say or do anything to get the media excited these days. It makes good television—but it's all a publicity stunt, nothing more."

Matt's expression remained set. "Okay, Sam, if that's what you wanna believe, fine. But we're doing this. For the chief. Victor Ballantyne's been on his back from day one to get something on Peter Munroe. If you're that opposed to seeing this psychic, then just let me do the talking. If she refuses, we can at least go back and tell Harrington we tried." He looked at the house again.

Sam followed his gaze.

Except for the immaculate lawn and flower beds, the house appeared deserted. The *Herald* lay where it had been tossed that morning and the blinds were still drawn. With any luck she wouldn't even be home.

"Look," said Matt, "maybe this woman *is* a fraud, okay? But you can't ignore her track record. She's worked on some pretty major cases, and if you ask me,

Van Horn is closer to the real thing than anyone I've ever heard about. Besides, what've you got to lose?''

A hot, early-July breeze worked its way sluggishly up the street and through the open window of the car. With it came the laughter of children followed by excited barking farther down the block.

Sam nodded, resigned. Matt was right—they had to try. Matt could do the talking, and considering that he'd never been the persuasive one in their partnership, maybe he wouldn't be able to convince Alessandra Van Horn to join forces with the Danby police. Then they could forget this ridiculous psychic business once and for all.

"Come on, Sammy." Matt slapped his shoulder and reached for the door handle. "What've you got to lose, hey? I'll even spring for beers at Morty's afterward, all right?"

"Well, you're probably going to need one after this," Sam remarked, taking Matt's lead as he opened the passenger door. And as he walked up the path to the front porch, Sam couldn't rid himself of the image of some heavyset woman with flowing garments and a kerchief wound around her head greeting them at the door and ushering them into a candlelit parlor.

ALI VAN HORN set the sweating glass of iced tea on the corner of the table and dried her hand on her shorts. She capped her drafting pen and wiped at the beads of perspiration on her forehead. By keeping the blinds drawn, she'd managed to block out most of the mid-afternoon heat, but even this seemed to have had only a minimal effect on the temperature inside.

Still, it was paradise compared to the top-floor apartment she'd left back in New York. She smiled, wondering how her friend Jamie was faring with the record highs she'd read about in yesterday's paper.

She studied the drawing on the table in front of her and picked up the pen again. In spite of the heat, her work was going well. Almost better than she'd imagined when she'd finally agreed to house-sit for six weeks while Vicki and her husband traveled overseas.

Now, two weeks later, Ali was beginning to realize just how much she'd needed to get out of the city. How much she'd needed to get away from the phone calls, the concerned friends, the endless nightmares and the memories. Especially the memories.

The laid-back atmosphere Danby offered was exactly what her tired mind had craved. The quiet, dead-end street on which her sister's house was situated lent itself to full days of uninterrupted work. Ali had Jamie to thank—he was the one who'd pushed her to accept her sister's invitation to Danby in the first place. And if all went well, she'd have four more drawings finished and sent by courier to New York before the end of the next week.

Tucking a stray curl behind one ear, Ali uncapped her pen and began working again. Her hand moved deftly, laying down the ink in bold strokes, outlining the characters of Jamie's next children's fantasy book in preparation for the color to be applied later. The pen danced along the surface of the paper, skipping from the goblin hiding behind a pile of boulders, to the dragon looming in the stormy sky above.

The success of Jamie's books over the past five years had launched Ali's career in illustration beyond anything she'd thought possible when she'd graduated from Parsons School of Design with her degree in visual arts almost six years ago. She'd considered herself lucky when she'd landed a job at Stinton Graphics upon graduation, but after signing a four-book contract with Jamie Ackerman, a friend from college, Ali had been able to go free-lance.

Within weeks of Jamie's first book hitting the shelves, Ali had found herself with so many offers she'd had to start turning people away. Children's books, magazine illustrations, advertisements—all were lucrative work. But none were as rewarding as illustrating Jamie's books.

Ali's hand jumped at the shrill ring of the telephone. In silent prayer, she looked from the phone back to the drawing, hoping that her pen hadn't skipped on the page. Releasing a long sigh of relief when she saw it hadn't, she capped the pen and crossed the living room.

"Hello?"

"Hey, Al, it's Jamie. Just thought I'd call to check up on you. Haven't heard from you in almost a week. How're you doing?"

Ali's lips curved into a smile at the sound of his voice. "Working hard, how else?"

"Well, that's good to hear. Any new drawings for me?"

"I should have some to you and Logan by the end of next week," Ali said, thinking of Jamie's agent, Logan Whitman, and the man's impatience once a project was under way.

"We got the first three drawings last Thursday. Logan loves them," Jamie told her. "In fact, he was so impressed he's given your name to one of his new writers. I'm sure you'll be hearing from somebody soon. Hope you can handle the extra work."

"It's not a problem, Jamie." Ali tucked the receiver under her chin and began pacing the length of the living room. "I can use the work right now," she admitted, knowing that Jamie understood full well what she meant. Drawing was the only thing that kept the memories at bay, the only activity that allowed her to forget the past and the emptiness that was now a part of her life. "Besides, I'm ahead of schedule on your drawings—I could handle another project right now."

"So you're really doing all right, then?"

"I'm fine, Jamie."

"The solitude hasn't gotten to you yet?"

"No. Besides, I'm not alone. I've got the dog," she said, looking over at the sleeping golden retriever Vicki had left in her care. Tash had taken well to Ali, unlike Hector, her sister's ungrateful tomcat who lived strictly by his own rules. Ali was thankful for the canine companionship while staying alone in the big two-story house.

"And the nightmares?"

Ali stopped. Unconsciously she sought the gold wedding ring on her left hand. Her fingers rubbed the smooth, warm band. Eleven months since Duncan's death, and still the dreams persisted—recurring nightmares, haunting images of his murder. She had them almost every night and sometimes she thought she'd go crazy. In desperation she'd decided to take Jamie's advice and get out of New York, out of the apartment she and Duncan had shared since their wedding only three short months before his death.

She turned and caught sight of the photograph of Duncan on the mantelpiece. His smile now seemed hollow, lifeless, nothing at all like the vibrant man she had loved.

"Ali?"

"Sorry, Jamie."

"I was asking about the nightmares. Have they stopped?"

"Yeah," she lied. "Yeah, they've stopped. I'm doing fine, Jamie, really. You were right. I just needed to get out of the city."

When Tash gave a sharp bark, Ali looked at the dog. Her ears were perked forward even before the doorbell rang.

"Listen, Jamie, I've got to go. There's someone at the door. I'll talk to you soon."

"I'll call. And I want to come and see you. Maybe in a week or so." Ali could hear him leafing through his daybook.

"Sure, Jamie. I'll talk to you then." She said goodbye and replaced the receiver.

During her short time in Danby, Ali had been grateful for the solitude. But she didn't mind the occasional interruption—Mrs. MacGregor next door, with her generous offerings of vegetables from her infinitely productive garden, or kids on a bottle-drive to support their Little League team. She'd welcomed these brief visits as breaks from the routine of drawing.

Fully expecting to see Mrs. MacGregor's round, jovial face beaming above a bundle of zucchini, Ali felt her staged smile disappear when she opened the door. Through the false protection of the screen, she saw two men on her front porch.

"Can I help you?" she asked, her voice wary as she pulled Tash back from the door.

"Ms. Van Horn?" One of the men stepped forward. At first Ali had thought he might be a salesman with his clean looks, his blond hair clipped short and his shirt freshly ironed. An awkward smile played on his smooth-shaven face. In one hand he held the morning paper. With the other he reached for something in his shirt pocket—a gesture Ali was only too familiar with.

In that instant she knew why they had come.

"Yes?"

"Good afternoon." He drew out his badge. "I'm Detective Matthew Dobson, and this is my partner, Detective Sam Tremaine. We're with the Danby Police Department."

Ali unconsciously took a step backward. With one hand still on the knob, she felt the room begin to spin. Through the blur of the screen she watched the detective's smile fade to an expression of concern.

She knew why they were here. She had tried to avoid listening to the news, tried to ignore the daily paper that, in spite of her request, Vicki had forgotten to cancel before she'd left. The Jacqueline Munroe case had been a major headline in the local news even before her arrival.

She'd read that there had been little development on the case that had caused a quiet panic to ripple through the small upper-state city. And Ali wasn't surprised to see the two Danby detectives standing on her front step. What was a surprise, however, was that they were seeking her help so soon. Jacqueline Munroe had been murdered only five weeks ago. It usually wasn't until all leads were cold and a case was considered practically unsolvable that the police pursued other alternatives to their standard investigative procedures.

"Could we come in, Ms. Van Horn?"

Ali hesitated, her knuckles turning white as she gripped the door handle. "Can I ask what this is about, Detective Dobson?"

"We'd only like a word with you. It won't take long. Just a few questions."

"What kinds of questions?"

The young detective shifted his glance to his partner and then back to Ali. "We're here about a case we're working on, Ms. Van Horn."

"And how does this case relate to me?" she challenged, hoping that the steady harshness in her voice would be enough to usher the detectives off her front porch.

"Well, it has nothing to do with you personally, but we were hoping you might offer us some assistance."

"Look, Detective, I have a pretty good idea why you're here, but I have to tell you there isn't anything I can help you with. I've just been in Danby for two weeks and—"

"I promise we'll take only a moment of your time, Ms. Van Horn," the other detective said, sincerity detectable in his firm voice.

Ali looked at him. Through the screen, she saw the flash of dark eyes, but the instant they met hers the detective turned his gaze to the street and fidgeted with the small notebook he gripped in one broad hand.

Had it not been for Detective Dobson's introductions, Ali would not have pegged the other man as a cop. He shifted his weight impatiently, hooking one finger through a belt loop of his creased slacks. His tousled hair was too long for what Ali would have considered police standards, and the rumpled shirt contrasted sharply with the immaculate appearance of his partner.

When he brought his gaze to hers again, offering a smile that seemed apologetic, Ali felt a strange tingle travel through her, and she shivered, despite the heat of the afternoon.

Her grip on the handle of the screen door began to relax, and reluctantly she swung it open.

"I have to warn you, Detectives," she told them as they stepped past her into the house, "you really are wasting your time."

"Perhaps you would just hear us out, Ms. Van Horn," Detective Dobson offered, loosening his tie as he looked around the ornate entrance hall and then up the winding stairs to the second floor. "So, you're house-sitting for your brother, then?"

Ali pulled the door shut and stepped back, suddenly aware of Detective Tremaine's closeness. "He's my brother-in-law, actually."

"Oh, right." Detective Dobson gave her a quick smile. "I haven't met your sister. I know Rick Nolan through the paper. What is he—senior editor now? Anyway, I heard they were heading off on a second honeymoon or something. It's a good thing they've got you to take care of this big place for them."

Ali cleared her throat. "So, what is it you've come to see me about, Detective Dobson?"

He took a last glance around the house as if checking for other occupants. "Please, call me Matt. And this is Sam."

Ali met the other detective's dark stare just before he looked away.

"Could we go and sit down, Ms. Van Horn?"

Ali stood her ground for a moment, crossing her arms over her chest. They wouldn't need to sit down. It wouldn't take her more than a minute to say no to the question she knew they'd come to ask. But when she caught Detective Tremaine's quiet expression, she found herself nodding. "This way." She motioned to the living room.

The two detectives walked in and sat on the couch, while Ali lowered herself into the large wing chair opposite.

Matt lifted a hand to wipe his forehead. "They don't have air-conditioning in this place?"

"It quit on me last week. I'm afraid I haven't gotten around to getting it fixed." She paused. "I take it this isn't a routine 'welcome to Danby' call on the department's behalf, am I right?"

"No, I'm afraid not. We've come to ask for your help." Matt moved to the edge of the couch. "Your reputation with the New York Police Department precedes you, Ms. Van Horn. Detective Tremaine and I found your track record extremely impressive."

Ali wondered just how many cases the two detectives had reviewed. Did they know about the times she'd failed. As was most often the situation, the police, even the NYPD after working with Ali and recognizing her success rate, usually came to her too late. They didn't dare consult some psychic until all possible leads were long dead, until all other procedures had failed to turn up anything, and until any hope of finding the perpetrator was lost. By then, it didn't matter if Ali wanted to help them or not—it was usually too late.

Not only that, the police were fanatical about keeping their occasional use of psychics off the record and definitely out of the hands of the press—especially when those cases had gone wrong. No doubt the two detectives sitting with her this afternoon had not read about the failures. No one wanted to hear about a missing child found too late or a serial killer stopped only after eight senseless murders, murders that might have been prevented had it not been for the police department's slowness to act on Ali's advice.

"I don't suppose that, after reviewing my track record, you took the time to contact the NYPD?" Ali asked, catching Sam's stare and then looking back to Matt.

He shook his head.

"Well, if you had," Ali went on, "you might have saved yourself a bit of time this afternoon. They would have told you I'm out of the psychic business."

"Ms. Van Horn, please, hear us out. Sam and I are only here as a last resort. If there was any other way…"

"As a last resort." How many times had she heard that line?

She let her gaze stray from Matthew Dobson to Sam Tremaine. He was silent, lounging back on the couch, attempting to appear comfortable as he let his partner try the persuasion game Ali was all too familiar with. She recognized that, under normal circumstances, Sam Tremaine would be the cop trying to persuade her. She could tell from the hardened expression on his face that he was the leader of the team. But for now, he remained silent, and Ali knew why.

She'd seen more than enough skeptics in the NYPD to recognize it. He had no more faith in her abilities than he had in winning the New York lottery.

Dark eyes met hers again. Ali held his gaze this time, intrigued by the secrets that seemed to lurk there. Eventually he turned away. A muscle flexed nervously along his square jaw as he looked around the room, obviously aware of her eyes still on him.

". . . and I'm sure you've seen the paper's coverage of the Jacqueline Munroe case." Matt's voice crept back into Ali's awareness and she pulled her gaze from Sam.

"Yes." She cleared her throat. "Yes, I have."

"Jacqueline Munroe was found suffocated in her mother's home five weeks ago. She's survived by her husband, Peter Munroe, and their five-year-old daughter, Cassandra. She was in her mid-thirties and a respected citizen of Danby. Her father, Victor Ballantyne, is one of our senior city councillors. We've yet to establish any motive behind the murder, but we're certain it wasn't the bungled robbery attempt it appeared. There was no evidence of sexual violence or even forced entry into the Ballantyne home. Other than Peter Munroe, who stands to get a healthy insurance claim, no one had anything to gain by Jacqueline Munroe's death.

"Right now, we've been working on the case for five weeks and we've still got nothing. No witnesses, no leads. We've been over everything a thousand times and we're still hitting dead ends."

Matt leaned closer to Ali. "You're our last hope, Ms. Van Horn. Our chief, Ed Harrington, is anxious to have you on the team with us. All we need is a direction. A different angle, something fresh to go on. Anything. Right now, we don't even have enough to get an arrest warrant for our chief suspect, Peter Munroe."

"Then perhaps he isn't the man you should be focusing your investigation on, Detective Dobson." Ali's voice was calm and matter-of-fact. Through all her work with the NYPD, the most important lesson she'd learned was that, from the onset, all predetermined theories surrounding the case had to be cast aside. Only after that would she submit to the impact of the visions and the draining migraines that accompanied them.

But she'd left all of that behind her now.

"I told you before, Detective Dobson, I'm not in that line of work anymore. You really are wasting your time."

But when Ali glanced at Sam Tremaine again, she felt compelled to offer him an apologetic look. For a moment she wondered if she might have agreed to help had *he* been the one begging her for assistance. There was something in his expression, something that made Ali realize that, for this detective, there was more than a professional interest in Jacqueline Munroe's murder.

He pulled himself up from the couch, either satisfied with Ali's resolve or, more likely, nervous from being near her, and extended his hand. "Thank you for your time, Ms. Van Horn. We're sorry to have interrupted your day."

"That's all right. I'm just...I'm sorry I can't help you." The warmth of his hand gripping hers lingered, and once again, Ali found herself meeting the detective's gaze.

She'd always been grateful for the limitations of her abilities, but now, more than ever, Ali was thankful that she couldn't "see" Sam Tremaine's thoughts. In his brooding silence, she recognized his commitment to this case. She sensed that, in spite of his obvious skepticism, he was oddly disappointed at her unwillingness to become involved. But what his true motives were she didn't know—and didn't wish to know.

"Yes, well, thanks, Ms. Van Horn." Matthew Dobson took her hand and gave it a cursory shake before following Sam to the front door. "If you do happen to change your mind, though—" he turned as Sam held the door open "—here's my card. Call me anytime, day or night. They'll page me if I'm not at the station."

"Right." Ali fingered the small white card, then slipped it into her pocket, making a mental note to throw it out when she did the laundry.

"Have a nice day, Ms. Van Horn," Detective Dobson said, following his partner down the wooden front steps.

Ali lingered in the doorway for a moment. A hot breeze tugged at Sam Tremaine's cotton shirt, outlining his muscular physique. His dark hair brushed the back of his neck as he glanced down the quiet street, and only when he looked once more at her did she turn away.

She couldn't make out their words, but she could tell the two detectives were arguing as they got into the Skylark.

When she closed the door, Ali heard the car's engine start up. She listened to it fade down the street and breathed a sigh of relief as she dropped a hand to stroke Tash's head.

But even as Ali returned to her desk and took up her pen, she knew she hadn't seen the last of Matthew Dobson and Sam Tremaine. It was not a premonition, just her own intuition. And for the first time during her stay in Danby, Ali regretted having followed Jamie's advice to leave New York.

CHAPTER TWO

"YOU COULD USE some sleep, Tremaine. You look like hell."

Sam's pen paused in midsentence. On the verge of finishing a double shift, he was hardly in the mood for motherly advice. Besides, he'd already paid for that with his last telephone call to Florida.

He tossed down the ballpoint. His gaze swung from his backlog of paperwork to the young detective perched on the only clear corner of the desk. Nancy Peterson gave him an enthusiastic grin, and Sam shook his head. There seemed no end to the energy Danby's newest detective had displayed in the short time she'd been with the department. On more than one occasion, Sam had been thankful she was Coleman's partner and not his. She'd been running circles around the older detective for six months now, and the guys were beginning to wonder if Coleman would file for early retirement, after all.

Sam shook his head again. He tried to remember if he'd ever been as optimistic as Nancy. If he'd ever possessed the faith that drove her, the belief that every case had an answer, that every criminal could be caught, and that through a conviction, the crime would somehow seem vindicated.

Nancy hadn't experienced enough dead-end cases in her young career to tarnish that vision yet. Even three years as a rookie with the NYPD hadn't hardened her. Soon enough, though, she would encounter the kinds of cases that had clouded Sam's own attitude—cases like Jacquie's murder. Nothing could make her death seem anything but senseless.

A phone on another desk buzzed, sounding more like a manic cricket than the latest in technology. Sam jumped. Hoping Nancy hadn't noticed, he got up quickly from his chair and began pacing the detectives' wing, empty but for him and Nancy. He was on edge, had been since Jacquie's death. That much he would admit to, but the last thing he needed now was to get the reputation of being a nervous cop.

"You're pretty edgy, Sam," Nancy noted, pushing herself from Sam's desk and crossing the floor to her own. "You really should get some sleep. I don't think I've ever seen you like this."

With an audible groan, he sank back down in his chair and rubbed his eyes. "Your concern is duly noted, Nance."

He reached for the paper cup that had been perched on the corner of his desk for the better part of the afternoon and tipped its contents into his mouth. Cold bitterness slid over his tongue. He grimaced and tossed the stained cup into the wastebasket.

"I mean it, Sam. Maybe you should take some time off. Even if it's only a couple of days. Maybe you could work on your house or something. Get your mind off the job."

"I can't right now, Nance. You know that. We're short-staffed as it is. Harrington would never agree."

"Oh, come on, Sam." She gave him a knowing smile as he spun his chair around to face her. "You know that's bull. Harrington would be the first one to agree that you need a break. Besides, Matt's off right now. What's he up to? Probably at the lake with the latest entry in that little black book of his. Is it still that babe from the *Herald?*"

Sam shook his head, grinning at Nancy's locker-room attitude, and looked up at the precinct's high ceiling. After two shifts, he had no energy left to argue.

"Not that it matters who he's with," she went on. "All I'm saying is the same kind of therapy wouldn't do you any harm. Maybe when Matt gets back you should let him handle your caseload for a couple of days. You could go up to the lake, kick back a bit, maybe even meet someone. It's not like you're past your prime or anything like that, Tremaine, but you're wasting precious years, if you ask me."

Sam gave a short laugh and let his chair snap into place as he turned back to his desk. "Nance, your concern is appreciated. So is your vote of confidence. But right now, as long as I have these cases hanging over me, I wouldn't be much good to anyone, anyway, all right?"

Nancy was silent—a pleasant change, Sam thought as he glanced at her one more time. Her blond hair was pulled into a ponytail, the few loose strands lending a softness to her sharp features. The smile on her thin lips faded slightly, as she leaned forward to look squarely at him.

"All I'm saying, Sam, is that maybe you need a change of pace for a couple of days. I don't care if you go out and get laid or not. I don't care if you work on that house of yours or do nothing but sit around on your couch for three days and watch Oprah and Donahue. But I do know that you need a break to find a new perspective on the Munroe case. It's been darkening your desk, not to mention your mood, for the past five weeks.''

Sam let out a long sigh of frustration. "Don't start about the case, Nancy, okay? For both our sakes.''

"For both our sakes?'' Nancy slid her chair and stood up abruptly, walking over to Sam's desk again. Her arms were crossed over her chest. "Sam, this isn't for both our sakes. I'm asking you to take a break for *all* our sakes. I doubt you've noticed, but you've been impossible these past few weeks. You're exhausted, short-tempered, impatient, on edge.''

The phone rang, and Sam knew Nancy saw him flinch.

"Look, Nancy. I'm all right.'' Sam reached over and squeezed her arm, hoping she understood his appreciation. "I'm sorry if I've been on a short fuse lately, but I can't let this one go, okay? Under different circumstances, I'd agree with you. But I can't drop this case right now.''

"You know you can, Sam. You know that a day or two isn't going to make any difference.''

He shrugged. There was more truth in Nancy's words than he cared to hear. "Trust me, Nance. I know my limits. I don't need a break.''

He looked at the unopened file on his desk. Jacquie's file. He had no idea what he was going to tell Harrington when he got back from the conference in Baltimore. They'd gotten nowhere with Alessandra Van Horn, and remembering the determination in her voice, Sam doubted there would be any convincing her. Then again, no matter how much he wanted to find Jacquie's killer, a part of him was relieved that Van

Horn had turned them down. The thought of having a psychic on the case—

"So you still haven't made any headway on the Munroe case, huh?"

Sam shook his head.

"And you didn't get anywhere with the psychic?"

"How do you know we went to see her?" Harrington had been adamant that they keep silent about using a psychic on one of the department's most talked-about cases.

"Hey, it doesn't take a rocket scientist to figure out where you guys were going the other day. And it certainly didn't take Freud to see that you'd been turned down by Van Horn when you got back in the afternoon."

Sam leaned back in his chair and laced his fingers together to cradle his head. "Well, if you hadn't gone to Harrington with Van Horn's name in the first place, we wouldn't have wasted our time the other day."

"Trust me, Sam, you're not wasting your time. Getting Van Horn on the Munroe case is probably your only way of closing it."

"And what makes you so sure? You know this woman?"

Nancy shrugged. "Not personally. But I did assist on a case with Gary Breckner when I was working with the twenty-first precinct in New York."

"Gary Breckner?"

"Guess you didn't get around to reading Van Horn's file, did you?"

"Guilty," Sam admitted, shaking his head. He'd had the file on his desk for two days and hadn't been able to bring himself to open it. Matt had filled him in on more than he wanted to know, anyway.

"Breckner's the guy who brought in John Fisher, that serial killer in New York two summers ago? He's also the detective who finally nailed Martin Burack after that killing spree."

"And you're going to tell me Van Horn helped crack those cases?"

"More than just those two. She worked quite closely with Breckner for a few years. The Burack and Fisher cases were only two of many she helped him with."

Sam studied Nancy as she slipped off her holster and walked back to her desk. After six months, he still hadn't figured her out. There was definitely more to her than the casual attitude with which she seemed to handle everything.

"Come on, Nancy. You're not going to tell me you believe in this psychic stuff, too?"

She slid her gun into her top drawer and looked up at Sam. "I've seen her work, Sam. That's all the convincing I needed."

"You've worked with her?"

"Not directly. She wouldn't work with anyone but Breckner. Whenever she was brought onto a scene, everyone had to clear out, and she and Breckner would be there for hours sometimes. Anyway, I was doing some legwork on the Fisher case when Breckner brought Van Horn to the apartment where the third killing took place. I wasn't aware they'd arrived, so I figured I was clear to enter the scene. Van Horn was already into her reading when I walked in on them. Breckner obviously didn't want to interrupt her, so I had to stand there and listen to the whole thing." Nancy shook her head and sank into her chair. "I tell you, Sam, it was the spookiest thing I've ever experienced."

Sam tried to picture the gentle woman he'd met on the scene of a brutal crime. He could still see her soft features, her almost innocent face and the fleeting but gentle smile she'd given him when she apologized for refusing to assist them. Alessandra Van Horn was a far cry from what Sam had expected when he'd stepped onto her front porch three days ago. It had taken great effort to mask his surprise when she opened the door, and even greater effort to conceal his attraction to the woman over the course of their brief meeting.

"She walked around that apartment," Nancy went on, "her face almost blank. And her eyes—she never really looked at anything but, instead, seemed to look *through* things. I don't know how to describe it. And then she stopped, right where we'd found the body, and she began talking to Gary. It was as if she'd linked with Fisher somehow, and she described to Gary everything that happened—absolutely every detail, every move Fisher had made—as if she'd been there. You'd almost think she'd killed the woman herself."

An eerie silence fell over the detectives' wing. Sam watched Nancy lean back in her chair and retie her ponytail.

"I don't know about you, Sam, but if I had the Munroe case still on my desk I wouldn't think twice about getting Van Horn's assistance. And the fact that she just happens to be in Danby for the summer... I just don't see how you can dismiss the possibility before you've even tried."

Nancy turned her attention to her own pile of paperwork and opened a folder to begin the laborious task of filling out forms.

"Well, we already gave it a try. She refused to help. What more can I do?" Sam rubbed the back of his neck with one hand. It was going to take a lot more than Nancy's story to break down the wall of skepticism that had kept him from opening Van Horn's file. Besides, this was *Jacquie's* murder he was investigating. Even if Van Horn's abilities were for real, he was not about to have Jacquie's death sensationalized.

"Maybe Harrington should go and talk to her himself. He's the one who wants to drag a psychic onto the case," Sam muttered, about to turn back to his own work.

"Well, why don't you ask him right now?"

Sam followed Nancy's nod to the front offices beyond the glass barrier. Ed Harrington had just arrived. He was leaning heavily against the counter, collecting his messages from the front desk.

"Damn. What the hell is he doing back so soon? Wasn't he supposed to be away until tomorrow?"

He caught the chief's nod and smile through the plate glass and answered it with a quick lift of his hand.

"Guess he's early, Tremaine. Good luck." Nancy winked and gave him a smirk.

But before Sam could comment on her lack of compassion, Ed Harrington stood in the doorway of the detectives' wing.

"Still here, Tremaine? I thought you'd be working on your house, nice afternoon like this."

"Paperwork. You know how it can pile up." Sam slapped his hand down on the stacks of reports on his desk, wishing he'd taken the afternoon off, after all. "How was the conference?"

Harrington moved to Sam's desk, settling his six-foot-three frame on the same corner Nancy had occupied only moments before.

"Just another conference, you know. Same people, different city." He dismissed further discussion of the trip with a wave of his hand, then reached up to straighten a few wisps of his graying hair, which was parted on one side and brushed over his balding pate. "There's another message here from Victor Ballantyne."

Sam averted his eyes.

"I take it you and Matt were unsuccessful the other day?"

"You could say that."

"So what's the story?"

"Look, Chief, there's no way this woman's going to cooperate with us. She's determined to stay out of any investigation, and if you ask me, I can't blame her. She's on vacation. She didn't come to Danby to solve police cases."

"We need her, Sam." Harrington bent closer. "Look, I know you don't agree with my decision to bring Van Horn into the investigation at this point. But right now I've got a major murder case on my hands and no answers. I've got Jacqueline Munroe's father, a senior city councillor, on my back about doing whatever's necessary to get Peter Munroe put away. I've got two of my best detectives tied up on a case that isn't going anywhere. You know this doesn't look good—for the whole department. We need answers, Sam. And we need them yesterday."

Sam leaned back in his chair, not so much to relieve the tension building along the muscles of his back but to escape the chief's intensity.

"The NYPD figures Van Horn is the best in the business, and I intend to have her on this case, no matter what it takes."

"Oh, come on, Ed. You don't believe in this psychic crap any more than I do. Ballantyne's got you so riled up you're grasping at straws."

"Look, Tremaine." The chief held up one thick finger. "It doesn't matter what I believe when it comes to this case. And frankly, at this point, I don't care what you believe, either. I don't want to tell you this again—you're going to have to file that skepticism of yours away for another day. I want you to get this woman for us and I don't care what it takes."

"Ed, she's not budging. You can ask Matt."

"Matt's no sweet-talker, you know that. I want you to speak to her, Sam. Go over to her house tomorrow and talk to Van Horn yourself. If you can't convince her, no one can."

Sam had worked for Ed Harrington far too long to consider hoping for a way out of this situation. He knew if the chief wanted something, nothing would stand in his way.

"Fine," Sam gave in. "I'll call Matt and ask him to come in tomorrow."

"No." Harrington planted his hand firmly on the Munroe case file. "I want you to talk to her alone, Sam. Don't you get it? It's less intimidating that way. Besides, you're the one with the good looks around here."

"And what the hell is that supposed to mean?"

"Read between the lines, Tremaine." Harrington stood up from the desk and checked his watch. "I have to get going. Can I count on you?"

Sam nodded his head in defeat. He knew the visit would be a waste of time. He'd seen the determination in Alessandra Van Horn's eyes. She wasn't about to become involved in any murder investigation, no matter how charming the appeal.

ALI LOOKED at the clock. She could just make it.

Flipping back a stray wisp of hair, she steered the grocery cart into the unfamiliar territory of the pet-food aisle. What was it Vicki had told her Hector ate? Tasty Vittles or something? Her eyes scanned the shelves of canned and boxed cat food, searching for anything that looked familiar.

In the couple of weeks she'd been at her sister's house, Ali hadn't needed to shop for the pets at all. But just this morning she'd poured the last hard morsels into Hector's bowl and now, even though she'd tried to make a point of remembering the brand name on the box, she drew a blank.

She stared at the shelves one last time and finally reached for the box with a picture that most resembled the antisocial tomcat. What the hell, she thought, old Hector wouldn't notice the difference.

Then there was dog food. If she hadn't gotten so involved with her drawings this afternoon and been in such a hurry to get to the grocery store before it closed, she would have written out a proper shopping list. But now, with the manager requesting over the PA system that last-minute shoppers take their items to the express lane, Ali supposed it didn't really matter which brand of food Tash ate for the rest of the month. She reached for a bright yellow bag of store-brand kibble.

"Purina's on sale."

Ali stopped, her grip slackening on the twenty-pound bag of dog food. She recognized the voice even before she turned.

Sam Tremaine, too, seemed to be using the last few minutes until closing time to buy his essentials. The basket in his left hand brimmed over with vegetables, but these didn't conceal the bottles of Coke he had tucked in the corner behind some green-topped carrots.

Ali's eyes were caught by the unsettling intensity of his gaze when she finally looked up at him. She pushed the hair back from her face, wishing she'd taken the time to tie it up properly.

"If your sister's dog is anything like mine, it probably won't touch that store-brand stuff." He smiled, and for a moment, Ali tried to imagine the type of dog Sam Tremaine owned. Perhaps she was influenced by the stereotypes of prime-time television, but a surly bulldog immediately came to mind.

In any event, Ali thought, if he was determined to give her advice, she'd rather accept the gesture gracefully and be done with it than get involved in a long-drawn-out discussion.

"Thank you, Detective Tremaine. I appreciate the advice."

With a shrug, he set down his shopping basket and reached for a bag of the brand-name dog food. Ali stood back as Sam placed the bag on the bottom carrier of her cart. She watched him from behind. The loose white cotton shirt he wore tucked into the faded blue jeans billowed slightly as he moved. Ali imagined the muscles rippling just beneath the soft fabric as he gave the bag one last shove and straightened up.

"Now, if the dog doesn't like that—"

"I'll send her down to the precinct," Ali finished for him and felt a momentary flush from the smile he gave her. She glanced away, uncomfortable with the peculiar familiarity she felt, and pretended to take inventory of the contents of her cart. "Well, thanks again, Detective Tremaine . . . for the advice."

"Please." He stopped her and extended his free hand. "Would you call me Sam? I hate formalities."

Reluctantly Ali took the hand offered to her, letting her fingers slide into his firm grip, and she heard her own voice repeat his name.

And then the sounds of the supermarket faded away, the price cards on the shelves began to blur, and the very floor she stood on seemed to sway until the feeling, the awareness, flooded in. Ali struggled to stop the "senses" that were overwhelming her, but the warmth of Sam's hand pulled her. She knew that only seconds were passing, yet they did so in slow motion.

There wasn't anything definable, no residue from Sam's day springing out at her. No images from his life. But then, she'd worked hard at suppressing these abilities over the years. Instead, there was a swell of emotions, both hers and Sam's, and in that moment, Ali couldn't separate the two. It had been a long time since she'd felt this kind of connection. A long time since she'd felt the pull on her senses from another person the way she felt now, pulsing through Sam's grip, as they stood in the middle of the pet-food aisle. And Ali knew that if she let it go on, if she continued to read from Sam's touch, these senses she felt beginning to stir would open up even further.

She couldn't let that happen.

Ali drew her hand away from Sam's and blinked. The shelves around her slowly came back into focus, and finally so did Sam.

His face had changed. His smile was gone and his forehead creased with lines of concern as he stared at her. Ali forced a smile and took a breath, hoping to alleviate the uncertainty revealed by Sam's expression.

She returned her attention to the shopping cart, determined not to let the brief encounter affect her. "Well, I'd better run these to the checkout before they close."

Even as she turned away from Sam, Ali felt his eyes on her.

"Are you all right?"

She felt his hand on her arm and turned to face him again. "Yes, I'm fine, Detec...Sam. Just in a bit of a hurry. I'd suggest you think about getting whatever else you need, as well. It's last call." She smiled again, uneasily, and pointed up to the PA system.

Sam seemed to catch the tail end of the manager's announcement and at last broke his stare to eye the contents of his basket. "No, I have everything I need. Listen, are you sure you're all right?"

"I'm fine, really. I, uh, have to run. I'll see you around, Sam." Ali wheeled her cart to the last open checkout where a cashier sighed impatiently. The woman rang in the food, zipping the bar codes across the plate of glass and then stabbing the prices into the register with ridiculously long-nailed fingers when the laser refused to read several items.

Ali watched her groceries move along the belt, aware of Sam's presence behind her. She fumbled through her wallet for change, hoping he wouldn't notice her trembling hands.

"Can I take these out for you, ma'am?"

Ali shook her head at the weary bag boy, about to thank him for his offer, when she heard Sam's voice behind her.

"I'll give her a hand with those."

She caught Sam's gaze for an instant just as she pushed the cart toward the doors. "I really think I can manage."

But before she could escape into the parking lot alone, Sam was at her side. "The Jeep's yours?" he asked, nodding at her sister's burgundy Cherokee parked beside what Ali guessed was Sam's Bronco.

"Good guess," she said, wondering if her response had sounded as sharp as she thought it had. "And I suppose the Bronco is yours?"

"Wow—" Sam let out a whistle "—is that psychic or what?"

Even Ali, as unsettled as she still felt from her experience only moments ago, was forced to crack a small smile as she opened the Cherokee and started to load the bags of groceries.

Sam heaved in the twenty-pound bag of dog food and dusted his hands off on his jeans. "Look, Ms. Van Horn—"

"Please—" she held up a hand before reaching for the next bag "—it's Ali, all right?"

"Okay, Ali. Listen, can I . . . can I buy you a coffee or something?"

Ali stopped, holding one brown paper bag against her hip as she stared at Sam. "I really don't think that would be such a good idea."

He held her stare and somehow Ali guessed that Sam would not be satisfied with a simple brush-off. But why did she feel so compelled to give him an explanation?

"Nothing personal, really," she said as she turned to ease the bag into the car. "It's just that I've got a lot of work to finish up tonight and I have to get to the library before it closes."

"Fine." He smiled. "Some other time, perhaps."

Ali nodded, wondering if there was something more personal to the audible disappointment in Sam's voice. Why couldn't she just believe he wanted to have a friendly conversation over coffee? Why did she have to immediately suspect some ulterior motive?

"Sure, some other time."

He helped her load the last of the bags into the Cherokee in silence. Only after slinging his own bags into the Bronco did he turn to her.

"Listen, Ali—"

She leaned against the side of the Jeep.

Sam looked down at his sneakers for a moment before letting his gaze lock onto hers again. Ali was struck by the sincerity in those dark brown eyes.

"I... I was going to come over and see you tomorrow, anyway," he stammered. "About the Munroe case."

"I already told you and your partner—I'm not interested," she said flatly as she opened the driver's-side door.

"I'm not asking if you're interested, Ali." Frustration sharpened his words. "I'm asking for your help."

When Ali turned to face him, Sam shifted his weight. She could see it was with a certain amount of reservation and skepticism that he asked for her assistance now. He looked down at the ground again, apparently struggling for the words he hoped would convince her.

"Look, I understand your not wanting to get involved. But all I'm asking is that you consider putting your past experiences—or whatever it is that made you leave New York—aside for one hour. A half hour. However long it takes you to get a reading, or whatever you call it. We need something, anything, that might give us a new lead, a new direction to investigate. I'm not asking you to get as involved as you might have with some of the previous cases you've worked on. Only that you give it a try. And I promise, if you don't come up with anything right off, you can dismiss the whole thing and forget we ever met."

Ali closed her eyes, taking a deep breath. She could feel the side of the car behind her, warmed by the late-afternoon sun. She didn't need this, not now. Not after Duncan and the horror of that night almost a year ago. She'd promised herself, as well as Gary and Jamie, that she was out of the business once and for all. And it had actually worked—for a while. For eleven months she hadn't had any visions. Nightmares, yes, but no visions, no images, no migraines. Nothing.

But now...Sam Tremaine had come asking for her help. There was something about the detective, something she'd "felt" unmistakably through their handshake back in the grocery store, something she couldn't quite put her finger on.

His request was sincere. Perhaps he had sensed something himself when she'd taken his hand. Perhaps he'd realized that she had "seen" something in him, and that alone was enough to convince him she wasn't a fraud.

She knew he wanted her help. Maybe he didn't believe, but he had enough faith to give it a try. Most of all, though, he wanted Jacqueline Munroe's killer. It didn't take a psychic to see that.

"Look at me, Sam." She waited until he looked up. "If I do this for you, if I try to help you out on this case, there are some ground rules you have to understand first."

"Name them."

Ali took another deep breath, collecting herself. If she agreed to help Sam, and if she learned anything from her reading, she knew she'd be committed to follow through on the case. Not by choice, but by the sheer fact that once she'd connected, once she'd plunged into the dark abyss of the killer's mind, there was no turning back. The pull would not release her, no matter how badly she might want to escape it.

The wind licked at a stray lock of her hair, and Ali raised a hand to push it away before continuing. "First off, I won't go to the precinct. If there's anything I can do, it will be done in my house. You'll have to either get authorization for the release of evidence so that you can bring it to me, or you'll have to find some other means. That's up to you."

She waited for Sam's nod and watched his face as these thoughts churned in his head.

"Second, I can't do readings with onlookers. People only create interference. And that includes your partner, Matt. You, alone, can be there. You can run a tape recorder if you want. I don't mind. But it's difficult to get accurate readings if there's more than one other person in the room."

Again Sam nodded.

"And last, no press. If there's so much as a mention in your local paper about my assisting with this case, I'll end my involvement immediately."

Sam's sober nod assured Ali that he recognized the importance of this last point. Still, she couldn't ignore her past experiences with police investigations—she knew the danger she was putting herself in.

She heard her own voice, low yet strong, and was surprised by its intensity. "I won't have my life put in jeopardy."

There was a moment of utter silence in the corner of the otherwise empty parking lot. In that moment, with Sam's eyes holding hers, Ali prayed that she could trust Sam Tremaine with her life.

CHAPTER THREE

SAM LEFT THE PRECINCT at nine-thirty. He hadn't called Matt. He hadn't told Joanne, the dispatcher, where he was going. And he'd made a conscious effort to leave the station before Ed Harrington got in from having his morning coffee at the doughnut shop.

Kicking a stone along in front of him, Sam crossed the Danby Police parking lot and wondered when the department would get around to paving the dusty, potholed disgrace. When he reached the old Skylark, he dug into his jacket pocket for the keys. His hand scraped against the sharp corner of a small box.

Jacquie's ring—still wrapped in the personal-effects bag marked 6-238 and then tucked into the box. He hadn't touched the ring. Not because he would actually admit to the waning of his skepticism about Ali Van Horn's abilities, but more so because he respected her request that he not handle the object he was bringing her this morning.

As he started the Skylark, Sam wasn't certain what was in store for the morning. After he'd watched Ali pull out of the supermarket's parking lot yesterday, he'd driven home, thinking about what he would bring her for the first meeting. He couldn't stop thinking about her, even as he unpacked his groceries, fed Ziggy and then fixed himself a sandwich. After three hours of putting up drywall in the second-floor bathroom,

Sam still hadn't been able to get his mind off Ali. Her words ran through his head over and over again, in spite of the blasting stereo. Even later, when he took Ziggy for his evening walk, Sam could still see Ali's pale eyes staring at him.

And in spite of turning in sometime after midnight, Sam had bounced out of bed at five, surprised at the almost boyish enthusiasm he was feeling. He'd gone for his morning run with Ziggy, urging on the Great Dane as he added another six blocks to his workout, and he was still at the precinct long before anyone else.

In the silence of the detectives' wing, he'd opened Harrington's file on Ali and briefed himself on the cases Nancy had mentioned—the Fisher murders, the Burack investigation and others. For close to five years, it appeared, Ali had worked steadily with Gary Breckner. And, as each case he read became more involved and more violent, Sam could only wonder at the effect this type of work might have on someone like Ali—someone without police training, without the experience or the detached indifference required for such inhumane work. No wonder she'd been so reluctant to become involved with the investigation of Jacquie's murder.

Now, despite all that, for some inexplicable reason he was looking forward to seeing her again. After reading the case summaries, he wondered if his beliefs were possibly changing. Or maybe it was something else.

He knew that whatever it was stemmed from yesterday in the grocery store. In that almost chilling moment when Ali had taken his hand, he had definitely felt an eerie sensation his analytical mind could not explain. A pull almost, as if a piece of him had been drawn out and examined.

They'd stood there for only seconds, really. Yet somehow it had seemed a lot longer. He'd watched her pale eyes darken—the pupils growing until they consumed the former brightness.

Then later, at the cash register, he'd seen her hands trembling as she fumbled for change. They'd still been trembling when she shook his hand later in the parking lot. Even now, as Sam rounded the corner of Blucher Street and pulled into the Nolans' drive, he felt the edges of his skepticism begin to push back. Inexplicable as it was, he could not deny that *something* had happened in the grocery store yesterday.

He pulled the key from the ignition and stared at the windows of the house. If Ali's file held any truth, then he supposed there was a slim chance she might come up with something that could help find Jacquie's killer. He could not deny that possibility, no matter how cynical he was.

"JAMIE, LOOK, I really have to go." Ali clenched the telephone receiver and turned to the hall clock. She'd told Sam ten, and it was almost that time now.

"What? You have a heavy date or something?" her friend joked, and then paused, as if waiting for a negative response before prying further. "Come on, Al. I haven't talked to you in days."

"Well, if you were home more often, I wouldn't have to discuss the progress of these drawings with your answering machine, now would I?" Ali smiled, rubbing her wet hair with a towel. She'd gotten out of the shower only moments before the phone rang. Foolishly she'd answered it. Now, fifteen minutes later, she was still standing in her robe with the receiver to her ear.

"All right, all right. So, what's the deal, then? Should I come up this weekend to take a look at these drawings or what?"

"This weekend?" Ali listened to the street noises outside, wondering if she'd heard Sam's car already. "No, Jamie. Not this weekend. I need another week."

"But you told me things were moving along and you wanted to show me some stuff as soon as I could get up there."

"Yeah, well, everything's on schedule, don't worry. I just think it would be better if I had another week. I'll have more to show you by then, and you can take a few pieces back with you."

There was a pause at the other end of the line, and Ali used the opportunity to shift the receiver to her other ear.

"Okay, Al, what's up?"

Jamie had known her too long. They'd spent four years together in college, and he'd even dated her best friend. Then, after graduation, they'd formed an unstoppable team of writer and illustrator, and Jamie had remained an important part of her life. After the car accident that had almost killed her and was responsible for her psychic abilities, he'd seen her through the beginnings of the visions and the turmoil of several police investigations. And then, last year, he'd been her only comfort when the world around her had become so suddenly and unbearably empty. They'd been through too much for Ali to hide anything from him now.

"Ali?"

"It's nothing, Jamie. Really. It's just that I've got someone coming over any minute and I'm still in my robe.'' Ali hoped her voice didn't reveal the nervous tension she'd been feeling from the moment she'd gotten out of bed this morning and remembered her promise to meet with Sam.

But there was a significant enough pause for her to realize that Jamie had recognized something. "I take it this isn't just a social visit?"

"Jamie—"

"You're not reading again, are you, Al?"

"Now why would you assume that I'm—"

"Ali, come on, this is Jamie you're talking to here, remember? Now what's going on?"

"It's nothing major, Jamie. Trust me."

"Ali, you can't do this anymore. You promised yourself you'd stay away from—"

"It's one case. One reading. I won't let it get personal," Ali said, trying to convince him. But Jamie knew as well as she did that keeping any case impersonal had been virtually impossible.

"And what about Duncan? You're just going to ignore everything that happened—"

"This has nothing to do with Duncan!" she snapped, and then took a deep breath to calm herself. "Jamie, listen to me." Her voice was firm now. "I don't have time to argue right now, okay?"

"I just don't want to see you get hurt again, Al."

"Trust me, Jamie. I know what I'm doing. I can handle it. Now I really have to go."

"You'll call me later?" The uneasiness in his voice was unmistakable. It was the same uneasiness she struggled to keep at bay herself.

"I will."

"Ali, I just...I just don't want you to have to go through that hell again."

"I'll be all right." And then, hoping to ease Jamie's worry, she added, "I promise."

But even as she hung up the phone, she wished she'd never agreed to meet with Sam. She should have said no, and yet... there was something about this case. Nevertheless, she'd already committed herself. And unless the item Sam brought held no connection for her at all, she was in for the ride.

She was still towel-drying her hair when the doorbell rang, and she cursed under her breath as she checked herself in the hall mirror. Of all the mornings to sleep in.

Sam, on the other hand, looked as though he'd been up for hours. His crisp denim shirt was tucked into freshly pressed slacks, and his face was clean-shaven. His bright eyes did a quick scan of the robed figure before him.

"Oh, I'm sorry. Looks like bad timing." He shifted his weight to one leg as if to turn and leave.

"No, not at all." Ali opened the door for him. "The bad timing is entirely on my part. I slept in."

"I can come back—"

"No, that's all right. Come in, Sam." Ali closed the door behind him, and becoming suddenly aware of the closeness of the detective, she pulled her robe more tightly around her. "If you'd like to make yourself comfortable, I'll just go upstairs and change."

"Sure, no problem. I'm not in a rush." He smiled, his eyes never leaving hers, and Ali once again felt that odd twinge of familiarity between them.

She'd have thought the close quarters of the front hall would have made her feel uncomfortable, but instead, there was something strangely comforting in Sam's nearness.

"Well," Ali said finally, pulling her gaze from his and looking down at her robe. "I'll, um, be right back. There's a pot of tea on the stove if you'd like to help yourself."

She nodded toward the kitchen and turned as Sam watched her climb the stairs. He watched the movement of her slender body beneath the terry robe until she disappeared into one of the bedrooms.

His memory hadn't been playing tricks on him last night when he'd thought of Ali, when her face had lingered in his mind hours after he'd talked to her in the parking lot. Even before he'd stepped through the front door just now, her pale eyes had captured him. Her full lips had curved into a soft smile, the same hesitant smile she'd given him yesterday.

Sam walked into the kitchen. His hand played with the small box in his pocket as he found the teapot and two cups already set out on a tray. Carrying these to the living room, Sam paused by Ali's drafting table. Intricate pen-and-ink drawings lay scattered across the surface, accompanied by preliminary pencil sketches, and Sam bridled the urge to lift a few of the top pages to examine the colorful creations beneath.

Instead, he set the tray down on the coffee table and scanned the rest of the room. Unconsciously his hand returned to his pocket, playing with the box as he crossed to the stone fireplace.

Photographs of the Nolan and Van Horn families lined the mantelpiece, and Sam's eyes wandered over these with only half interest—until he caught Ali's face among them.

He stopped. In a polished brass frame, Ali looked back at him, her smile frozen in time. The man who stood beside her with his arm thrown over her shoulders was also smiling in the happy moment caught on film. His dark hair, framing his tanned face, blew back in a breeze that Sam imagined smelled of salt from the ocean behind them.

The photo looked recent. Ali's dark curly hair was cut in the same blunt style she wore now. But she looked younger, Sam thought as he leaned closer to the photo. There was no trace of the worry lines Sam had seen etched in her face only moments ago. And in the photo, there was no sign of the strain he had seen in the smiles she had given him.

He was still examining the photograph when he heard Ali clear her throat behind him. He turned quickly, embarrassed. She had changed into walking shorts and a loose, white cotton shirt. Her still-damp hair, hung in soft curls.

Sam nodded toward the drafting table in the corner of the room. "Your work's impressive."

"Thank you."

"You illustrate children's books?"

Ali moved to the couch, her hands buried in her pockets. "Mainly just the one series. My friend, Jamie Ackerman, writes them. I do advertising work, as well. Magazine illustrations, brochures, posters."

"I guess psychic work doesn't pay that well, huh?"

She managed another one of her half smiles before lowering herself onto the couch. "It does if you sensationalize it. But then you end up sensationalizing the crime more than the method by which it was solved. Not exactly my idea of a solution." She poured the tea. "So, I take it you were able to bring something?"

Sam was struck by her cool, businesslike approach. No small talk, just straight to the task at hand. And, no doubt, as soon as Sam left, Ali would be back at her drafting table drawing more dragons and demons.

He sat down in the wing chair next to the couch and took the small box from his pocket. Ali watched him open it and pull out the plastic personal-effects bag. Her eyes didn't leave the bag as she wiped her palms on her shorts and reached out to take it from Sam.

The light caught the ring on her own finger and he was taken aback. He wasn't certain why he hadn't noticed the gold wedding band before. He thought of the picture on the mantelpiece, the man at Ali's side, the laughter in their faces.

"You asked me for something of Jacquie's that was personal," he said at last, forcing himself to concentrate on the business at hand.

Ali sat on the edge of the couch and passed the bag from hand to hand, rubbing the surface with her fingers.

"She'd worn that since high school."

Ali was silent, her eyes fixed on the bag in her hands.

"You can take the ring out, if you like," Sam said.

She gave an almost indiscernible shake of her head— a gesture that seemed like an attempt to dismiss his presence. He fell silent. From the hall, a clock chimed and then continued its sluggish ticking. The motor of the ceiling fan above them whirred. The only other sound was the rustle of plastic in Ali's hands.

Then her voice broke the silence—low but steady.

"She's been staying with her mother. An argument between her and her husband." Ali paused, her eyes lifting from the bag no more than a fraction as she seemed to focus on some unknown plain, piecing obscure and fleeting images together. "There's something about a divorce. That's why she's been staying with her mother. She's been there a few weeks. And her daughter is staying with them, as well—Cassie, I think. The girl is there that night.''

Her voice became deep, slow, methodical. ''Jacqueline's mother isn't home, though. She's gone out to her bridge club and doesn't get home until after eleven. It's obvious there's been a struggle—a few things knocked off a side table, the TV and stereo are by the door. She rushes to Cassie's room, but the girl's still asleep. Then she finds Jacqueline.''

Ali's slender fingers continued to rub the ring through the plastic.

''You're one of the first men on the scene.'' Ali turned to Sam briefly but seemed to look right through him. The silvery gray of her eyes was gone now as her pupils enlarged. Sam wasn't sure if it was her eyes or her distant voice that made him uneasy.

''Matt is there, too. You radioed him as soon as you found out and he arrives shortly after you. You're trying to talk to Cassie when he comes in, but you already know you aren't going to get anything out of the girl—she's too frightened, too confused. You go back to the guest bedroom.''

Another long pause as Ali took a deep breath and turned the bag over in her hands.

''The other officers are collecting whatever they think might be evidence. There's black powder everywhere—dusting for prints. They haven't moved the body yet. She's still lying on the bed, half under the sheets. Anybody can see it was suffocation... but they're talking about doing an autopsy, anyway, since she's Victor Ballantyne's daughter.

''The rest of the house seems untouched except for the TV and stereo. No sign of a forced entry, but you figure the front door lock could have been picked since it hadn't been chained. The police dust for prints...but they come up with nothing. From all accounts it looks like a bungled robbery, but you don't believe that. You still don't.''

Ali looked up after another pause. Her hands, still holding the bag, lay motionless in her lap. She stared at Sam and he shifted uncomfortably.

''You don't believe me, do you?'' Her voice was still low but now it possessed a coldness that sent a chill through Sam.

Had he not been thinking that very thought? While he listened to Ali laboriously describe the scene of that unforgettable night, had he not been questioning his own rationality for sitting here listening to a description of the crime scene that anyone could have put together from the press it had received over the past few weeks?

''It's not a matter of belief, Ali. It's just that you haven't—''

''You think I'm reading this entirely from you, from your memories of that night.''

Sam shook his head. ''To tell you the truth, I wasn't even giving you credit for that.'' He held up his hand to stop her as she was about to return the bagged ring to him. ''Please, Ali, don't get me wrong. It's nothing personal, trust me. It's just that you're dealing with a real skeptic here, and quite frankly, you haven't exactly told me anything that hasn't been on the six o'clock news.''

He watched Ali's lips tighten. A muscle along her jaw flexed a couple of times, and even though Sam prided himself on his honesty, this was one time he truly regretted having said anything at all. He fully expected her to toss the bag with Jacquie's ring back at him and demand he leave.

But instead, her icy stare was broken and Ali looked down at the bag in her hands. She opened it. Her fingers trembled slightly as she reached for the ring. Slowly she removed it from the bag, tumbling it through her fingers. She rubbed the ruby-colored stone and the embossed high-school motto before sliding it over her finger.

Sam shuddered. Whether by coincidence or some unknown means, Ali had slipped the ring over the second finger of her right hand—the same finger he had seen Jacquie wear it all those years.

Ali twirled it. Her eyes focused on that same unseen plain. Her pupils widened further still, her eyes almost black now. She was silent for a long time. Motionless, except for the turning of the ring.

"Are you getting anything?" Sam didn't know why he'd bothered asking. But as he watched Ali now, he came closer to believing in her ability than he had since the moment Ed Harrington first mentioned her name almost a week ago.

After a long silence, Ali answered him. She spoke slowly, meditatively, as if trying to put some hidden image into words for him. "She cherishes this ring. I don't know why." She shook her head. "She wears it every day. Her husband doesn't like it. I can't tell why, but she refuses to take it off even for him.

"She turns it around her finger...whenever she's nervous. She doesn't even realize she's doing it, she's done it for so long."

There was no way Ali could have known that. Sam sat forward in the chair, moving closer to her, wanting to touch her for some reason but not daring to break the delicate connection she seemed to have acquired. Instead, he only stared at her, his heart beating faster.

"Can you tell me anything about the night Jacquie was killed?"

Ali shook her head and continued to twirl the ring. "She's nervous. Turning the ring...around and around. She's put Cassie to bed already. The house is quiet. In the living room, she's switching off the lights, wearing her robe. She's worried about something. Anxious."

"What, Ali? Can you tell what she's thinking?"

Again she shook her head. "No, just a sense. There was a phone call. She's thinking of her husband. She called him earlier tonight. They talked. Something about trying to work things out. Moving back tomorrow...but she hasn't told her mother yet."

Ali took another deep breath and Sam waited patiently as she slowly continued. "There's someone else, though... She's thinking about someone else. Another phone call. After her husband's. I don't know who. It's upset her. An angry phone call. She's thinking about the other caller. And she's thinking about her husband... In the bedroom—she's getting ready for bed. Her hands are cold even though it's a hot night. The ring slips and she turns it so that it's straight again. She looks at the ring, but doesn't take it off right away. Just looking at it...touching it. She's still worried but not so much now. She's staring at the ring on her hand. She's thinking about..."

Sam barely restrained himself from reaching out to Ali then. From reaching out and shaking the answer from her. It seemed so close....

His hands clenched into fists. "What is she thinking, Ali? Who is she thinking about?"

Ali looked up slowly, her still-dark eyes following the lines of Sam's tense body until they met his. Her lips quivered briefly, her fingers trembled. She continued to hold his gaze while, in one deliberate motion, she removed the ring from her finger.

When she finally spoke, her tone was flat. "She's thinking about you, Sam."

"What?" Sam's heart seemed to stop in his chest.

"You gave Jacqueline this ring, didn't you?"

His breath caught in his throat. How could Ali have possibly known? He'd given her no indication there had ever been anything between Jacquie and him. Something like that couldn't be found in the paper or on the news. Only a handful of people knew about him and Jacquie. How could someone just new in town possibly...?

He shifted in the chair again, wanting to snatch the ring back, but instead, struggled to retain his composure. "I don't see how that's relevant to the case."

Ali held his stare until Sam was forced to look away. "No, I suppose you're right," she said finally. "It was a long time ago."

Silence.

Sam concentrated on the whir of the ceiling fan, the ticking of the grandfather clock out in the front hall, the honking of a horn in the distance.

It was Ali who spoke first. She sat forward on the couch and reached out to return the ring. "There's nothing more I can get from this."

She dropped the ring into his hand, her fingertips lightly brushing his palm. When he looked at her again, he could almost see the suspicion in her eyes. He looked away, tucking the ring back into the plastic bag and putting it into the box.

"Jacquie took the ring off just before she went to sleep that night. There's nothing on it that's going to be directly related to the crime."

"That's it, then?"

Ali nodded and stood up from the couch as if needing to put distance between herself and Sam. "I can't see something that isn't there. The link I'm establishing is through the victim, and it's extremely limited. I'm sorry. It's also been a while since I've done this kind of thing."

Sam slipped the box into his pocket. "So where do we go from here?"

She shook her head and turned her back to him as she opened a blind and looked out the bay window. "I don't know. If I'm to get anything on this case, I'll need something else. Something more related to the murder."

"Like what?"

Her voice was still shaky but not as hesitant as it'd been moments ago when she'd held the ring. "In other cases there have been weapons—guns, knives, objects that were either used in the murder or at least touched by the killer. If Jacqueline had been wearing the ring when she was killed, maybe then I might have had something more to go on. But right now, as I said, I'm linking only with the victim. That's not how I usually work. I need to be able to pick up on the killer directly if I'm going to be of any use on this case."

Sam nodded slowly. "I'll work on it."

"What about the child?" Ali asked, turning to face Sam again.

"Cassie?"

"Maybe she saw or heard something."

"I've already talked to her several times. She was asleep when her mother was killed. She didn't see or hear a thing."

"Yes, but maybe she knows something else, something that doesn't seem relevant to your questions. You're talking about a five-year-old here, Sam."

Sam stood up, as well, and ran a hand through his hair. "I don't know, Ali. I don't like the idea of dragging her into it any more than she has been. She's just a kid."

"She doesn't have to talk about it, Sam. All I need is to sit with her."

Sam didn't respond. He paced to the fireplace, catching another glimpse of the photograph of Ali and her companion.

"What about the husband?" she asked.

"Peter Munroe?" He shook his head. "There's no way his lawyer would agree to it. We've already pushed as far as we dare." He turned to look squarely at her. "Okay, Ali, listen. If you're willing to go the distance on this one, I'll see what I can do about setting something up with Cassie's grandmother. As far as getting a hold of something that might have come into contact with the killer, I'll do my best."

Ali nodded once and then headed for the front hall. "That's it, then," she said as Sam followed her. "If you can find something, if I can link with the killer, even briefly, I might be able to come up with something. But I'm not making any promises."

Sam paused at the front door.

"What is it?" she asked, obviously noting his apprehension.

"It's nothing. Just thinking," Sam lied. What else could he tell her? That in spite of her telling him things no one else knew about Jacquie, he still couldn't swallow the idea of psychic powers? That he didn't believe her when she told him she might be capable of linking with Jacquie's killer?

"Don't worry about not believing, Sam," she said as if she had reached into his mind and pulled out his very thought. "Not everyone does. Even when I'm able to give them something to go on."

She offered him another gentle smile. "I've given up trying to prove myself. It's not important. What is important is that we're both looking for the same thing. We're both looking for answers. It shouldn't really matter how we get them, should it?"

Sam shook his head, impressed by her candor. "I suppose not."

"Trust me, Sam, even if you don't understand what it is I do. Just concentrate on convincing Mrs. Ballantyne to let us meet with her granddaughter. That'll be the biggest start we can hope for."

"I'll see what I can do. Can I give you a call, Ali?" His hand played with the box in his pocket as he lingered in the doorway, surprised by his reluctance to leave. Why did he feel like some teenage boy asking for a date or something? It was just police business, wasn't it? If he hadn't been here today, Matt would have been.

She nodded, her smile strained, and Sam thought again of the photograph on the mantelpiece. He wondered what had happened to cloud Ali's former happiness.

"I'll be in touch." He went out, crossed the porch and headed for his car.

Ali watched him leave. His hair, caught by the wind, blew across his forehead, and he lifted a hand to brush it back as he got into the Skylark. She watched him start the car and back out of the drive. Long after he'd pulled away from the curb, Ali stood in the open doorway.

She massaged the finger where the ring had been. If she hadn't looked down to be certain, she'd have believed the ring was still there. She could feel its warmth radiating against her skin, pulsing its secrets.

At first, when she'd held the plastic bag in her hands, Ali had picked up on residue from Sam and even from the other responding officers that night. But when she'd taken the ring out, when she'd slipped it on her finger, she had seen more than she'd dared admit to Sam.

In a flood of images, Ali had watched a much younger Sam Tremaine nervously standing on a bridge. He was waiting, his hand in his pocket, fidgeting with something there. And then she saw Jacqueline. Ali had expected a gangly seventeen-year-old, not the beautiful woman who walked along the bridge to meet her young lover. She was radiant. Even through time, Ali had been able to catch snatches of their conversation. Sam going to college . . . how he wanted Jacqueline to go with him . . . telling her he could support her and love her. There was mention of marriage and talk of waiting . . . and then there were loving promises as Sam had given her the ring.

But these weren't the images that bothered Ali.

There had been darker shadows in her visions—the affair that had crushed Jacqueline's marriage, the other man, the other phone call. He was the reason Jacqueline had left her husband. And he was the man who'd been in the forefront of her mind the night she'd been killed. Jacqueline had been thinking about him as she'd turned the ring on her finger, thinking of him as she switched off the bedside lamp.

Even though Ali's connection with her had been broken the moment Jacqueline had taken off the ring that fatal night, Ali knew, with growing certainty, what Jacqueline was afraid of when she lay down to sleep for the last time. It had nothing to do with her phone call to Peter Munroe or with the decision to go home and renew her relationship with her husband.

It was the other man Jacqueline feared.

And now, standing in the doorway, looking out into the street beyond, Ali began to feel that same fear.

CHAPTER FOUR

A LIGHT CLOUD of plaster dust shimmered in the sunlight that flooded through the open front door and reached across the hardwood floor to the living room as Sam sank onto the sheet-covered couch. With a satisfying crack, he opened a chilled can of Coke and pushed aside stacks of books to find a coaster on the coffee table. He swept a hand over his T-shirt, releasing another dust cloud, and reached for the open book on the floor.

He'd spent his Sunday morning finishing putting up the drywall before giving in to Ziggy's pleas for a run at noon. Now the Great Dane lay in an exhausted heap by the front door soaking up the afternoon sun. Sam took a swig of Coke and began reading again.

Yesterday morning, Sam had been one of the first people in the public library, and after an hour of scouring the shelves, he'd left with a couple of armloads of books on the paranormal. He was hoping to find something that might explain what he had seen Ali do Friday morning when she'd slipped Jacquie's high-school ring onto her own finger. After almost three hours of reading about psychic detection yesterday afternoon, Sam had needed a break from the haunting accounts. He'd mowed the lawn, talked to his neighbor about the heat wave and finally managed to take his mind off of his latest research by cranking up the stereo and plastering the cracks in the ceiling of the upstairs bathroom.

When he'd bought the house almost two years ago, he had initially viewed the two-story "fixer-upper" as a blessing in disguise. Not only was it the answer to solitary evenings and the occasional empty weekend, to the surges of pent-up energy that had to be released, but it had allowed him to come home and lose himself in repair work, forget about the cases that had consumed his thoughts all day.

Sure, there had been occasional breaks in his loneliness—a few dates, even a couple of longer relationships in the past few years. But no woman was willing to put up with the erratic and endless hours he gave to his job. Then again, no woman had ever made him want to question his own priorities—why he chose work over everything else.

As he turned the pages of the book and took another swig of Coke, he had to admit that, as unsettling as the cases outlined in the books were, there had to be at least a fraction of truth in them. The coincidences were simply too numerous to ignore. And through the details of each account, Sam grew to realize that what he had seen Ali do the other day was not unheard of— strange perhaps, inexplicable, but not entirely unique.

"Hey there, Sammy!"

Sam jumped at the sound of Matt's voice and the book snapped shut. Ziggy gave a lazy, muffled bark before getting up to inspect the arrival.

"I have a doorbell, you know, Matt." Sam watched Matt brush off the Great Dane's friendly advances and struggle through the door with a large pizza box in one hand and a six-pack in the other.

"You're not going to tell me you fixed that thing?" Matt nodded to the wires dangling from the hole above the door.

"I guess it's next on the list."

"Yeah, well that list just keeps on getting longer, doesn't it?"

Sam nodded and studied Matt. He was wearing his typical Sunday attire—a Mets cap and T-shirt, shorts and a pair of high-tops—and as usual was freshly shaved with not a hair out of place. Scratching his own two days' growth of beard, Sam wondered where Matt got the energy to keep himself so immaculate.

"I told you before, Sammy. You should be looking at condos. I haven't had to do a thing to mine in what? Four years. In fact, I think there's one for sale in my complex. Just lemme know. I'll put in a good word for you. They love cops." He winked. "Keeps the neighborhood safe. And it sure beats the hell outta playing slave to your house."

Matt set the pizza on top of the books stacked on the coffee table and pushed Ziggy's massive head out of reach. "So what's all this?" he asked, picking up one of the books and turning it over in his hands. "Some light weekend reading?"

"Just doing my homework."

Matt pushed Ziggy away again before finally giving in to the Great Dane's demands for attention and reaching down to scratch the big dog's belly. "Anything interesting?"

Sam shrugged and opened the book where he'd left off. "Pretty spooky stuff, a lot of it."

"Don't tell me Sam Tremaine, the great skeptic, is actually thinking twice about psychic detection," Matt said, cracking open a can of beer and handing it to

Sam. "So you've persuaded Van Horn to assist on the case and now you're trying to convince yourself she might actually be able to help?"

"I don't know. Some of this stuff is awfully convincing. There's one case in here where a psychic picked up enough from a suspect's house to tell the police exactly where the twelve bodies of his victims were buried across an entire state. Another guy could tell the police about murders that hadn't even taken place yet. There was still another the police locked up, thinking he was responsible for the killings—until he provided them with enough information to nail the real perpetrator."

"I don't know, Sam." Matt paused to tilt back his beer and drink deeply. "Part of me wants to believe this kind of stuff—the same part of me that wants to see Jacquie's killer behind bars. But I gotta tell you, I wouldn't want to work with a psychic on a regular basis. You'd always wonder if they're reading your mind or something." Matt shook his head and reached for the television's remote control. "I don't think I could take it."

Matt clicked on the TV and after searching several channels, found the Mets' game, which was already into its first inning.

"Now come on, Sammy, it's Sunday. Time to put away the books and get your mind off work for a while. We got a game happening here." Matt reached for the pizza box and gave Sam one of his boyish grins. "Relax for a change, okay? Quit playing super cop twenty-four hours a day. The case isn't going anywhere. You can worry about it tomorrow."

"YOU'RE PULLING MATT from the case?" Sam sat down on the other side of Ed Harrington's desk. A low whistle escaped through a crack along one side of the vinyl-cushioned chair, and the chief paused as if waiting for the accustomed sound to finish.

"Sorry, Sam." He shrugged and Sam recognized the chief's rare form of an apology. "The decision's already been made. I need Matt to pick up the slack on your other cases so that you can work exclusively with Van Horn. Victor Ballantyne is too important in this city for us to drag our asses when his only daughter has been murdered. People are watching us. They want action. They want answers."

Even through the closed door of Harrington's office, Sam could smell Monday afternoon's burned coffee from the front of the station mingling with the familiar staleness of the precinct. He grimaced. The stench of old coffee grounds and rancid cigarette smoke was as much a part of the Danby police station as the officers behind the front counter. But when the humidity levels outside reached record highs like today's, it didn't matter that the building had been declared smoke-free for almost four years now. Even the odor of pine cleaner did little to camouflage the age-old stench that lingered in the air ducts and vents, Sam thought as he leaned back in the chair.

He sighed. "But Matt's as much a part of this investigation as I am, Ed. You can't pull him now. Not after all the legwork he's done on this already." Sam shook his head. "Listen, Ed, a lot of us knew Jacquie, Matt included. He wants this guy as much as any of us. Probably more."

"I know how much this case means to Matt. He made his position quite clear earlier today. In fact, I was a little surprised at his reaction." The chief leaned back and laced his broad fingers behind his head. "That's not the point here, though, Sam. You know that. I need this case closed, and given the circumstances, it's best done by one person."

Sam bit his lower lip. His back muscles had long ago stiffened into tight knots. There was no sense arguing. In his six years of working under Ed Harrington, Sam had come to recognize the chief's bullheadedness. He saw it now in the man's face, in the way the corner of his eye twitched just slightly, the way he clicked his pen several times in quick succession.

No, he wouldn't argue. He'd let Harrington believe that he agreed with the decision to pull Matt and carry on as usual. He owed his partner that much.

Harrington's chair groaned as he shifted his weight. "Listen, Sam, I called New York this morning. Talked to a guy by the name of Gary Breckner—one of NYPD's finest. He's also worked with Alessandra Van Horn. He had a lot to say about the little lady."

"Little lady" was not the term Sam would have used to describe the woman he'd dealt with only three days ago. Not the woman who had lingered in his thoughts all weekend. And certainly not the woman whose hesitant smile sought to cloak the true strength of her determination.

"You might want to talk to him sometime," Harrington added. "I left his number on your desk."

"What did Breckner have to say?"

"Well, from the sounds of it, we'll be damned lucky to get her assistance. According to Breckner, she's refused to take any cases in almost a year now. And if we *do* manage to get her, she's quite specific on what she will and will not do."

"And what are these specifics?"

"Mainly that whenever Van Horn assists on a case, she won't work with more than one detective. And she doesn't do her readings, or whatever they are, with more than one other person in the room. Basically she calls the shots."

Sam nodded and Ed leaned forward. He rested his wide midriff against the edge of the desk and closed his hands together in front of him.

"I take it you know all this already?"

Sam took a breath and eventually nodded. "I had a brief visit with Ms. Van Horn Friday morning."

"And?"

"You could say that similar stipulations were made."

"So she'll work with you?"

Sam hadn't wanted to discuss Ali with Harrington until they'd come up with something more promising, but it was impossible to avoid the issue now. "As long as we don't release her involvement in the case to the press."

Sam leaned forward himself now, hoping to emphasize the gravity of this request. "Ed, we can't let this thing leak. If there's so much as a whisper of her involvement, she'll drop it cold."

Ed studied Sam for a long time, until Sam shifted his position to break the stare.

"All right," the chief said finally. "It's settled. You're working with Van Horn—alone. I don't care how pissed off Matt is. I want this entire thing kept quiet."

Harrington clicked his pen again and scrawled his signature at the bottom of a release form. He didn't look up again, and Sam knew he was being dismissed.

"Let me know the minute you've got something, Sam."

Sam nodded and reached for the doorknob. "I'll work on it, Chief."

But Harrington didn't look up. He opened the next dog-eared folder, his thick fingers leafing through crisp pages. Even as Sam closed the chief's door, he could see the strain on the older man's face. There was a lot more at stake with this case than the department's reputation. Ed Harrington's position was on the line.

Nothing like a little added pressure, Sam thought as he crossed the almost-empty detectives' wing.

A fluorescent lamp buzzed and flickered on the battered oak desk that Sam had called home for the past three years. Beneath the lamp's failing glow, two pillows sat on top of a stack of files and reports, still wrapped in their plastic evidence bags.

Sam looked from the glare of the white pillows to Nancy Peterson. She was hunched over an open folder on her desk.

"You work too hard, Peterson," Sam offered as he approached.

She looked up and squinted. "Yeah? Well, you're one to be giving lectures on overtime, Tremaine."

Sam shrugged and leaned against the corner of her desk. "Listen, thanks for getting the pillows for me. Did Jacobson give you a hard time about taking them out?" he asked, referring to the head of Forensics.

"No, he just wants them back in the morning." She removed her glasses and tossed them onto the papers in front of her. "So, you working a new angle on the Munroe case?"

"Just with an idea. I don't know if it'll come to anything."

Nancy leaned closer and lowered her voice so that the two other detectives in the wing couldn't hear them. "Then I take it your first session with Van Horn was a success?"

Sam shook his head and smiled, darting a watchful eye toward the door as the two detectives left for the evening. He gave them a quick wave before turning back to Nancy. "Boy, you don't miss anything, do you, Peterson?"

She returned his smile with a knowing smirk. "Not much."

"Well, I'm sorry, there's nothing to fill you in on. We didn't really get anywhere."

"And the pillows?"

Sam pushed himself off Nancy's desk and crossed to his own. "They're just an idea." He rested his hand on the top pillow.

In fact, the pillows were far more than that, Sam thought as the plastic evidence bag crinkled under his palm. They were his only hope. After Ali had asked him for something that may have been handled by Jacquie's killer, and after he had read case after case in the library books, it hadn't taken much for him to realize that the two pillows from Jacquie's bed were their only hope.

He shoved the pillows aside and sat down. "Listen, Nance, I need a favor—"

"No way, Tremaine. Don't even think about asking me. You can see the paperwork Coleman's left for me."

Sam gave her a baleful look.

"And don't give me that big, brown-eyed puppy stare, either. It won't work on me." Nancy pointed her finger at him in a way that reminded Sam of his mother.

He smiled and leaned back in his chair. "It's just a little one."

"Bull," was her only response.

"Come on, Nance. It'll only take a half hour. I promise."

She looked at him, her eyes narrowed. "And what's in it for me?"

"I'll buy you lunch."

"I already ate."

"So, I'm good for a rain check."

She shook her head.

"I promise, Nance. It's not much. I just need you to help me set up a meeting with Jacquie's kid."

"Get Matt to do it. He's your partner."

"I think it would be better if the request came from you."

"You just want me to talk to Mrs. Ballantyne because she can't stand the sight of you. Is that it?"

Sam nodded. "Pretty much, yeah."

"So send Matt. There's no, uh, history between the two of them, is there?"

"No, but I still think we'd have a better chance of convincing her if you went with Matt. You know, woman to woman. What do you say?"

Nancy weighed her options. Her gaze shifted from the mass of paperwork consuming her desk to Sam's pleading eyes. "And you'll buy me lunch?"

"I promise."

"All right, then," she answered. "But that's it. I can't spare any more time after that."

"Thanks, Nance," Sam gave her a quick smile and turned back to his desk. He picked up the top file and rubbed his face with one hand. Sleep was what he needed. A good ten hours of it.

He opened the file. In front of him lay a complete set of photographs from the Ballantyne house—the yard, the front drive, the entrance and Jacqueline's bedroom. Sam looked at the case notes. They were in Matt's handwriting. Interviews with people related to the case. Even documentation of the questioning of every neighbor on the street. Everything they had worked on together in Jacquie's case was here, and Sam could imagine the frustration Matt must have felt when he'd tossed the file onto Sam's desk after his meeting with Harrington this morning.

He'd have to give Matt a call tonight and talk to him.

Sam flipped through several more pages, stopping only when he reached the transcription of Peter Munroe's interrogation the night of the murder.

Ali's words rang through his head again. Somehow she'd known about the phone call between Jacquie and Peter that night—a fact that hadn't been released to the media. Her knowledge of the phone call wasn't logical, but her conviction that Peter and Jacquie had decided to revive their marriage confirmed what Sam had suspected all along.

"What's your impression of Peter Munroe?" Sam's voice broke the lull that had fallen over the empty wing as he closed Matt's file and leaned back in his chair.

Nancy looked up from her work. "What are you talking about, Sam? I haven't read the file."

"I know you haven't." He spun around in his chair to face her and wedged his sneakered feet against the edge of the next desk. "But you were here when they brought Peter Munroe in the night Jacqueline was killed. You saw him. What did you think?"

Nancy shrugged.

It had been raining that night. Raining hard. Sam could still remember the downpour he'd driven blindly through on his way to the station. He remembered the nauseating disbelief that had clutched his insides from the moment he'd gotten Harrington's call, the shock that had held him in its grip during Peter Munroe's interrogation. But most of all, he remembered the anguish on Peter's face.

The man's hair had been soaked with rain, his face drawn and pale as he sat on a hard metal chair in the interrogation room waiting for Matt and Sam's arrival. And when Sam finally entered the small room, Peter's eyes had turned on him—vacant and desperate, as if pleading with Sam to tell him it wasn't Jacquie's body he had just identified.

"Are you asking me if the man looked guilty, Sam?"

"No, Nance, I'm asking you what you thought. What was your immediate reaction to his behavior? What would your impression have been if it had been *you* in the interrogation room with Peter Munroe?"

Nancy drummed the top of the desk with the end of her pen for a moment. "I guess I might have pegged him as innocent," she admitted eventually and nodded her head as if to convince herself. "The man was shattered. Either that, or one helluva actor."

The lull was broken as the door swung open to the bedlam of the rest of the station, and Sam turned to follow Nancy's gaze.

"Matt." He watched his partner's dour approach. His tie was loosened, his hair windblown, and his jacket was slung over one shoulder. "I thought you'd called it a day."

"Charlene's running late at the *Herald*," he said with a shrug, and dropped into his chair across from Sam. "I thought I'd try to straighten up a few things here while I waited."

"Well, you can stick this in your pile of things to straighten up." Sam swung his feet down from the desk and tossed the Munroe case file back onto Matt's desk.

"Right, Sammy. Have you forgotten? Harrington's pulled me."

"Yeah? Well, I still need you on this one, Matt." Sam looked toward Harrington's office. The chief was on the phone now, cradling the receiver under his chin as he scribbled notes on a pad. "Unofficially, that is," he added, giving Matt a wink. "I'll still need you to pick up my half on both the Herborth and the Rainer cases, though. I may be tied up a fair bit with Van Horn for the next few days at least."

"So when are you going to fill me in on things?" Matt asked, straightening the contents of the file.

"Tomorrow morning. But listen, Matt, you have to promise me you won't talk to anyone about Van Horn. Especially to Charlene. She's the last person who can know we're consulting a psychic. If she gets wind of this, you can bet she'll have the entire front page of the *Herald* plastered with the story, and Van Horn will drop the case like a hot potato."

"Mum's the word, Sammy."

Sam nodded approvingly, but at the same time worried about how far Charlene Evans, the *Herald*'s leading reporter and Matt's latest conquest, would go for a tip on the Munroe case.

"Tremaine."

Sam's head shot up. A junior officer stood in the doorway and nodded to the front of the station.

"Someone here to see you. Wouldn't give me her name, but she says it's important."

Sam feigned a puzzled look as he stood up and headed for the door because he suspected he wasn't going to be surprised by the visitor. It was just a feeling.

ALI SHIFTED AGAIN in the straight-backed chair. She lowered her arms to the cold chrome armrests and shivered. But it wasn't the metal against her skin that sent the chill through her. Rather, it was the immediate and queasy familiarity of her surroundings—buzzing phones, impatient voices, clattering typewriters and printers, and that blend of burned coffee and stale air that seemed unique to every police station she'd ever been in.

She lifted a hand to the back of her neck and massaged the tense muscles there. She took a deep breath and let it out slowly, then wiped the beads of perspiration from her face. She had to try to relax.

People bustled up and down the corridor past her. If they looked at her, she didn't notice. All that registered was the blur of the station spinning around her, the voices and phones sluggishly melting into a single yet constant hum.

She'd sat in a chair just like this one when Gary had brought her into the precinct the day of Duncan's death. It had been cold and hard, too, as unyielding and impersonal as the rest of the precinct that dark night. Her clothes had been drenched—the rain and Duncan's blood had soaked her shirt and jeans.

Closing her eyes, Ali rubbed her forehead as if this might abate the intensity of the memories. But she could still see the concern in Gary's face as he'd removed her bloodstained jacket and put his cardigan over her shoulders.

Ali exhaled and shivered again. The dull gray of the precinct walls seemed to close in on her as she gripped the chrome armrests with sweaty palms. She had to leave. She'd been wrong to think she was ready to deal with this again so soon. To cope with the memories. It was too early.

Eleven months ago, it hadn't taken much to convince her to abandon that part of her life. But then, after the shock of Duncan's death, she'd felt too numb to consider the possibility of "reading" again. Even much later, when Gary had persuaded her to help with a case concerning a missing child, she'd come up empty. After that, she'd turned down all requests for her assistance. She'd turned off everything, all links with Gary and ties with the police force.

But it was happening again. Now. With Sam Tremaine and the Munroe case. He was drawing her in, and Ali felt helpless under the intensity of that pull.

She had to get out.

Pushing away from the chair, she stood up on shaky legs. It would be easy enough just to turn and leave. But Sam's face filled her mind. There was something about his smile, about his eyes, that drew her toward him. Something she couldn't explain and something she desperately wished was not there.

She began pacing.

Through the reinforced glass of the station's main doors, a patch of sunlight washed the floor of the front foyer. If she could make it to that bright blur, she could make it outside. And once outside, she could forget she'd ever agreed to assist Sam Tremaine with his case.

WHEN SAM PAUSED to glance through the glass barrier that separated the side corridor from the main offices, Ali was pacing the hall like a caged animal. He could see the tension in her rigid shoulders and in her stride. But as she turned, he was once again struck by her softness—a softness that seemed foreign to the harsh sterility of the station.

So she'd come, after all. Somehow he'd felt she would, but after what he'd seen last Friday as Ali had turned Jacquie's ring around her finger, he was reluctant to label the feeling as cop's sixth sense. Perhaps it was just that he'd hoped she'd come. Hoped she would at least call.

It was when Ali turned the second time that she saw Sam behind the glass partition. She stopped abruptly, as if startled, and he watched a tentative smile start to form on her lips. Nodding to her, he reached for the door.

"I wasn't sure you'd still be here," Ali admitted as Sam ushered her from the corridor and closed the door to the din of the station.

"Just doing some clearing up. So what brings you here? I thought you hated precincts." He smiled, hoping to ease the anxiety that was deeply etched in her face.

"I do." Her voice was little more than a hesitant whisper. She brushed back a stray wisp of hair and turned to look at him. "But I thought I should see you."

Sam nodded. "Would you like to sit down? Someplace a little more private perhaps?"

"I suppose, yes."

"So, what's on your mind?" he asked, leading her through the wing, hoping she didn't notice the ogling stares from several of the officers behind their desks.

"Well, it's just an off-chance idea," she said as they rounded the hallway of interrogation rooms. "I don't even know if I'd get anywhere with it, to tell you the truth. But after you left on Friday, I got to thinking about Jacquie's ring. About how removed it was from the murder, from what really happened that night. And I just kept thinking that there had to be something else. Something else for us to look at."

Sam held open the door to one of the hollow, uninviting interrogation rooms and ushered Ali in.

"Anyway, I ruled out the possibility of walking through the crime scene itself. As far as my abilities are concerned, by now it's more than likely lost any connection to the murder. So really, the only option left to us is the murder weapon. Since she was suffocated, then perhaps there was a pillow...."

Sam couldn't suppress the slight smile that crept to the corners of his lips. Ali had been thinking along the same lines he had for the past three days—thinking like a cop. "Hold that thought, Ali," he said, holding up one finger and then heading down the hall to the detectives' wing. When he returned with the two pillows, Ali was sitting on the edge of one of the metal chairs. She had pulled it up to the table and was staring at her hands, folded together in front of her. She flinched when Sam closed the heavy door. There was definitely more to her dislike of precincts than she was letting on, he thought.

He tossed the pillows onto the table. "Looks like we were working on the same angle. Does that make me psychic or something?"

The tension in Ali's shoulders eased visibly and she smiled.

"Now I realize this is a long shot," he explained. "I know about metal objects—you know, being easier to take readings from—and I just want you to understand that I'm not expecting any miracles." He pushed the pillows toward her but she didn't reach for them right away. Instead, she leaned forward and rested her arms on the battered table.

Her lips broke into one of her strained smiles, but its sincerity was obvious. "I'm impressed, Detective Tremaine."

Sam shrugged. "Just a little weekend reading. I like to keep abreast of things. So—" he pulled up a chair "—how can I help?"

Ali shook her head. "You can't, Sam. If there's something here, I'll find it. If there's nothing...I'd have to say that the likelihood of my helping with this case was dwindling fast."

She fell silent. Just reached for the first pillow, slipped it from the plastic bag and ran her slender fingers along its surface. Sam saw them tremble once or twice just before she closed her hands on one of the sides.

For what seemed like five minutes or more, Sam sat quietly, watching Ali's expression darken. He could think of no other word to describe the shadow that passed over her face as she clutched the pillow. Her brow creased, her lips pursed, and her eyes, those silvery eyes, grew wider and darker as she stared beyond him.

Only when he was about to break the dead silence did she finally speak.

"It's not very clear. Dark. Blurred." She blinked, but her eyes never strayed from the unknown plain she peered into. "It's Jacqueline's bedroom. The lamp from the nightstand is on the floor. Must have been knocked down. And the sheets are all pulled back...crumpled up at the end of the bed. There's a pillow on the floor."

Sam watched as Ali's knuckles whitened from her grip.

"He's got the other pillow in his hand. Kneeling on the bed, holding it. And he's got Jacqueline's wrist in his other hand. She's pinned beneath him."

Sam swallowed hard. Nothing, not all the books he'd read this weekend, nor all the case studies he'd reviewed, could have prepared him for the chilling portrait of Jacquie's murder laid out for him now.

His voice was only a whisper. "Can you see Jacquie?"

Ali took a few shallow breaths and nodded slowly. "She's on the bed. Staring up at him. Her eyes are wide, glassy. She'd been crying. Her cheek is red and there's a smear of blood on her chin. I think...I think it's from her lip. He hit her and that's why her lip is bleeding. That's why her cheek is red. She's not struggling now. But she was."

Ali shook her head. "His heart...I can feel his heart racing. He was struggling with her, fighting, holding her down. But she's quiet now. Limp. Her body...her head...so limp. It falls to one side as he reaches for her neck. He's...he's feeling for a pulse. Pressing his fingers against her neck, moving her head, touching her neck again."

Ali shook her head again, her eyes squinting.

"What is it, Ali? What do you see?"

"Gloves. Black leather. Why is he wearing gloves unless he knew he was going to—"

"Ali." Sam fought the urge to touch her, unwilling to jeopardize the fragile connection she seemed to have established. "Ali, try to go back. Can you see how it happened? How did they wind up in the bedroom?"

She was silent for a long time, then gave a slight nod. "He followed her in here—into the bedroom. They were arguing. Fighting. She tried to get away from him and he came after her. He... he hit her once with the back of his hand and that's when the lamp fell. Then he pushed her onto the bed. Now he has her pinned down."

Ali's knuckles were white now. "He's got the pillow in his hand. Jacquie is beneath him on the bed. She's trying to push him off...trying to scream, but his hand is clamped over her mouth. He's pushing her head back into the mattress, pressing against her mouth, covering her screams... his hands... black leather gloves. She's gulping in breath through his fingers. He has to keep her quiet, but she keeps resisting, keeps fighting, trying to force him off of her. And he knows if he takes his hand away, even for a second, she'll scream."

Ali shook her head forcefully now, as if trying to deny the images she was seeing.

"The whole bed is shaking. She's still trying to scream. Her eyes are wet with tears... wide with fear. She's twisting her head, trying to get away from his grip but she's powerless and he... he knows she is." Ali stopped speaking.

The soft creak of Sam's chair threatened to break the suspended silence as he leaned closer. He licked his lips.

"Ali, can you see the killer? Try to focus on him. Can you see his face at all?"

"No...no, I can't see him." Her voice was flat and distant, and her eyes glistened with tears. "I *am* the killer."

CHAPTER FIVE

"WHAT DO YOU SEE?"

Sam's voice whispered along the periphery of her awareness. Ali sensed his concern. She could feel him drawing closer to her, wanting to touch her. But she knew he wouldn't.

No one could touch her here. Not when the connection was this intense, this vivid. She was a prisoner here, on this gray and fatal plain, and there was no escape until it was over. Until she had seen all there was to see.

For now, she embraced Sam's voice. It was her only link with the reality she longed for.

"Ali, what do you see? What are you doing now?"

She took a deep breath, trying to relax, letting the vision draw her in. The fog cleared again. The grayness slipped away until only the edges of the image remained blurred. Her body tensed, her muscles tightened. And then she plunged forward once more.

The heat of the bedroom prickled along her skin. The darkness closed in around her. Long shadows convulsed across the walls and ceiling as the fallen lamp cast its strange and harsh light along one side of Jacqueline's face. Ali took another gulp of air. Beneath her, she could feel the bed rocking fiercely.

"Ali, where are you?"

"I'm on the bed. With Jacquie." Her own voice, like Sam's, sounded hollow and distant, unreachable. "She's beneath me. Fighting me." The bed continued to shake. "She's strong, but one of her arms is pinned beneath my knee and the other... she's trying to pull my hand from her mouth."

Ali looked down at the arms that pinned Jacquie to the bed. Powerful arms, muscles as taut as iron. A man's arms, and yet they felt as though they were hers. They forced Jacquie back into the mattress, bearing down on her, overpowering her. And his hands—her own now, too—were clad in tight, black leather gloves. She felt the leather, soft and slick, against her skin. And, through their suppleness, she felt Jacquie's mouth crushed beneath the pressure of her hand. Felt her struggle to breathe between the gloved fingers.

"She's frightened. She knows she's going to die. I can see it in her eyes. They're wide... desperate... staring up at me. She's jerking her head back and forth, trying to get out of my grip... trying to scream."

"Where's the pillow, Ali?"

The haze cleared a little more. The contours of Jacquie's terrified face grew sharper. Ali felt the gloved hand grappling for the pillow.

"In my other hand. I'm pulling it over... still holding Jacquie down. She won't stop struggling. I'm yanking the pillow toward her... taking my hand off her mouth and shoving the pillow over her face... covering her face with it. Covering the screams."

Ali swallowed hard.

"And she is screaming. It's muffled, but she is screaming. I can hear it through the pillow. I'm press-

ing down with both hands now. Smothering her...
killing her." Ali gasped for air herself.

"Ali, let go now. It's not you." Sam's voice pulled
her away from the horror long enough for her to take
a breath. "Let go of him, Ali. Ease back."

She felt the pressure in her head begin to slacken, the
grayness slip back around the edges of the images that
whirled before her. And she felt herself draw away,
stepping out of the killer's mind but remaining in the
room, standing in the far corner, observing.

"What about Jackie? Can you see her?" Sam
watched Ali. Her knuckles were as white as her waning complexion. But even as he resisted the urge to
touch her, to wrench the pillow from her grip, her face
changed. He watched the tension lessen to a small degree and her grip on the pillow ease.

She shook her head. "I can't...feel Jacquie anymore. She's gone."

"What's he doing? Can you follow him?"

Ali tilted her head to one side as if struggling to understand something. Another long minute passed before she spoke again. "The pillow is still in one hand.
He leans over her now, touching her face, her eyes, her
lips, her cheek. He brushes her hair from her face with
the back of his hand—fine blond hair. He brushes it a
few times...caressess it. His hand moves to her neck.
He's feeling for a pulse...but there isn't one. He just
stares at her...looks at her on the bed. Her nightgown is bunched up along one leg and...he reaches
down to pull it straight."

Almost savagely Sam wiped at the tear that threatened to roll down his cheek. Jacquie.

In the deathly silence of the room, he watched Ali as she seemed to take another step into a world he could only imagine.

"He's...he's looking for something. I don't know what. He checks her hands, and then turns away from the bed. Looking at the nightstand. A box. On the nightstand there's a small box—a jeweler's box. It's covered with dark blue velvet. He picks it up and opens it."

"What's inside, Ali?"

"A bracelet...glittering. But he doesn't take it out. He just stares at it. Diamonds, I think. I can't tell—he's closed the box. He's looking back at Jacquie. He tosses the pillow back onto the bed."

"What's he done with the bracelet, Ali?"

"I think he slipped the box into his pocket."

Ali's back pressed rigidly against the frame of the chair, and her hands still clenched the pillow. Perspiration shimmered on her forehead, a vein in her temple had swelled and now pulsed beneath her pale skin. She hadn't looked nearly this drained after their first session.

Sam glanced up at the wall clock. Six-fifteen. For almost an hour he'd sat here with Ali—listening to the vivid details of Jacquie's brutal death as if he himself had stood by helplessly. He rubbed his face and let out a long breath before looking at Ali again.

Leaning forward, he laid his hand over hers, surprised at its coldness. Eventually, as he felt her grip loosen, Sam drew the pillow from her grasp and pushed it farther down the table. Ali closed her eyes. Her hand trembled once in his, but Sam didn't let it go until she opened her eyes.

"Can I get you anything, Ali? Coffee? Some water?"

She nodded slowly and wiped her forehead with the back of one hand. "Water would be great, thanks."

"I'll be right back."

The detectives' wing was deserted now. The lights in Harrington's office were off, and even Nancy's chair sat vacant, Sam noticed as he crossed the wing to the water cooler. In the fringes of his perception, he was aware of the noises around him—the buzzing phones, the traffic on the boulevard outside, people talking in the precinct—but his thoughts were still haunted by what he'd just witnessed.

Equipped with the knowledge extracted from the books he'd read, he could find no rational explanation for what had happened in the interrogation room where Ali sat now, pale and exhausted. If he hadn't seen it with his own eyes, heard Ali's voice whisper every detail of Jacquie's murder as if she herself had committed the crime, he never would have believed it possible. And yet, in spite of the lack of explanation, she'd done it. Ali had suffered the killer's brutality as if she'd been there herself.

But at what expense?

Sam saw his own hand tremble slightly as he held the paper cup under the spout and watched bubbles rise to the top of the cooler.

It was no wonder Ali had broken her contacts with the police force in New York. And he understood why she'd been so reluctant to assist him on Jacquie's case. In fact, even now Sam felt a pang of guilt as he turned back to the interrogation room. If each case she accepted entailed what he'd just seen her go through, then whatever it was Ali Van Horn possessed, it was no gift. It was a curse.

She turned to him when he stepped into the room, and again Sam was shocked at the exhaustion in her face. She massaged her temple with one hand and accepted the cup of water with the other.

"How are you feeling?"

Ali shrugged and gave a half smile. "I'll be all right." She reached for her purse and pulled out a bottle of pills. Snapping off the cap, Ali shook out a single blue capsule and swallowed it with a mouthful of water.

"Are you sure?" Sam asked.

Ali nodded. "Honest, I'll be fine. It's just a migraine. Goes with the territory."

"You get migraines every time you do a reading?"

"Usually, yeah." Ali shrugged again as if to minimize what seemed an unjust payoff for the work she'd done. "It's not that bad, Sam, really. I'm used to them."

Still concerned, Sam reached across the table for the pillow, its sides creased from the intensity of Ali's grip. "I take it there's nothing more we can get from this?"

She shook her head as Sam stuffed both pillows back into the evidence bag. "I really doubt it. I'm surprised I got as far as I did, given the object and the time that's passed." Ali rested her elbows on the table and rubbed her temple again. "A good coach always helps. It makes a big difference when there's someone there to lead me. It keeps me on track. You've been doing your research, Sam."

"Goes with the job." He sat down across from Ali and returned her smile.

"I'm still impressed—coming from a skeptic. I wasn't expecting any kind of encouragement during the session."

Sam held her gaze, watching the color slowly return to her cheeks. "How's the headache?"

"It'll pass." She nodded and looked around the interrogation room with the same trapped expression he'd seen on her face when he'd found her pacing the main corridor. "If you don't mind, though, I think I'd rather be outside. I need some air."

"I'll walk you to your car," Sam offered, handing Ali her purse and opening the door.

Outside, a breeze had picked up from the west, drawing with it cooler air from the lake. Miniature whirlwinds of dust danced across the station's parking lot and disappeared behind the crumbling building. Sam walked Ali past the patrol cars to her Cherokee, parked at the far end of the lot.

"I'm sorry I haven't given you more to go on, Sam." Ali turned to him when they reached her car. "I'd hoped there might have been something more definite."

He caught her brief smile and recognized the apology behind it. "Well, I wouldn't say we've hit a complete dead end. There *is* the bracelet. That's something we didn't know about before," Sam said, burying his hands in his pockets. "And there's still Cassie, Jacqueline's daughter. With any luck we'll be able to meet with her before the end of the week."

Ali dug out a set of keys from her purse and unlocked the Jeep, but she didn't get in. She leaned back against the side of the vehicle and Sam was immediately aware of how much more at ease she seemed now, free from the confines of the precinct.

"Listen, Sam, I'd hate to see you get your hopes up about the girl. There may be nothing there, you realize."

"I understand."

"I just don't want you getting too optimistic. I got lucky in there tonight. There may be nothing else I can do for you." She shook her head and looked down as she kicked at a stone. "I really don't think you should abandon any other investigative means you may have going at this point. I didn't exactly have an exceptional success rate on the last few cases. That, coupled with the fact that a fair bit of time has passed since Jacqueline's death, isn't exactly a formula for success."

"Well, after what I saw in there today, I have to admit maybe I'm a little more hopeful than I have a right to be. But I'm still willing to try. One step at a time. Maybe things'll come together, maybe they won't. As long as you don't mind trying, I'm willing to arrange for anything you need."

He watched Ali and waited for her nod. He wouldn't have blamed her if she'd turned him down, he realized now as she attempted a reassuring smile—especially after what he'd witnessed in the interrogation room.

But he hoped she wouldn't.

"You may be in for a long haul, Sam. Cases like this can drag on for weeks before I come up with anything concrete. Sometimes a link is established almost immediately. Other times... I can go through a whole series of readings before I link with the perpetrator. And—" she shrugged "—there are times when it just doesn't happen at all."

"So what are your feelings about the case right now?"

Ali shook her head and looked across the parking lot. A breeze whispered past her cheek and played with a stray wisp of hair. "I don't know. I picked up on the killer's emotions during the reading. That in itself is promising. But... it wasn't as strong as it usually is. I couldn't stay with him. And I couldn't get into his head. I couldn't tell what he was thinking—only feeling."

She looked down at the brass key ring she rubbed in her hands. "It's been a long time for me, Sam. I... I haven't been any good on a case in almost a year."

"I'm not expecting miracles, Ali."

"Good." The corners of her mouth lifted into a soft smile. "I don't think you're about to get any."

"Why did you quit, Ali? Was it the Farthing case?"

She looked so taken aback, so violated, that Sam immediately regretted having brought up the case. It was the last case in the file Harrington had given him on Ali, a case that hadn't been closed. At least not that the brief records showed.

"What do you know about the Farthing case?" she asked.

"Nothing. I mean, not much. No details." Sam heard his own voice, defensive and apologetic. "I'm sorry, Ali. It's just... I know it was the last case you worked on."

"The last *successful* case," she corrected him.

"Was it the reason you stopped working with the NYPD?"

"There were other reasons."

She seemed to withdraw then, the congeniality of only moments ago shattered. She shifted her position against the Jeep as if to leave.

"Listen, Ali, I'm sorry. I didn't mean to dredge up any bad memories. I know this can't be easy for you, and believe me, I understand your reluctance to help with this case."

"You couldn't begin to understand the half of it, Sam."

He shrugged. What else could he do? He'd witnessed the physical toll the session had taken on her, but there was no comprehending the true price she paid for those visions.

"No, you're right. I can't," he said. "And I wish I could tell you we don't need you on this case. That we can close it through some other means. But right now we have absolutely nothing else to go on. Right now we need you, Ali."

He caught her gaze again and held it. "I need you, but most of all, Jacquie's kid needs you. If Peter Munroe isn't responsible for Jacquie's death, then we have to close this case even sooner. Cassie needs to be with her father. Especially now. And until he's cleared of suspicion..."

Ali shook her head. "I can't give you the answers you want, Sam."

"I'm not asking for any. I'm only looking for a different angle. And I think you're the only one who can provide that."

Sam gave her a smile he hoped was reassuring, and waited for her eventual nod. It came. In the glow of the late-afternoon sun, her skin appeared to have regained its natural color. Her eyes lost their former intensity and her lips curved into a more relaxed smile.

All weekend he'd thought of her. All weekend her face had filled his mind. He'd blamed it on his obsession with Jacquie's murder, on being presented with a new avenue of possibilities at last. But only now, standing next to Ali, did he realize that it wasn't just the investigation.

Right now Jacquie's case was the farthest thing from his mind.

"Can I buy you dinner, Ali?"

She was shaking her head even before he'd finished asking. "I don't think that would be such a good idea, Sam." But he knew her reaction was too immediate to be anything but defensive.

"Ali, after what you just went through in there, it's the very least I can do. We'll call it business and charge it to the department. We don't even have to discuss the case."

Ali held Sam's gaze. Then her lips parted in a hesitant smile and she nodded. "Okay. I suppose dinner would be all right."

"Great. There's a pub just around the corner. A bit of a watering hole for the guys at the station, but since it's Monday, it shouldn't be very busy."

IT WAS NINE O'CLOCK by the time Ali and Sam walked out of Morty's, leaving the half-empty pub to the dozen baseball fans who warmed the stools in front of the bar's television. With the end of the day came an end to the blistering heat. The gentle breeze that had whispered up from the lake earlier had mounted into a cool wind that threatened to stir up a storm before morning.

Stepping out onto the sidewalk, Ali shivered against the chill that tingled along her skin. But she had no more than a second to regret her lack of a jacket before she felt Sam bring his own coat gently to her shoulders. The smell of worn leather mingled with a subtle trace of cologne, and Ali welcomed it as much as the warmth of the jacket.

"So, you were telling me about the accident," Sam said. "You said you were twenty-one when it happened?"

Ali nodded. She wasn't certain why questions that usually made her uneasy seemed natural when coming from Sam.

Through a haze of cigarette smoke, Sam had led her to a booth at the back of Morty's, away from the cheering ball fans at the bar. And by the time dinner had come and gone, they had exhausted all the safe topics of conversation—books, movies, music. There had been no more than a moment's lull in their dialogue before Sam opened with his first question on Ali's background, as though he had waited all evening to ask her.

And as the questions came, Ali had found herself surprisingly open to answering them. Perhaps it was the glass of wine she'd had with their meal. Or perhaps it had something to do with the familiarity she felt in the surroundings of the small sports bar, she thought now as she fell in step with Sam's easy stride.

She'd spent hours at O'Reilley's, a similar Mets-devoted bar that catered to some of the men of the twenty-first precinct. And her time there hadn't always been business with Gary Breckner. Maybe at first, but when Duncan had entered her life, her visits to O'Reilley's had become more frequent and far more personal.

It seemed a world away, a lifetime ago.

Now, walking outside, away from the smokiness of the bar, Ali knew it had been more than the comfort of Morty's that had made her open up to Sam. There'd been more to the closeness she felt between them, to the pull she felt toward him as they'd laughed and talked through the evening. And there'd been something inexplicable in the almost instinctive way she'd nearly reached out to take his hand when they'd stepped out of the bar only moments ago.

She buried her hands in the pockets of her shorts, resisting the strange urge to slip her hand into Sam's as if it were Duncan walking beside her down this quiet street so far away from everything she'd known before—from everything that had hurt.

"You mentioned it was a car accident...." Sam's voice reminded her of where she was. Ali nodded, watching their shadows creep back from the glow of the street lamps.

"It wasn't anything terribly dramatic, really. Just a patch of black ice on a back road in northern Vermont. We were coming back from a ski trip during study week. My friend Cheri was driving. We hit the ice, the car did a couple of three-sixties and ended up nose-first in a ten-foot snowbank. I cracked my head, not to mention the glass on the passenger-side window, and that was that."

"So then what? You were in a coma or something?"

Ali laughed, momentarily surprised at the unfamiliar sound. "No, I'm afraid that, despite the Hollywood stereotypes, a coma is not necessarily a prerequisite for acquiring psychic abilities." She saw Sam shrug. "No, my recovery wasn't nearly as glamorous—or painless. Two broken ribs, seventy-eight stitches to my face, not to mention some minor reconstructive surgery. I wasn't a pretty sight for a few months."

"And then what? You just started 'seeing' things?"

"It took some time," she replied. "At first I figured it was the painkillers I was on. I started having these visions, like daydreams or something, almost hallucinatory. Images entirely unrelated to my own life, of people I'd never seen before, places I'd never been. And yet there was always a weird familiarity about them. After I left the hospital they became even more frequent. And then increasingly violent."

Ali still remembered the foreboding brutality and rage that had lingered after each vision. An aftertaste, almost, of the crime she'd witnessed before snapping out of it in a cold sweat.

"It just went on for weeks, until finally, I realized that unless I got some help I'd have to quit school. I went to a counselor on campus, and eventually we started making the connections. Once we came to terms with the fact that these waking dreams—'blackout visions,' we called them—were in fact images of real crimes that had already taken place, crimes the counselor had read about in the papers, we went to the police."

Ali felt the gentle pressure of Sam's hand on her elbow as he guided her around the corner of the precinct and toward the parking lot. "It wasn't easy at first—working with the police. We were met with the usual skepticism, the typical disbelief, and even suspicion I was somehow connected with the crimes I described. And then someone took a chance and believed in me."

"Gary Breckner?"

Ali glanced at Sam. "You've certainly been doing your homework, Detective Tremaine."

He shrugged. "Policy, I'm afraid. You didn't think we'd approach you without checking your credentials?"

"No, I suppose not. It's just...well, being tossed from one case to the next, with different investigative teams, I hardly expect to walk into any precinct a complete stranger anymore."

"So you worked with Breckner a lot, then?"

Ali nodded. "He's a good man. He always believed in me. That was important in the beginning. But most of all, he's not afraid of me."

"Afraid of you? What do you mean?"

"Come on, Sam. I think you know what I mean." They'd reached her Cherokee and Ali turned to face him. In the shaft of light from a street lamp, she saw a muscle flex in his jaw. She saw his quick black-brown eyes dart away from hers and then back again, and she watched him shift his weight from one foot to the other. "You've been on edge all night. Feeling a little vulnerable perhaps?"

"I don't know what you mean."

"Sam, I don't need psychic ability to see how threatened you feel by me. I've seen it enough times in the past. But honestly there's really no need for it. You can relax." She curbed the desire to reach out and touch him to emphasize her point. "Trust me, Sam—I can't read your mind."

He crossed his arms over his chest and turned the full force of his dark gaze on her as if searching for the proof he seemed to need. "Then how did you know what I was thinking?"

"Like I said, I see it all the time. I walk into a precinct, onto a crime scene, anywhere my reputation is recognized, and I see it. People are afraid. Believe me, after you've been stuck in a stuffy interrogation room with half a dozen cops, scared to death you're going to reach into their minds and pull out their darkest secrets or their deepest sexual fantasies or maybe just the fact that they yelled at their wife before coming in for their shift that morning, you get to recognize the signs pretty fast."

Ali watched Sam study her. No, she couldn't read his mind, but there was something about the way he looked at her—so uncertain, so cautious—that made the corners of her mouth curl into an amused smile.

"So you really can't tell what I'm thinking?"

"Really." She nodded. "Reading minds is not something I was ever keen on developing. In fact, over the years, I've done everything possible to keep the potential of that ability suppressed."

"Yeah, but . . . that's what you do, isn't it? Get into people's heads?"

"Sure. Unfortunately it's not the minds of people like you and me I often get into. It's the criminal mind—minds that harbor anger, hatred, the violent rage that carries them through their crime.

"I act like a receptor to their passions. When I walk onto a scene or handle an object related to the crime, I pick up on these residual destructive energies. I can often relive the crime in great detail—as you witnessed earlier. And once I've done that, I sometimes develop a link with the assailant. I get a fix on them and then they just . . . they kind of stick to me. Sometimes I'm able to see where they go, where they live, the places they frequent.

"It's difficult to describe. There's no single explanation for the way these things work. Different people have different abilities. Some have dreams about events that have yet to occur, others work strictly from past occurrences, while others still only link psychically in real time. Each person learns to hone one or more of these abilities and direct them in their own way.''

Ali noted Sam's attentive expression. ''It varies a lot from person to person. For me, it even varies from reading to reading. I don't have premonitions or images of future events. Mostly I connect with heightened emotions from situations or crimes that have already taken place. From there a real-time link may or may not develop. It's never the same twice.''

''And you never have any kind of connection with the victim?''

''Once. In the beginning.'' Ali shook her head, remembering the horror she'd experienced during one of her first cases with Gary. ''It wasn't anything I'd want to go through again, believe me. I think that's why I channel into the attacker rather than the victim—a kind of self-defense mechanism. The fear of going through the victim's fate instinctively pushes me toward the attacker, the force in control. I also pick up much stronger images when fed by more hostile energies than those of desperation. They're clearer somehow, sharper, more vivid.''

Ali pulled Sam's jacket more closely around her, shivering once against the cool air whispering over her exposed legs. ''Often the link with the perpetrator lasts only long enough to give me an image of what went on during the crime. And sometimes that brief link is enough—sometimes it's as simple as the victim calling out the attacker's name. Other times, the connection can last for weeks.''

''And after they've been caught? What then? Are they still 'with' you?''

"No, it kind of dies after that. I usually only connect with the criminal during acts of intense and violent emotion. So, once they're convicted, if that's the case, the connection seems to fade."

"And if the criminal is released?"

"Fortunately I haven't had to deal with anything like that yet."

Sam held Ali's stare long enough that she felt compelled to look away.

"So, it could be possible for you to link with Jacquie's killer beyond what you did tonight, develop a connection with him to the point where you can see where he lives and works?"

"It's too early to tell, Sam. It may develop in time or may take several more readings from other objects related to the murder before I'm able to give you anything more. Or it may not happen at all."

"How will you know?"

Ali shrugged and looked past Sam. In spite of her desire to help him now, she wasn't looking forward to the possibility of psychically linking with the man who'd smothered the life out of Jacqueline Munroe.

"If it happens, it happens. But don't worry, Sam, you'll be the first to know," she assured him before opening the door of the Cherokee.

"It's getting cooler," Sam observed, as if sensing the shiver that Ali had attempted to suppress. "Why don't you return the jacket some other time?"

"You're sure?"

Sam nodded, and Ali wondered why saying goodnight to him should suddenly feel so awkward. A breeze played at his hair and she watched him brush it back.

"Listen, Sam, there's not going to be a problem keeping my involvement with this case quiet, is there? I mean, if the local television station or the paper was to get hold of this... I just don't want to run those risks again."

Four years ago, it had taken an actual threat to her own life, a situation that culminated in a suspect's standoff with police outside her apartment, to convince the NYPD to put an absolute ban on any statements involving Ali's participation in a case during its investigation. And Gary had always done his best to keep her shielded from the press, to keep her name out of potentially harmful situations even after the fact.

"If Jacquie's killer finds out about my assistance..."

"I've already spoken with the chief, Ali. We're keeping this as quiet as we can, especially given the nature of the case. Jacquie's father is a prominent resident of Danby. This case is hot news for the media, but I promise you, Ali, your involvement will be treated as confidentially as possible."

She could see the sincerity in Sam's eyes. She could hear it in his voice. "All right," she said finally, taking a breath and hopping up into the Jeep. "We'll see what happens from here. I'll wait for your call about Jacqueline's daughter."

She closed the door and rolled down the window as Sam stepped up to the side of the vehicle.

"I may be able to arrange for something as soon as tomorrow afternoon, if that's all right."

"Just give me a call. And thanks for dinner."

"It was my pleasure." The easy smile that curved his lips played at the corners of his eyes, as well. Again she felt an urge to touch him, to put a hand on the strong forearm that rested on the frame of the driver's window.

Instead, Ali turned the key in the ignition. She looked at him one more time and arranged his jacket over her shoulders. "I'll talk to you soon, then. Good night, Sam."

"Good night, Ali."

As she pulled out of the Danby precinct parking lot, Ali knew Sam was watching her.

CHAPTER SIX

"Jamie shouldn't have called you, Gary. I'm sorry." Ali wound the phone cord around her fingers and glanced through the open blinds to the quiet street. "There's nothing to worry about."

"Ali, it wasn't only Jamie who called." Gary's gruff voice held that impatient tone of concern she was only too familiar with.

When she'd picked up the phone minutes ago, Gary Breckner was the last person she'd expected to hear from. It had been weeks since they'd spoken, months since she'd last seen him. Yet, one concerned phone call from Jamie and here he was, looking out for her again. Even on a one-week vacation at the cottage, he couldn't shrug off his concern.

"I also got a call from the chief of the Danby police, Ed Harrington," Gary went on. "He sounds pretty serious about getting your help on this homicide of theirs."

"Gary, really, it's a straightforward case. I can handle it."

There was a pause, and in the brief silence Ali could hear Gary's two boys laughing in the background. "Al, listen to me, you couldn't even handle that case involving a missing child a few months ago. Do you really think you're ready for this again?"

She didn't need to answer that one.

"Well, there's no sense in warning you. You're going to do what you're going to do, anyway. I just hope you don't get in too far."

"How are the boys?" Ali asked, recognizing the need for a topic change.

"Tearing up the beach and glad to be out of school."

"And Diane?"

"She's fine. Ali, listen to me, you have to promise you'll be careful, all right?"

"Gary, trust me."

"I do trust you. I just don't like it when you're working with a bunch of cops who don't know what it's like."

"Gary—"

"Al, I'm serious. It's not like you've got Duncan or me around to look out for you if things get too deep?"

"I think I can manage."

There was another long pause, and she wondered if she'd been able to convince him at last.

"Do you have your gun?"

Ali felt a shiver go through her. She never liked the idea of owning a gun. But after her life was threatened working on the Burack incident, Duncan had bought her a compact semiautomatic as a gift. She didn't know what she'd initially thought the box had contained, but Ali remembered the icy queasiness that had swept through her when she'd unwrapped it.

"Gary—"

"Do you have it?"

"Yes, but I don't think—"

"Just as long as you have it. That's all I need to hear."

He paused, and Ali imagined him standing at the window of the beachfront cottage she'd visited a few times with Duncan. The last weekend she'd been there, she'd noticed a photo of Duncan and her on the windowsill overlooking the lake. She guessed it was this photo Gary was looking at now.

"Listen, Al, I promised Duncan I'd look out for you. You know that. But there's more to it than that."

"Gary, you don't have to—"

"Ali, I'm the one who got you into this investigative shit to begin with. I'd never forgive myself if anything happened to you because of it."

"Nothing will happen, Gary. Everything's being kept as quiet as possible. They assured me of that."

"Promise me you'll call if things get out of hand." There was an unmistakable older-brother tone in his voice, and Ali knew Gary's insistence went deeper than his promise to Duncan. If it hadn't been for Gary, she never would have agreed to assist with as many cases as she had over the years—nor would she have ever gained the reputation that had directed the Danby police to her. "If you need me, call. You've got the number at the cottage?"

"Yes."

"Good."

Ali couldn't tell who was more reluctant to hang up the phone when they finally said goodbye. She knew Gary missed Duncan. She knew that every time he saw her or spoke to her, he felt a certain pang of guilt for not having been there with his partner that night eleven months ago.

But for now, as Ali's hand lingered on the receiver, she felt a sudden and familiar emptiness wash through her, as if Gary's voice alone had transported her back to New York, back to Duncan and to the undying memories.

SAM RUBBED his eyes and looked back at the cold blue glow of the microfilm machine. He lifted a hand from the controls and massaged the stiff muscles along the back of his neck before scanning ahead several more issues of the *New York Times*.

He'd sat in the cool basement of the Danby library for more than an hour now and was still no farther ahead in his search. His eyes skimmed quickly over the fresh screen, searching for names, for photos. Unless he had more to go on, he could be here all evening.

From the file Harrington had given him last week, Sam had gleaned very few details or dates surrounding the Farthing investigation—the case that had obviously upset Ali enough for her to discontinue her work with the NYPD. All the file indicated was that the case had been the last one she'd worked on and that it had gone from a double-homicide to a hushed-up internal investigation. Sam had even called New York this morning, hoping to gain a little more insight into the case, but the call had proved useless—Gary Breckner was on vacation until next week.

Sam exhaled a quiet groan and reeled forward another two editions, promising himself that this was definitely the last film he was looking through. He searched the headlines. And then, just as he was about to throw in the towel, the name jumped out at him. There it was: Gabriel Farthing.

He adjusted the zoom lens and leaned forward.

The facts were few but still enough for a *Times* reporter to stretch the story on the police shooting eleven months ago to three columns. The killing was thought to be directly related to the eight-week investigation of an earlier homicide—the murder of Gabriel Farthing. Farthing, a prominent industrialist, had been found dead in his Manhattan penthouse, and with only broken leads and time against them, it was thought that the NYPD's investigation had come to a dead end.

Until the shooting of Detective Duncan Carvello.

Sam read through the rest of the article. Another familiar name leapt out—Detective Gary Breckner. His eyes swallowed the text of the report, extracting what little there was. Carvello had been assisting Breckner on the Farthing homicide for almost six weeks before the shooting. Following an anonymous lead, Carvello had ended up in the garment district where he was shot by an unknown assailant and later pronounced dead at the hospital. No direct link had been made between the Carvello murder and the Farthing homicide at the time of the shooting, although a statement from police later indicated there was a connection.

Sam's eyes darted from this last allegation to the two photographs at the top of the screen. He worked the dial at the base of the time-worn microfilm reader, struggling with the focus. From the first frame, an unsmiling Gabriel Farthing glared back at him, his corpulent features oozing financial gluttony.

Adjusting the blowup further, Sam stared at the second photo. As the picture slid into focus and he read the caption beneath, Sam realized he was not looking at Duncan Carvello's face for the first time. He'd seen that smile before, those animated eyes, that alert expression.

Piercing through the silence of the library, Sam's watch beeped insistently, bringing him back with a start.

Seven o'clock.

He cursed under his breath as he fumbled with the reel of microfilm. He'd promised Ali this morning over the phone that he'd pick her up at quarter-past seven. Even with traffic lights in his favor, he'd still be pushing it to get there on time.

Leaving the air-conditioned library, Sam was struck by the stifling heat of early evening. In moments he'd rolled down the car windows and nosed the Bronco into traffic heading north.

Several times throughout the day, Sam had recalled his hurried telephone conversation with Ali that morning. Even now, as he overtook several cars, he remembered how out of sorts Ali had sounded when he'd told her about the meeting Matt and Nancy had arranged with Jacquie's daughter. He'd even been about to ask Ali if she had changed her mind about seeing Cassie, but fearing she might say yes, he'd kept the phone call brief.

Now, as he drove across town, he hoped that Ali hadn't changed her mind, that she wasn't having second thoughts about her involvement in Jacquie's case.

For three days he had thought of Ali and little else. Remembering their dinner the other night, the way he had managed to bring a smile to her face, to make her laugh, Sam realized it had been a long time since he'd felt the way he had when he was with Ali. He could still see her leaning against the Cherokee as they'd talked, the soft glow of the street lamp playing on her honey-colored skin. And he remembered how he had wanted to kiss her right there in the precinct parking lot.

Then this morning, when he'd heard her voice over the phone and felt his heart quicken, Sam knew for certain there was more than Jacquie's case behind his desire to see Ali again. A day had never seemed longer.

He was only five minutes late when he steered the Bronco into the Nolan driveway. Ali was already at the front door, switching on the porch light and locking up behind her. She wore a pair of cotton pants and a simple silk top that flowed over the slender curves of her body. Her hair was drawn back from her face with a fabric band, but gentle curls escaped to frame her delicate features.

Sam climbed out the Bronco and approached her. "Sorry I'm late. I lost track of the time," he confessed, taking in Ali's casual beauty as she pulled the door shut behind her.

"That's all right." Her smile assured him that five minutes made little difference to her. "I had a phone call, anyway. So, how are you doing, Sam?"

He shrugged, surprised at the sudden restlessness he felt when she lifted those gray eyes to his. "Fine. I'm fine, thanks."

"Your jacket," she said, handing him the leather bomber jacket he'd lent her. "With many thanks."

"No problem." He took it from her and draped it over his arm, catching the delicate trace of her perfume rising from its folds.

"I brought my own this time," she said, following him to his car. "The weather forecast doesn't look too promising. They're calling for quite the thunderstorm tonight. I hope you've got your windows closed at home."

He cast her a defeated look as he unlocked the passenger door. "You couldn't have told me that earlier, could you?"

"Sorry." She shrugged, and Sam caught her smile before he walked around the Bronco and hopped in.

"So, how have you been?" he asked, backing out of the drive. "You look tired." He'd noticed the shadows beneath her eyes when he'd greeted her. Her face was pale and her smile strained.

"It's nothing. I just haven't been sleeping well the past couple of nights." She looked out the open side window, and Sam studied her profile for a moment.

"Yeah, well, this heat wave's getting to everyone lately, I guess," Sam offered.

"It's not the heat."

Out of the corner of his eye, Sam saw her shake her head, and once he'd maneuvered the Bronco into the southbound traffic, he met her gaze.

"No, it's not the heat," she repeated.

"It's not this case, I hope."

"I'm . . . I'm not sure." She still didn't look at him. "It could be. I really don't know yet. I just keep having the same dream night after night. Voices, sounds, smells, places that seem familiar but that I've never seen before."

Sam stopped at a light. "You think they might be related to the case?"

"Could be," Ali said. "I can't tell yet. They're disjointed, but definitely nothing I can associate with my own surroundings."

"Well, what are they about? Would it help to talk about them?" Sam followed the flow of traffic across the Weston overpass, avoiding the downtown traffic.

"It's nothing, Sam. Really. Sometimes I get dreams that have some relation to a case I'm working on. Other times they're just dreams. They probably don't mean anything. They just wake me up sometimes, that's all." She paused. "So, Matt's going to meet us there?"

Sam nodded, respecting Ali's wish to change the subject. "Yeah, he'll be there. He and one of the other detectives set up the meeting, so he wanted to be there."

Ali looked out the side window again and remained silent for the rest of the drive to the outskirts of the city.

When they pulled into Marilyn Ballantyne's drive fifteen minutes later, the Skylark was already parked out front. Sam backed the Bronco in beside it and ushered Ali up the porch steps.

"Listen, Sam—" She stopped him when they reached the front door "—I hope you're not expecting too much."

"We already went through this the other night, Ali." He gave her a quick smile. "Believe me, I'm not expecting anything. Hoping, maybe. I just want you to get what you can, all right? I'm not expecting miracles."

Ali's smile assured him she understood his position, and he reached down to rap against the tin panel of the screen door.

"If nothing else, I can guarantee you're about to meet the cutest five-year-old you've ever laid eyes on."

ALI INHALED DEEPLY, trying to relax. She pulled up a hard wooden chair next to the child's bed, which had been ornately covered in pink and lace. From the moment Cassie had looked up wide-eyed at Ali, there'd been a hesitancy in her innocent gaze, and Ali guessed that the five-year-old had already met her share of strangers since her mother's death, all claiming to want to help.

Ali looked at the girl again. Cassie lingered by the closed bedroom door, uncertain of her new visitor. Children were rarely easy reads, and as Ali watched her look up from her hands, clutched together in front of her, she realized Cassie Munroe was no exception to the rule.

Marilyn Ballantyne, Jacqueline's mother, had greeted them at the door with a definite air of forced hospitality that only grew colder when she saw Sam. She'd held the door for them while brief introductions were made, and after the woman's frigid handshake, Ali noted Sam's apologetic glance as they stepped into the lavish split-level bungalow.

Now, with Cassie nervously eyeing her from the other side of the small bedroom, Ali wished that Sam had joined her in spite of her request to be alone with the child. Cassie seemed to know Sam, perhaps from the investigation into her mother's death or maybe through some other means. Either way, she appeared to like him, Ali recognized, as she recalled the glowing reception he'd received from the little girl. But even as she was considering changing her mind and asking Sam to join them, Cassie took a couple of brave steps forward.

"D'ya like my room?" Her voice wavered softly.

"Yes, I do," Ali said, looking around the room again, trying to sound suitably impressed with the pink surroundings. "Did your grandmother fix this up for you?"

Cassie's blond braids bounced on either side of her round face as she nodded and reached for a stuffed Ninja turtle. She pulled the toy to her chest and took another step closer to Ali. "Are you a friend of my mom's?"

Ali shook her head. "No. I didn't know your mom."

"You know Uncle Sam, though."

"Yes, I do know Sam. But I didn't know he was your uncle."

"Well, he's not really." Cassie's lips quivered into a tentative smile as she took a few more steps and leaned against the footboard of the bed. She fidgeted with the turtle's bright blue bandanna. "He just lets me call him that, and Mom said it was all right."

"How long have you known your uncle Sam?"

"Oh, I don't know. A long time, I guess."

"And you like him, do you?"

The girl's face broke into a bigger smile. "Yeah, he's funny. And he gave me this." She held out the green stuffed animal for Ali to inspect.

"It's very nice. What's his name?"

Cassie looked from the Ninja turtle back to Ali, her nose wrinkling up in what Ali could only guess was disbelief.

"He's Leonardo. Can't you tell?"

Ali nodded, giving the girl an apologetic smile. "So, do you see a lot of Sam?"

Cassie's narrow shoulders lifted in a quick shrug. "Not as much as I like, but sometimes. Only when Mom visits him, though. Daddy doesn't like Uncle Sam."

"Oh? And why is that?"

"I don't know. Just doesn't." Her smile faded again. "Are you here to ask me questions about my mom?"

Ali shook her head. "No, I'm not going to ask you any more questions, Cassie. I promise."

"I don't know anything. People keep asking me things, and I don't know. Even Uncle Sam was asking me stuff."

"Well, I just want to visit with you for a little while, Cassie. Would that be okay?" Ali waited for the hesitant nod. "Good. Then how about you sit with me here," she suggested, patting the side of the bed.

"Are we going to play a game or something?" Cassie asked, hesitation still in her voice.

Ali smiled. The girl was bright. She knew something was up. "Yes, I suppose it is a game of sorts," she answered.

Cassie pushed herself up onto the edge of the bed and faced Ali. "What's it called?"

"That's a good question. You know, I don't exactly have a name for it."

"What do I hafta do?"

"Well, let's put Leonardo here beside you, okay? And I need you to sit quietly and hold my hands like so." Ali took the small hands in her own. "Now all I need you to do is think."

"'Bout what?"

"I need you to think about your mom, Cassie." Ali felt the child start to pull her hands away, but her smile must have given Cassie the shred of confidence she needed to continue. She remained where she was. "I'd like you to close your eyes and think about the last time you saw her. Can you do that for me?"

Ali watched Cassie nod and her bright blue eyes close. "That's good. Now just keep them closed and think about that night, okay? You don't have to say anything. You don't have to answer any questions. Just try to remember."

FOR FIFTEEN MINUTES Cassie had sat stock-still on the edge of the bed, her hands in Ali's, and hadn't spoken a word. As far as children went, she'd been a good subject. If Cassie had actually heard or seen anything the night of Jacqueline's death, the girl would have been an invaluable source of information.

As it was, Ali had come up empty-handed. There was nothing in the child's memory of that night beyond what they already knew through Ali's reading from Jacqueline's ring.

Jacqueline had come into her daughter's room sometime before Cassie had fallen asleep and told her about their move back home the next day. She had tucked her in, kissed her good-night and turned off the light. In the dim light from the corridor, Cassie had lain awake in bed for a while, thinking about her father, about her old bedroom and returning to their house.

She'd heard the phone ring a second time, heard her mother's voice from the living room, at first barely audible and then, eventually, arguing. But through the childlike perceptions and memory, Ali was unable to pick up any of the words—there was only the angry tone of her mother's voice and then the discomfort that Cassie had felt before finally falling asleep. Beyond that, there was nothing. Nothing until her grandmother's arrival, followed by the police and finally Sam. He'd come into Cassie's bedroom after her grandmother and the female police officer had left. He'd closed the door and sat on the bed beside Cassie and told her, for the first time, that her mother was gone.

The girl hadn't understood her grandmother's distress. She hadn't understood what she'd been trying to tell her. It was Sam who explained that her mother was not coming back. It was Sam who comforted her in his embrace and promised her that things would be all right. She saw a tear on his own cheek and then felt the security of his strong arms around her when she finally cried herself.

The rest Ali knew. There'd been no point in going on.

Now, as Ali left Cassie to serve tea to Leonardo and the rest of her stuffed animals, she closed the bedroom door and followed the carpeted corridor out to the living room. Sam rose from the couch, and as she approached, Ali was greeted with the expectant faces of Marilyn Ballantyne and Matt Dobson.

"She's in her room playing," she assured Mrs. Ballantyne before turning to Sam's hopeful expression and shaking her head. "She doesn't know anything. She was asleep until Mrs. Ballantyne came home and woke her. I'm sorry."

However brief, Sam could see that the reading had taken a certain toll on Ali once again. Her complexion was pallid, and he guessed that another migraine was setting in. He fought the impulse to reach out and take her hand in support. "How are you doing?"

Ali shrugged. "I'm all right."

Matt stood up from the easy chair he'd been relaxing in for the past fifteen minutes. "So, I guess that's it, then, huh?"

Ali nodded to him and Sam recognized his partner's desire to keep his word to Marilyn Ballantyne. Matt had promised her repeatedly they would take only a few minutes of her time. They were pushing their luck staying any longer, but still...

"Listen, Ali, is there any sense in going into Jacquie's bedroom? Do you think there's a chance you might pick up on something there?"

"I suppose it wouldn't hurt."

"Mrs. Ballantyne?" Sam turned to the woman and caught the full force of her scowl. "I promise we won't be more than a moment. Matt will wait with you here

if you're uncomfortable going in.'' But Sam didn't wait
for her nod of consent. He knew he'd never get one.

Placing his hand at the small of Ali's back, Sam
ushered her down the hall. He could feel the tension in
the muscles of her back even before he stopped at the
closed door and reached for the knob.

"Are you sure you're up to this right now, Ali?'' he
asked.

She nodded and took a deep breath.

"I wouldn't ask you to do this if it wasn't for Mrs.
Ballantyne. Somehow I doubt we're going to have this
opportunity again if we don't take it now.''

"It's all right, Sam,'' she said, touching his arm as
if to reassure him she was okay.

Sam gripped the doorknob. Jacquie's room. He
found himself taking a deep breath, as well. How many
times had he been in Jacquie's bedroom? Years ago,
when her parents weren't home, when they'd had the
house to themselves for the weekend, when they were
young and eager to spend every moment together.

He hadn't been here since they'd taken her body
away. And when he'd stepped into her room that night
weeks ago, he'd been surprised at how little it had
changed in all those years. Now, however, as he opened
the door for Ali, he saw that everything had been re-
decorated, the furniture rearranged and the bed made.
Even so, Sam could still picture Jacquie's lifeless body
lying on the crumpled sheets.

He closed the door and leaned back against the
frame as he watched Ali walk slowly around the room.
The light from the street outside cast long shadows
across the room until Ali moved to the nightstand and
switched on the lamp. The soft yellow glow did little to
warm the cold memory of that terrible night for Sam.

For almost ten minutes Ali moved through the room—from the nightstand to the window, from the bed to the chair in the corner, then back to the nightstand. She touched the furniture, ran her fingertips over different objects, stroked the frame of the bed and the top of the nightstand until, eventually, she stood in the middle of the room. She turned to face Sam.

"Anything?"

"It's too clean. There's nothing here. At least, nothing distinct." She looked around the room again. "I don't know, Sam. Maybe it's me, you know? It's been a long time."

"It's all right, Ali." Sam tried to conceal his disappointment with a smile. "You tried. Who knows, maybe between the two of us, we'll come up with something else to go on. I'm not throwing in the towel yet."

But as he crossed the room to turn off the lamp, he could tell from Ali's expression that she didn't hold the same enthusiasm he'd tried to muster in his own voice.

"Come on, I'll take you home."

Matt was doing his best to lighten the mood when Sam followed Ali back to the living room.

"Once again, thank you for your time, Mrs. Ballantyne." Matt shook the woman's hand and gave her a hearty smile.

"I suppose whatever it takes..." she responded, treating Ali to another one of her disapproving once-overs.

Matt followed her stare and reached for Ali's jacket. "How are you doing?" he asked Ali, helping her with her jacket and letting his hand briefly linger on her shoulder as he opened the door.

"I'm fine, Matt. Thanks."

Sam motioned for him to lead Ali out, noting his display of concern with an approving nod as he followed them to the door. But at the threshold, Ali stopped.

From behind, Sam saw her sway, almost staggering forward. Her hands groped for the door frame, her fingers slipping across the slick surface of enameled wood.

In a flash Sam's arms were around her. She sank back against his chest, her body going limp for a moment as he felt her warmth through his shirt. "Ali? Ali, what is it?"

But she only shook her head.

"Ali?" Sam tried to see her face, easing his grasp when he felt her regain her footing. "Matt, get some water." He was vaguely aware of Marilyn Ballantyne's gaping expression as Matt stumbled past Ali, back into the house and toward the kitchen.

"Ali, tell me what it is."

She shook her head again, pushing away from Sam to support herself against the doorjamb. With one shaky hand, she rubbed her forehead and looked at him with wide eyes. "I don't know, Sam. Just . . . kind of a flash or something. Like a surge." She took a deep breath and accepted the glass Matt offered her.

"I'll be fine, really." She turned to Sam after taking a long drink. "I just need some air. Can we go?"

There was no mistaking the urgency in the fleeting glance that passed between them, and Sam knew that something had happened in the instant Ali had stepped over the threshold.

"Sure. Sure, we'll get going. Mrs. Ballantyne, again, thank you very much. We'll be in touch," Sam said hurriedly, and led Ali down the porch steps to the Bronco.

The storm that had been forecast was beginning to display its full potential. In gulping gusts, the wind sucked at the tops of the trees that lined the otherwise quiet street. The temperature had dropped several degrees, and the thick odor of rain saturated the air as the first heavy drops pelted down.

"Is she all right, Sammy?" Matt asked, raising his voice above the increasing gale as Sam closed the passenger door behind Ali.

"I don't know. You think I know how this psychic stuff works?" Sam dug into his pocket and fished out his car keys. Cold rain splashed his face, and he watched Matt squint against the heavy drops as the first roll of thunder rippled through the night. "Anyway, look, I'm going to take Ali home. I'll talk to you in the morning?"

"Yeah, I'll see you at the station." Matt nodded and climbed into the Skylark as Sam jogged around to the driver's side of the Bronco.

Sam waved once to Matt as his partner revved the Skylark's engine, steered the sedan out the drive and turned right.

"So what happened back there?" Sam asked Ali once he'd shut his door to the churning storm. He jerked his seat belt across his chest and wiped the rain from his face.

Ali stared out the windshield as rain pelted against it. Only once the headlights of the Skylark were out of sight did she speak. "I'm not sure, Sam."

"Did you see something?"

"I think so. I couldn't tell—it was just a quick flash." She massaged her temple with one hand and closed her eyes. "I saw the glove again. On the door frame. It was just so brief, I almost can't be sure. But there was this surge. I've never—"

"A surge?"

"I've never had it happen like that before—with so little to go on, so little energy."

"What do you mean, Ali?"

"There was a link, a connection somehow. It lasted only a split second, but it was there. Any energy that might have been left at the house is so residual, and yet...I picked it up."

Sam turned in his seat. "Are you telling me you linked with Jacquie's killer? That you might be linking with him now?"

Ali shook her head and let out a long, shaky breath. "I have no idea, Sam. I mean, it shouldn't be possible at this point. There hasn't been enough for me to go on. I'm out of practice. And yet..."

She stared out at the pounding rain. In the fragmented light of the porch lamp through the rain-covered windshield, Ali looked tired, worn. He'd take her home. They'd done enough for one evening. If he had to come back and ask Marilyn Ballantyne himself to allow Ali access to the house again, he would. But for now he had to get her home.

He reached over and gave her hand a gentle squeeze, not understanding why it was so important for him to make physical contact with her.

"Listen, Ali, don't worry about it right now, okay? It looks to me like you've had enough for one night." He started the Bronco and sent the windshield wipers flapping against the downpour. "We can talk about this tomorrow."

Sam turned on the headlights and shifted the car into gear, but he hadn't gotten to the end of the drive before he felt Ali grip his arm.

"Turn left." Her voice was flat, mechanical almost, and when Sam looked over, he was surprised at the change in her posture. Her back pressed severely against the curve of the seat, and her eyes were fixed straight ahead.

"What is it, Ali?"

"Turn left," she instructed him.

"What?"

"Turn left."

"But that would take us out of town. I really think I should get you home before—"

"Sam, please, just turn left."

With a shrug, Sam obliged. He steered the Bronco out onto the wet street and headed away from town. For almost ten minutes he drove in silence, flicking on his high beams as the last street lamp fell behind them into the turbulent darkness.

When he snatched another quick glance at Ali, the amber lights of the dash cast a warm glow on her skin, but her expression remained as cold as stone. "Ali? Can you tell me where we're going?"

She massaged her temple again, and when she finally spoke, Sam had to look over to be sure the detached voice was indeed coming from Ali's lips.

"I don't know yet," she said, "but this is the way the killer drove."

THE HANDS GRIPPING the steering wheel wore black leather gloves. In quick flashes, residual images, Ali saw the hands as if they were her own. As if *she* were driving through the night, not Sam. Sounds of the storm faded until there was only a low, constant buzz. It intensified, blocking out the sound of the car's fan, the engine, the wipers and the wind.

And then there was a momentary calm—that split-second lull that came before any direct connection.

It had been hot that night, thick and muggy. There was the smell of imminent rain. He was driving from Jacqueline's house. Driving, because he didn't know what else to do. Driving, because it helped him think.

"What do you see, Ali?" Sam's voice filtered into her awareness, drawing the two worlds together.

She shook her head, her eyes closed as she tried to sort out the fleeting images from that night. "He's driving. He's...he's just killed Jacqueline and he doesn't know what to do, so he's driving."

"You can tell what he's thinking?"

"No, not exactly. Only feelings. Emotions. He's calm, thinking things through, trying to figure out what to do next. But he's calm."

She reached out, opening her eyes now, and placed her hand on the dash. "Slow down. It's here somewhere." The connection was weak now, easing off, but she'd sensed the jeweler's box in his pocket, tumbling through his fingers as he pulled over to the side of the road and got out of the car.

"Right here. Pull over here."

The tires chewed on gravel as Sam pulled onto the rough shoulder and turned off the engine. Outside, the wind raged, battering the tops of the trees. Rain drummed hollowly on the roof of the Bronco.

"Is this it, Ali? Is this where he pulled over?"

She nodded and at last broke her stare. Silently she reached for the door handle and stepped out into the night, oblivious to the storm.

"What is it, Ali? What are you getting?" he asked when he reached her side.

She stopped at the edge of the muddy embankment that extended from the side of the road into the darkness. The wind whipped her hair and tore at her thin jacket. Needles of rain lashed her face.

"He stopped here," she shouted above the gale, shivering when another tenuous connection flared.

"Why did he stop?"

"He's angry." Her hands clenched into fists and she closed her eyes again. It was slipping. She was losing the link. It was no longer direct, but instead, played like a memory. *As if she had been here* at the brink of this slope, looking through the darkness. As if she had reached into her pocket to pull out the jeweler's box with the bracelet and hurled it into the swampy brush below.

"The bracelet's down there, Sam," she gasped at last. "He threw it right down there!"

CHAPTER SEVEN

SAM PLUNGED through the clinging undergrowth, wrestling it from his path. Water, thick with mud, oozed into his sneakers, and he let out a groan of defeat.

"It's no use," he yelled above the wind. His hair was soaked from the rain, his shirt was drenched, and cold droplets trickled down his neck. "We'll never find it this way!" he shouted, sweeping the flashlight beam back toward the embankment where Ali stood.

"I'm coming to help," she called out, her words swallowed by another blast of wind.

"No. No, stay there, Ali. We'd only trample everything down here, anyway." He swore under his breath when his foot sank into another pocket of mud. Fifteen minutes he'd spent thrashing through the tangle of dogwood and goldenrod with nothing to show for it but a pair of ruined sneakers and soaked clothes. "We'll come back tomorrow—in the daylight."

He looked up to see if Ali had heard him. She stood on the edge of the slope, her hair matted by the rain as she clutched the edges of her jacket around her. Flashes of lightning ripped across the sky and low rumbles of thunder drew nearer.

"I'm coming back. This is crazy." He gave up trying to avoid the mud now and headed toward the embankment.

"Watch out for the fence, Sam," Ali called out just as he felt the barbed wire against his shin.

Sam held the two strands apart and ducked between them. But even as he did so, his foot began to slide and he lost his grip on the wires. The top wire whipped back, one of the barbs snagging his shoulder, gouging his skin through his shirt. Sam pulled himself free of the tangle, swearing.

"What is it?" Ali yelled.

"Nothing." He cursed again, reaching the bottom of the slope. "It's nothing."

"Here," she offered, extending a hand. "It's really slippery."

He felt her fingers wrap around his hand, and then her strong pull as she helped him to the top.

"Listen, Ali, we'll come back tomorrow," he said once he stood beside her. "In the daylight. I'm only trampling the box more into the mud by crashing around down there—that is, if the box is even there."

She nodded her head and looked from the darkness beyond the slope back to him. "You're right. We'll come back."

"Well, I don't know about you, but I need a hot shower and some dry clothes." He wiped the rain from his face. "Come on. I'll take you home."

Ali turned to follow him to the Bronco, but before he reached the trunk to put away the flashlight, he felt her hand on his arm.

"For God's sake, Sam. What did you do to yourself?"

"It's nothing, Ali. Just got caught on that damned wire."

"Like hell it's nothing. You're bleeding." She snatched the flashlight from his grip and shone it at his shoulder. A dark, crimson stain washed across the sleeve of his white shirt. "Let's go get that cleaned and dressed."

"YOU'RE GOING to have to take off the holster, Sam, and the shirt." Ali turned her attention to the first-aid kit and rummaged through it until she found a bottle of iodine.

Sam watched her as he unbuckled the gun holster, surprised at her apparent indifference to the weapon that had become a permanent fixture in his life. Jacquie had always been jittery when he'd had the .38 around. For that matter, so had the few women he'd periodically been involved with over the past five or six years. That was one reason, he imagined, those passing relationships had never amounted to much.

Ali, on the other hand, didn't even glance up from the contents of the first-aid kit when he lowered the heavy gun onto the bathroom counter. As she worked, a small puddle grew on the floor of her bathroom. She was every bit as soaked as he was. Her hair hung in dripping, weighted curls. Her silk top clung to the enticing curves of her figure, and her skin glistened with beads of rain.

They'd dried out a bit in the Bronco during the drive back into town, but by the time they'd pulled into Ali's driveway, the full force of the storm had caught up with them. Rain washed the streets in torrents, and lightning streaked the sky. They'd raced through the downpour across the lawn and up the porch steps, and now, inside the house, only the thunder was a rumbling reminder of the storm.

"Ali, I really don't think this is necessary." Sam inspected his shoulder. "See, it's already stopped bleeding. I'll be fine."

But Ali wasn't listening to his arguments. He could tell by the stubborn set of her chin and the way she continued to ransack the first-aid kit that she was not about to be deterred.

"All right, look, *I'll* do it, okay?" he said. "Just give me the stuff and I'll clean myself up."

"Sam—" Ali shook her head "—the cut's too far back. You can't reach it." She pointed to the ragged tear in his shirt.

"Ali, trust me, it'll be fine. It's not like I haven't been cut before."

"Look, it's either this or I'm taking you to Emergency for stitches, which you should probably have, anyway, with a gash like that."

"All right, all right. You win." He surrendered and began unbuttoning the blood-soaked shirt as she reached past him to wet a washcloth. "But it's not that bad. I guarantee you're going to be disappointed. It's only a scratch."

"Humor me then." Ali flashed him a quick smile and handed over the damp cloth. "I'm going to find a fresh towel. I'll be back in a sec."

She headed down the corridor.

Standing squarely in front of the mirror, Sam removed his shirt, wincing as he pulled it away from the cut. It really wasn't bad at all, he decided, examining the injury. He'd had stitches more times than he cared to remember, and this certainly did not merit any doctor's needle.

"So what do you think?" he called out to Ali as he lifted the washcloth up to his shoulder. "You think we might be onto something with this bracelet?"

"Sure," came the muffled reply from down the hall.

"You think it's still out there somewhere in that muck?" He stifled a curse as he dabbed at the wound. "Because if we can find it, there's the possibility it can be traced back to the retailer and, with any luck, the purchaser."

He could hear her coming back down the hall.

"It could definitely give us something to go on, don't you think?"

But Ali didn't answer him.

Sam saw her in the mirror. She stood behind him in the doorway, motionless. She stared back at him through the mirror, her face framed by dark, wet curls, her gaze unswerving. He followed her hard stare, watched her eyes lock coldly on his chest and the savage scar that marked his closest brush with death.

"Ali?"

She hadn't expected this—the sudden, almost nauseating, flood of familiarity. When she'd stepped into the bathroom, her eyes almost involuntarily went from the revolver at the edge of the counter to his tanned, muscled back, from his reflection in the mirror to the well-developed, sculpted lines of his chest. And then her gaze had locked onto the scar.

She'd seen the scars left by bullet wounds. Duncan had tried to hide his from her as long as he could when they'd first met. She still remembered the shock of seeing it that first time. And she remembered the sleepless nights, fraught with worry, from the moment her fingers had brushed the ragged ridges of scarred skin.

"Ali?"

But this was Sam, Sam Tremaine, not Duncan. He wasn't a part of her life the way Duncan had been, that part of her life she'd believed she could not possibly exist without. And despite the inexplicable pull Ali felt toward Sam now as he stood before her, she could not ignore one glaring fact—Sam was a cop. His scar attested to that. A chilling reminder that he ran the same risks Duncan had, lived by the same hand of fate that had steered Duncan to his death.

It wasn't going to happen again. She would never spend sleepless nights worrying about anyone again. She'd promised herself that eleven months ago when she'd felt Duncan's touch for the last time, when he'd whispered her name and then was silent.

"Ali, what's wrong?"

She shook her head, her gaze inching up to meet his in the mirror. "Nothing, Sam," she said, hoping her strained smile was sufficient to quench the concern on his face. She forced herself to focus on the gash on his shoulder and not the scar that marred his otherwise perfect chest. "Here, give me the cloth for a second."

She turned him so that he faced her, and standing on tiptoe, she reached for the top of his shoulder.

"See, I told you it wasn't that bad," he said.

As he spoke, she could feel the warmth of his breath against her cheek, his skin radiating an almost electric heat that tingled against her own as she dabbed at the cut.

"This really isn't necessary, Ali."

She felt his eyes on her as she finished cleaning the wound, but resisted the urge to look at him. She couldn't be certain what to expect if she met those dark, penetrating eyes.

Instead, she turned to the first-aid kit again, taking out gauze and tape. He was silent as she cleaned the cut with iodine and applied the salve. And throughout, Ali knew that Sam watched her. Even when she asked him to hold the gauze so she could tape it, she felt his gaze on her.

"That should do for now," she commented, inspecting her handiwork. "Let's just pray you don't get an infection."

"I'm sure I'll be fine. Thanks, Ali."

"You're welcome," she said, and wondered if Sam recognized the uneasiness behind her smile. She felt the pull toward him now more than ever. Felt the urge to reach out and lay her hand on his strong chest to feel the inviting warmth of his skin.

She looked away, but only for a moment.

It had been too long since she'd felt this kind of longing, the tug of intimacy that caused her to reach up now and trace the lines of his chest with trembling fingers. Sam said nothing. There was only the sound of his breathing, slow and steady. And when Ali's hand reached the scar, she circled the ragged mark with one fingertip.

"How . . . how did you get shot?" Her voice trembled as much as her finger against the ridge of tissue.

When she studied Sam's face, his eyes seemed to question her recognition momentarily. "Some punk in a back alley. I don't think he even meant it. He panicked and I was stupid. It happened a long time ago."

He lifted a hand. His fingers, broad and strong, covered hers, pressing them lightly against the scar. A shiver traveled through her at his touch.

"Does it bother you, Ali?"

She shrugged and was about to shake her head when he lifted his hand to her cheek. His finger teased one damp curl and then traced her jaw.

She should have pulled away, but didn't. She should have turned from him, but couldn't. Instead, she stared up at him—losing herself in the mesmerizing depths of his eyes, wanting what he wanted, submitting to the mysterious pull that had beckoned her from the day Sam had first stood on her front porch.

Slowly he closed the narrow gap between them, his bare chest radiating a heat that seemed to call to her, drawing her to him. His lips brushed her cheek first, sending an explosive tingle racing along her skin as a warmth washed through her and called out a deep and distant warning. She ignored it.

"Can you read my mind now, Ali?" he whispered, his breath caressing her ear.

She didn't respond. Couldn't respond. She drew in a shaky breath and brought her other hand up to touch his cheek. Her fingers caressed his strong jaw. And then Ali closed her eyes, surrendering to the gentle brush of his lips. She shifted closer to him. The heat of his body burned through her thin silk shirt. His breath mingled with hers, and her heart raced as his lips embraced hers.

She wasn't thinking now, only responding. Responding to desires that had been dormant for months until she'd met Sam. Her hand fluttered back, feathering through his damp hair, feeling the play of muscles along the back of his neck as she pulled herself closer still. Her previous calm was shattered by the desire for his kiss.

Tentatively his lips parted hers. The familiarity that had burned within her from the first time she'd held

Sam's hand called out to her now, and this time she answered it. Answered the hunger that surged through her body.

Sam's arms encircled her, drawing her into an embrace. And Ali felt the scar shift beneath her palm. An iciness shivered through her, gripped her the way a cold day catches a person's breath. The warning she'd tried to ignore called out to her again—a stronger beacon than Sam's desire this time—reminding her of the fear, the sorrow, the loss, and of the vow she'd made to herself.

Ali dragged herself from the circle of his arms. Her lips still tingled warmly from their kiss, but not enough to thaw the icy chill of those lingering memories.

"Ali?"

She couldn't look at him. He lifted her chin, forcing her to meet his gaze, but she closed her eyes and twisted away.

"Ali, I'm sorry."

"No, Sam. Don't be. It's not you." She raked a hand through her wet hair and shook her head. "It's me. I'm...I'm sorry. It's been a long time. I just don't think I'm ready for anything like this yet."

"I understand, Ali. Really I do."

Even when he took her hand, Ali still could not bring herself to look at him. She felt his stare for a long moment before he finally reached for his damp shirt.

"I'll get you some fresh clothes," she offered. Anything to break the awkwardness of their closeness now, anything to distance herself from the unsettling familiarity she felt swelling between them. "There should be something of Richard's in one of the closets." Her eyes fixed on his and she felt her heart skip. "I'll just check."

Once in the privacy of the master bedroom, Ali released the breath she'd been holding. As she searched through her brother-in-law's closet for a fresh shirt and jeans, she could still feel the heat of Sam's lips on hers, still taste their kiss. She could not shake the sense of betrayal she'd felt from the moment their lips had touched.

She'd crossed a barrier tonight—one she'd never intended to cross again—yet somehow, it had seemed inevitable.

After Duncan, Ali had not thought it possible to feel anything for anyone again, and yet she could feel something growing inside her, like a dormant seed after a gentle rain. With the passion and affection of Sam's kiss, it had broken through the dark earth and lifted toward the light.

But she could not allow it to flourish.

A NOISE MUST HAVE woken Sam. He didn't jerk awake but, instead, lay on the couch, his eyes still closed, listening.

Silence.

He rubbed the sleep from his eyes—not that he'd had much sleep to speak of. The couch in the Nolans' den had proved far too soft. That, coupled with the fact that he generally slept lightly in strange places, had insured him no more than four hours of intermittent dozing.

Sam closed his eyes again and listened. The house was quiet.

After Ali had left him in the upstairs washroom with a pair of Richard's jeans and a fresh shirt, he'd changed and eventually wandered downstairs. At the breakfast bar in the kitchen, he'd sat on a stool and

watched Ali pour the tea. When she joined him, they'd
cradled the steaming mugs and talked. By the time they
were onto their second cups, they'd moved into the
living room where, bit by bit, Ali had begun to open up
to him even more. She described some of her early
cases with the NYPD, those first nightmarish visions,
and how, with Gary's help, she'd learned to hone and
direct her psychic abilities. But not once did she mention the Gabriel Farthing case or Duncan Carvello.

Sam had sat and listened, savoring her company and
admiring the inner strength she seemed to possess.
He'd watched her, studied her—her eyes, her lips, her
fine features—remembering their kiss and thinking
about how easy it would be to reach over and caress
gently her lips with his once again.

It was well after midnight when they finally realized
the time and Sam had suggested he leave. By then, the
storm had turned even more violent. Sheets of rain
swept through the black night, and the wind beat at the
windows as if challenging anyone to venture outside.

It hadn't taken much persuasion by Ali for Sam to
accept her offer of the couch for the night, but in spite
of its initial comfort, Sam was beginning to wonder if
he should have braved the elements and driven home,
after all. He'd spent the past few hours tossing from
one side to the other, watching the rain stream down
the tall windows. And as he lay there, wishing for sleep,
a single thought had pulsed through his mind—Ali.

Only one floor separated him from the guest bedroom where he knew she slept. Only one floor between him and the woman whose tender kiss had
stirred emotions he hadn't addressed in years.

There was the sound again. Sam's eyes flew open. A
muted footfall from the next room. So he hadn't

imagined it. It was clearer now—a movement from the living room. He heard something, a mug perhaps, being set down on the glass top of the coffee table, and then the creak of a floorboard.

Rising from the couch, Sam pulled on his shirt and left the den. Barefoot, he padded noiselessly down the corridor to the front hall and stopped in the doorway of the living room.

The storm had passed a couple of hours ago, and now soft moonlight filtered in through the partially open blinds. In vague shadows of gray, he saw Ali.

She stood by the fireplace, her back to him, as she leaned with her arm against the mantelpiece. One hand was buried in the pocket of the robe that was drawn about her slender figure, and the other held back her hair as she stared at a photograph on the mantel.

Sam knew which photo she looked at even before he stepped into the room.

"Can't sleep?" he asked, approaching her. His voice was little more than a whisper, but Ali still jumped. She turned to look at him, her eyes wide. "I'm sorry, Ali. I didn't mean to startle you."

She stepped back from the fireplace, pulling her robe tighter around herself as she shot him a nervous glance. "No, no. It's all right. I...I guess I didn't hear you."

In the bands of moonlight that slipped through the blinds, Sam noticed the shimmer of tears glistening on one cheek. And then, when he stepped beside her, he saw her body shudder as she drew in a long breath. "Ali, what is it?"

She lifted a hand, avoiding eye contact, and wiped her cheek. "It's nothing, Sam. Honestly, I'm fine."

"No, you're not, Ali. You're shaking." He reached out and grasped her shoulders, surprised at how deli-

cate she felt. He turned her to face him. "Do you want
to talk about it?"

"No, Sam, really." She shook her head, yet did not
pull away. "It's nothing." But there was more than the
drying tears. He could see the pain that clouded her
expression.

With Ali at only arm's length, Sam fought the urge
to pull her to him, to feel the thirst of her lips again, the
softness of her skin and the heat of her body against
his. He denied the impulse to take her into his arms, to
crush her sorrow with his embrace.

But then, even as he struggled with his own emotions, he saw the photograph on the mantel—the one
Ali had been staring at before he'd interrupted.

It was the man he'd seen on the microfilm. From the
photo in the *New York Times*. The Farthing case. The
shooting.

"Do you want to talk about him, Ali?"

She pulled back and moved away from him. "I don't
think so, Sam."

"He's Duncan Carvello...your husband? Am I
right?"

Ali stopped. She didn't turn to Sam but stood with
her back to him, rigid and tense. "How do you know
Duncan?"

"I didn't know him, Ali." Sam shook his head and
tucked his hands into his jeans pockets. "But I do
know about the Farthing case."

Still she didn't move. He watched another gentle
tremble go through her body.

"And I can only guess he meant a lot to you."

When she turned, a shaft of light touched the fine
angles of her face, highlighting the clenched muscle
along her jaw.

"I don't think it would hurt to get it out into the open," he said, taking a step toward her. "I mean, we're working on this case together now, Ali. With partners on the force, when we're working a case, it always helps if things are out on the table, if you know what I mean."

She only held his stare when he took another step toward her.

"I just think that if what happened to Duncan Carvello has anything at all to do with your potential to assist with the case, it might be best to talk it out. Get it off your chest."

"This is not something I can just get off my chest, Sam. I'm sorry." The tension in her voice hung in the air between them like breath vapor on a frigid winter day, and before she could turn to stalk from the room, Sam caught hold of her arm.

"Ali, please. Listen to me. I'm sorry. The last thing I want to do is dredge up your past. And I certainly don't want to cause you any unnecessary pain, but at the same time I can't help thinking that there's something here holding you back. And . . . I'm not referring only to your readings."

She studied him before replying, obviously comprehending his reference. "Look, Sam, you're right, okay? It does affect the way I do, or don't do, any case readings now. In fact, it has everything to do with it. Duncan's the reason I haven't engaged in any psychic work in almost a year. His death is the reason my readings have been so inaccurate, so damned limited." She looked away, biting her lip. "But there is no way that sitting down and talking it out is going to change any of that."

Her words struck out at Sam—sharp, stinging blows that defied him to challenge her. But he refused to let her anger or her pain push him away. He stood his ground, squeezed her arm gently and tilted his head so that he could look her in the eye even as she tried to turn away from him.

"You could at least try, Ali. I know there's absolutely nothing I can say or do to take away the loss you've gone through or the pain you're still feeling. But if you'd only let me listen . . . I know it's not much, but it's all I can offer right now. And it might help—it might help both of us."

"He's dead, Sam. How can that be helped?"

Sam shrugged, wishing he could find the words, wishing he knew Ali Van Horn better, wishing he knew what it would take to help her forget the sorrow of her past.

"There's nothing more to talk about," she said flatly.

"Tell me how you met him."

Ali lifted her eyes to meet his. Fingers of moonlight touched his face, outlining the strong angles of his jaw and nose. She held his gaze, amazed at his persistence and yet neither surprised nor uncomfortable with it.

"I really don't see how that bears any relevance on my potential to function within this investigation."

He shrugged. "It's a start, that's all."

Ali felt distinct comfort in his touch as he took both of her hands in his and guided her to the couch under the bay window. It felt natural, the way she sat beside him now, the way he kept her hand in his as she curled her legs beneath her, always maintaining a physical contact with her—a contact she had missed over the months.

Through the blinds, beyond the glistening lawn and the street, Ali could just make out the first breath of dawn. Delicate hues of amethyst brushed the early-morning sky with a wavering hesitancy that seemed to reflect her own.

There was a lot to dredge up. More than two years' worth. And yet sometimes it seemed like only yesterday that Gary had introduced her to Duncan, his new partner. She could still see the look on his face when he'd returned her handshake—the same nervous, suspicious expression she'd seen on the faces of many people when mention of her abilities accompanied her name. But there'd been something different in Duncan's eyes. Something that had captured her. A curiosity that went beyond what she represented to the precinct and to Gary.

They had started working on a missing-persons case that had developed into a homicide investigation, she explained to Sam as he held her hand. Gary still worked with her on the readings, but Duncan was always close at hand. She'd been amazed at his willingness to accept her work, at his interest and his respect.

They were always together whenever they worked a case—the three of them. And it was only a few weeks before Gary had begun to feel like the proverbial fifth wheel.

Sam listened patiently, giving her hand a tender squeeze every so often to reassure her.

She told him about the apartment she and Duncan had shared for four brief months before his death, and she tried to imagine it now—empty and lifeless. It had been difficult living there without Duncan. It had never been the same. She'd found that out the hard way. And still she hadn't been able to let go of the apartment. It was her only link to the man she'd dreamed of sharing the rest of her life with.

"We'd gotten married only three months before he died," she whispered, her former control slipping now as she stared out the window, unable to meet Sam's sympathetic gaze. All she could see was Duncan's smile.

On the deck of the sailboat they had rented in Maui for their honeymoon, he'd made a vow to be with her forever. They'd made love on that same deck—the place where their child had been conceived.

She pulled her hand from Sam's.

He didn't need to know this. This was the secret she'd shared only with Duncan. No one had known except Gary—he'd taken her back to Emergency only two hours after she'd left Duncan there. He'd been the one holding her hand through the night. He'd stood at her side during the funeral, and afterward, he'd called her every day for weeks just to be certain she was all right.

Ali got up from the couch and turned from Sam.

"Ali?" Sam got up, also, and put his hands on her shoulders. "He was shot, wasn't he? In the line of duty."

She was silent for a moment, and then, as her own voice slipped into the milky darkness of the living room, she thought it might break. Instead, it was strong, disjointed and impersonal, like the front she'd put on from the moment they'd lowered Duncan's casket into the damp earth that cold, drizzly day.

"He was shot point-blank in the chest with a .38," she explained, "and thrown back through a second-story window."

Sam squeezed her shoulders. For almost a year she'd not allowed anyone to touch her. And yet now, under Sam's firm caress, she found a strange and welcome solace. She did not pull away.

"If the gunshot hadn't killed him, the fall did." Even when the medics had raced through the rain toward Duncan, Ali had cradled him in her lap, rocking him, stroking his face with trembling hands as if, by sheer will, she could have brought him back. And when the medics demanded she give them room, Gary had dragged her from Duncan's body. She'd clung to Gary then, the cold rain washing over them as he held her, as she watched the medics try to bring Duncan back.

But she'd already known he was dead. She'd already felt his life slip from her grasp when he'd whispered her name for the last time. And no matter how many friends and family told her that she had to put everything behind her, that she had to go on with her life, Ali knew that a part of her had died that night. On that dark and miserable street, something in her heart had withered when Duncan had gasped her name with his final shuddering breath.

"He was dead before they lifted him off the pavement," she heard herself say.

Sam's breath brushed the back of her neck. She felt his body move closer, solid and real, pressing against her. She felt his arms encircle her with a new and comforting strength.

"Were you there?"

She took another deep, shuddering breath. "I saw it all. Through the visions. I may as well have been there. I saw him take the bullet. I saw him smash through the window. I saw him fall to the street."

She was silent again. Remembering. In the blink of an eye, she could still see it all so vividly, so clearly—a permanent image in her mind. "I was too late, though. I could have warned him. I saw what was happening. But I got there too late. All I could do was hold him in my arms—and watch him die."

There was no energy left for tears. For eleven months she'd cried. For eleven months she'd tried to find a reason to live. And now, as a dry lump in her throat dammed her tears, Ali submitted to the comfort of Sam's embrace.

Through her thin robe, she felt the heat of Sam's chest against her back. She felt his strength surround her and his tenderness nourish her as he held her. Lifting her arms, she wrapped them around his, taking his hands in hers.

"Duncan wasn't the only one I lost that night, Sam," she confessed, feeling an even deeper pain now. "Three hours later...I had a miscarriage."

The silence of the house covered them now, encircling them just as their arms encircled each other when Sam turned her to face him.

"I'm sorry, Ali," he whispered as he pulled her closer. "I'm so sorry." And he rocked her tenderly as the dawn's cleansing light washed over them.

CHAPTER EIGHT

SAM HAD MANAGED to dodge Ed Harrington all morning. As he glanced up from his desk at Harrington's office, the chief was in the throes of bawling out Bobby Groff, one of the junior detectives on the force. And judging by the vivid red flush on Harrington's face, Sam doubted Bobby would be out of the office for some time.

Harrington had known yesterday afternoon about the meeting Matt and Nancy had arranged with Cassie Munroe. It was only a matter of time before he pinned Sam down long enough to grill him on the results of Ali's session with the girl. And informing an already heated Ed Harrington that they had once again come up empty-handed was the last thing Sam wanted.

He looked across his desk to Matt, but his partner seemed unperturbed. He only took a swig of his Coke and paged through the file on his desk. Sam leaned back, propping his feet on the edge of his desk, and stared at the file in his lap. But the meticulous, typewritten reports were not registering. He hadn't been able to concentrate all morning.

Shortly after his and Ali's talk, he had left her house, slipping on his jacket in the hushed calm of the early morning as they stood on her front porch. The sky had begun to lighten in the east and Sam could still remember the subtle blush the sun had given Ali's skin as she'd seen him off. He'd wanted to kiss her again or at least hold her one more time as she stood with her arms wrapped around herself against the morning chill. But instead, he'd reached out and touched her arm only briefly.

All morning Sam had thought about what Ali had confided. All morning he remembered the feel of her body as he'd held her in his arms, her gentle curves melting into his. From the moment they had met, he had recognized Ali's strength, her independence and determination, and yet, when he'd cradled her in his arms, feeling her restrained sobs, he was surprised at how fragile she had seemed.

He'd left her on the porch, promising to pick her up in the afternoon to look for the bracelet again. He had watched her as he backed the Bronco down the drive, and as he'd driven home, the scent of her perfume emanated gently from his own skin.

Sam sat up, his chair springing back into place. He tossed the file onto the pile of paperwork stacked on his desk. This wouldn't do. He had to keep his mind on his work.

He rubbed his eyes as if to wipe Ali from his thoughts.

"So what's new with the Rainer case these days?" He looked across to Matt again and was greeted with a lazy shrug.

"Haven't had a chance to look at it for a couple of days. Besides, we're still waiting to hear from that lawyer, Budsman, or whatever his name is." Matt took another swig of Coke and turned back to his own work.

"It's Bergsman," Sam said. "And why don't you just give the guy a call yourself?" In their years of working together, Sam had grown to appreciate and respect Matt's keen investigative sense, his almost photographic memory of crime scenes and the way he could unearth the smallest detail or the most unthinkable angle in almost any case. Between the two of them they had the highest success rate on the force, but when it came to speed, Sam had to admit that Matt Dobson did need the occasional prod.

Matt pulled his gaze from his work and looked at Sam. He loosened his tie and leaned back in his chair. "Fine. I'll call the guy."

There was more to Matt's irritation this morning than the seemingly endless string of dead ends they'd met on the Rainer case. Sam had detected his partner's short fuse from the moment Matt had dragged himself into the precinct at eight-thirty this morning. The shadows beneath Matt's eyes had indicated Sam hadn't been the only one who'd experienced a lack of sleep the night before. Sam wondered if Charlene Evans was the cause of those dark circles.

"So, what about Van Horn?" Matt tossed his pen onto the desk along with the case file, and Sam recognized his partner's ploy of evasion.

Sam took a quick survey of the detectives' wing. Besides Bobby Groff, who was still bearing the brunt of Harrington's wrath, there were only three other detectives in the wing. And, not including Nancy, who knew about Ali's involvement, anyway, all were out of earshot.

"What about her?" Sam asked.

"Did she tell you what the hell happened last night?"

"When?"

"When she almost passed out on Mrs. Ballantyne's front step. I mean, if you hadn't caught her when you did, she would have been out for the count. What was it, low blood sugar or something?"

Sam shook his head. He couldn't say anything, not yet. Until he and Ali had something more concrete to go on, until they had the bracelet in their own hands, he couldn't discuss their drive out of town last night with either Harrington or Matt.

"I don't know what it was, Matt. A fainting spell or something. It seems like her visions really drain her. She was fine by the time I got her home."

"So you think you'll actually get anywhere using her? She didn't come through with anything last night obviously."

"I think it's still too early to tell."

"Well, you'd have thought she'd have found something by now. I mean, if she's going to pick up on vibes or whatever, she should have done it already."

Sam shrugged. He drummed his pencil against one knee and leaned back in his chair. "I guess you can't really tell with stuff like this. Ali says it could take anywhere from a few days to a number of weeks. I'm just trying to be patient."

"You got faith, Sammy. I'll give you credit for that. Quite a different story from a few days ago, though. What's she done to convert you?"

Sam looked across in time to catch Matt's wink. Had his attraction to Ali been that obvious last night at Marilyn Ballantyne's house? "I've done some reading, that's all. Maybe you should take a look at some of those books yourself."

Matt shook his head and reached for another case file. "No, thank you. That kind of stuff gives me the willies. I mean, whatever works, that's what I always say. But I have to admit, I'm just as happy it's you working with Van Horn. I only hope you don't have your hopes up too high with her, Sammy."

Sam caught Matt's quick smile and knew his partner wasn't referring strictly to the case. He also understood that Matt was refraining from further comment for the time being when he opened the file he'd reached for and began fingering through the typed reports.

Still, Sam thought, Matt suspected something between him and Ali. Even if there was a certain truth behind his partner's hunches, Sam knew he had to be scrupulous when it came to Ali. This morning, when she'd told him about her loss, Sam knew she hadn't told him about Duncan's death because they were working on the investigation together.

There was more to it than that.

In spite of her initial hesitancy, Ali had *wanted* to tell Sam about Duncan. She'd wanted to share her painful secret, and she'd sought his comfort in the same way he'd sought her touch.

She'd suggested they wait until the afternoon to resume their search for the bracelet so that the ground would have a chance to dry after last night's storm. Sam had agreed, promising to pick her up at twelve-thirty. He checked his watch—eleven-fifteen.

"Anyone feel like an early lunch?" he asked, wheeling his chair back and looking over at Nancy. She'd been rooted to her desk all morning and Sam doubted she'd need much coaxing.

"Sure, why not? You owe me anyway." Nancy tossed her glasses onto her desk. "You hungry, Matt?"

He waved a hand in their direction. "Naw, you guys go on without me. I'll catch up in a bit. You going to be at Morty's?"

"Where else?" Sam reached for his jacket from the back of his chair. "See you later, Matt. And listen, why don't you give Bergsman a call before you come over, okay?"

"Yeah, yeah. Sure. I'll see you guys later."

Sam held the front door for Nancy, thankful for a breath of fresh air as they left the precinct and walked down the street to Morty's.

"So last night was a wash, then, eh? Van Horn didn't get anything from the girl?"

Sam shook his head as they walked. "No, nothing."

"So, what? You going to work a new angle or something?"

"We're considering a couple of possibilities."

Nancy stopped at the newspaper box beside Morty's and fished through her pockets for change. "Hang on a second, Sam. I want a paper. You got a quarter?"

"Here," he said, flipping her the coin. Nancy caught it in midair, but before she'd put the change into the slot, Sam spotted the headline halfway down the front page of the *Herald*. And as soon as Nancy opened the box, Sam snatched the top paper.

She didn't say anything, only watched Sam's face harden to an expression of violent anger.

"I'm sorry, Nance. I've gotta go. I'll talk to you later." His voice was cold and she saw a muscle flex along his jaw.

Only after he had stalked around the corner to the precinct did Nancy turn back to the open newspaper box. It was then that she, too, saw the bold, front-page heading.

ALI SET DOWN her pen and stretched. Progress had been slow and she blamed it on her lack of sleep. After Sam had left this morning at five-thirty, Ali had gone back to bed, but she couldn't seem to relax. She'd lain awake and watched the sunlight finger through the blinds and creep slowly across the bedroom floor.

Eventually she'd pulled herself out of bed and taken Tash for a walk before buckling down to do some drawing. But filling in the pen-and-ink drawings with color wash was mindless work, and her thoughts wandered to Sam.

This morning when he'd held her and she'd told him about Duncan, Ali had been moved by Sam's tender understanding. It had been a long time since she'd spoken openly to anyone about her loss. Now, having told Sam, she was reminded again of how empty her life seemed without Duncan.

Somehow, with the apartment behind her in New York, Ali had been able to block out the fact that she and Duncan had ever shared a life, however brief. She'd buried herself in her work, believing it to be the best way to overcome the emptiness that had haunted her for eleven months.

But she wasn't over it. Not yet, anyway. And as Ali looked up from her drafting table to the mantelpiece where Duncan's picture sat, she guessed it would take much more than a comforting embrace from Sam Tremaine to make her forget her shattered past.

Still, there was no denying the comfort she'd felt when Sam had taken her into his arms and held her close. There was an honesty in his affection, a sincerity Ali did not doubt.

No, she couldn't deny she was attracted to him, that she'd thought about him from the moment she'd held his hand in the grocery store only last week. Yet she could not ignore one fact. The familiarity between them, her attraction to him, stemmed from one very obvious parallel—Sam, like Duncan, was a cop. And it was this very thought that set off Ali's warning bells.

The clock in the front hall chimed noon. Sam would be by in a half hour. Ali capped her pen and walked to the front hall. She'd just have time to leaf through the paper before they set out to resume their search for Jacqueline's bracelet.

Outside, a few straggling clouds scurried across the slate-gray sky, and in spite of this morning's sunshine, Ali guessed they were in for another storm before the day was through. With any luck, though, another storm might be just what they needed to break the last of the late-July heat wave. Ali reached for the *Herald* on the front step, closed the door and carried the paper into the kitchen. She tossed it down on the ceramic top of the counter and pulled a bottle of water out of the fridge.

Only when Ali turned, with the bottle lifted to her lips, did she see the headline. She froze. The bottle met the countertop with a heavy thud. Water splashed onto the newsprint and the tiles, as Ali read the glaring headline—Danby Police Seek Aid of Renowned Psychic in Munroe Murder.

SAM'S HARD GAZE shot from the folded *Herald* on the passenger seat back to the red light. He ran a hand roughly through his hair and stared straight ahead.

When the light turned green, he gunned the engine and accelerated through the intersection. Cursing, he prayed that Ali had not yet seen today's paper.

Matt had still been at his desk when Sam had stormed into the detectives' wing. His partner had looked up in surprise when Sam slapped the paper on his desk, demanding an explanation. Sam had given him a few seconds to look at the headline, and when Matt didn't look up again, Sam snatched the paper back, spilling several case files to the floor.

"You want to tell me that this has nothing to do with you?" Sam had tried to keep his voice down, but Harrington came to the door of his office to check out the commotion. Matt shook his head, mumbling something that sounded vaguely like an apology.

"Damn it, Matt, I told you this had to be kept quiet. I warned you about Charlene, didn't I?"

"Sam, listen, I—"

"Do you realize what this little leak of yours means? Not only have we likely lost Ali's assistance, which, may I remind you, is the best chance we've got for getting a lead in Jacquie's case, but you might have just put Ali's life at risk. You may as well have rented a billboard and advertised to Jacquie's killer personally."

"I'm sorry, Sam."

"Sorry? For God's sake, it's a little late for 'sorry.'"

"Look, I'll go over and see Van Horn myself if you like. I'll talk to her, explain what happened."

"I hardly think it matters who talks to her, Matt. She already told us she'd drop the case if anything like this happened. Shit, she hasn't even been helping us for more than a couple of days, and Charlene's already gotten it out of you. Just how the hell do you expect—"

"Sam." Ed Harrington cleared his throat. "Is there something we should talk about?"

Sam let out his breath in one frustrated rush and jammed the paper under his arm. "It's all right, Ed. I have to see someone right now, anyway. I'll be back later."

Sam watched the chief close the office door and retreat to his desk before he looked at Matt again. He wondered if it was regret he saw shadowing his partner's blue eyes.

"Listen, Sam, I swear I don't know how it happened. Charlene promised me she wouldn't—"

"And you believed her? Damn it, Matt, just what the hell *were* your priorities last night, anyway?"

Sam shook his head, stared at his partner and finally spun on one heel. He hadn't really expected an answer. They were nowhere near finished with the topic of Charlene Evans as far as he was concerned, but for now, Sam knew that seeing Ali was far more important than discussing codes of conduct with Matt.

Nancy had caught up with him by the time he barged out of the detectives' wing. He brushed past her, muttering a hurried apology as he headed toward the main doors.

Now, as Sam swerved the Skylark into Ali's drive and brought it to a lurching stop, he grabbed the paper from the passenger seat. He wouldn't blame her if she pulled out of the investigation, even refused to talk to him. He wouldn't blame her if she didn't answer the door, for that matter.

Sam took a deep breath and reached for the bell. But before his finger touched the small glowing button, the front door swung open.

He was too late. He could see it in her eyes first. Then he saw the *Herald* in her right hand. She said nothing, only stared at him, shaking her head as if in disbelief.

"Ali, listen—"

"You promised me, Sam."

In that instant Sam knew her trust in him had been broken. It didn't matter who had leaked the story to Charlene Evans. It was Sam's word to Ali, *his* promise, that had been broken.

She turned from the doorway and Sam bustled in after her. "Listen to me, Ali. It was an accident." The screen door banged shut behind him as he followed her into the kitchen. "Let me explain."

"What's to explain, Sam?" She spun around to face him, anger flaring in her eyes as she threw the paper down onto the kitchen bar that separated them. "It's all there on the front page."

"Ali—"

"I told you what would happen if there was a leak. I warned you about the dangers. But no, you assured me you would keep my involvement quiet. You promised there wouldn't be any publicity. Damn it, Sam, I trusted you!"

She turned away, crossing her arms in front of her and resting her back against the bar as she looked out the window. Even when Sam stepped in front of her, Ali refused to look at him.

"Ali, I'm sorry." He reached out to touch her arm, desperate to make her understand. But when he felt her muscles tense beneath his touch, he withdrew his hand.

"Look, I know it doesn't matter how the story was leaked. It's my case. I'm responsible."

Sam took a deep breath. Whether she dropped the case now or not, he owed her an explanation. "Harrington wanted me to work the case alone. He even pulled Matt off a few days ago because he didn't want too many people to know the extent of your involvement. But Matt's put a lot of hours into this case. It means a lot to him. We both...we both knew Jacquie. And we both want the guy who did this to her."

"So how does Matt fit into this?"

Sam followed Ali's unbroken gaze out the window to the backyard. The trees that bordered the Nolans' property swayed in the wind. "I've been keeping Matt posted on the progress of the case over the past couple of days, hoping for extra input from him. I know I shouldn't have involved him, but he's my partner."

"So it was Matt who leaked the story?"

Sam nodded. "It wasn't intentional," he said, surprised at his willingness to defend the man who had, only moments ago, borne the brunt of his anger. "He's been dating Charlene Evans for the past couple of weeks. She's...uh...she's a reporter for the *Herald*, the one who wrote the story."

Silence. Still Ali didn't look at him.

"Ali, listen, I'll understand if you don't want to help me now. I just want you to know I'm sorry." He reached over and put his hand on her arm. This time she did not tense up, and Sam did not withdraw his hand. "I'm going to talk to Matt. If you do continue to assist on the case, I can promise you this won't happen again. He made a mistake, Ali. He knows that. And I know he won't let it happen again."

She turned to him at last, her eyes searching his for the assurance she could put her faith in him again. "You trust him, Sam?"

"Like a brother."

Finally she nodded and stepped away from the kitchen bar. "Then I think we'd better find that bracelet. If Jacquie's killer is still in town, I want us to find him—before he finds me."

THEY'D SEARCHED the marshy underbrush for close to an hour, and all Sam had to show for it was another pair of mud-soaked sneakers. Ali had had the right idea with rubber boots, he thought as he stopped to watch her squelch through another thick puddle. He heard the mud suck at the once bright yellow boots, but Ali didn't seem to take any notice. Intently she studied the soupy ground in front of her.

"Ali, I hate to be the one to suggest this, but if the box was out here I think we'd have found it by now."

Ali took another wary step forward. Black water shot up from beneath her boot, spraying her left leg. A grimy smear of mud already graced her bare knee below the cuff of her walking shorts, and when she finally spared Sam a glance, he saw another smudge along her cheek.

"Maybe some kids were out here and picked it up. It was weeks ago, Ali."

"I don't think that's likely, Sam," she said, returning her attention to the wet ground.

"Or maybe I trampled it deeper into the mud last night."

Ali straightened up at last, stretching her back and looking around. "Or perhaps we're not looking in the right place."

That was a possibility Sam had considered but did not venture to suggest. At this early point in their collaboration, he had to display faith in Ali's abilities, not question them.

"Come on, let's take a break." He nodded to the dusty Skylark parked beyond the embankment. "I need a drink."

Holding the strands of barbed wire apart for Ali, Sam attempted a reassuring smile, but his hope was rapidly dwindling. When they reached the car and Sam pulled out a bottle of water, he was ready to call off the search entirely.

He uncapped the bottle and gulped the cool water as he paced the shoulder of the road. He stopped when he saw Ali. She sat on the passenger seat of the car, her slender, tanned legs splaying out through the open door, her elbows resting on her knees, and her chin cupped in one hand as she looked out beyond the sagging wire fence.

Other than Jacquie, Sam couldn't remember ever being as attracted to a woman. A breeze scurried along the lonely strip of road, pausing long enough to play with the few curls that had strayed from her short ponytail. Mindlessly, Ali raised a hand to brush them from her face, and when she looked up and caught Sam staring at her, she offered him a smile—so gentle and yet so hesitant that he found himself wanting to kiss her, to extinguish all of her doubt and pain with his desire.

She got out of the car, stretched again, and leaned against the hood. Taking a few steps closer, Sam offered her the water bottle and followed her gaze out to the marsh.

"You know, we can come back tomorrow if you want to call it a day. We've been at this awhile. Maybe we need a break."

"No," she said quietly, her voice sounding weary. "We're here now."

She met his gaze again, and Sam was immediately aware of how close they were standing.

"Look, Ali," he said, needing to break the strained silence, "I really am sorry about the story in today's paper. Danby isn't like New York City—it just isn't big enough for anonymity, you know? Even for a city this size, it still has that small-town flavor. Everyone seems to know everyone else. It's hard to keep certain things quiet sometimes. I shouldn't have promised you that nothing like this would happen."

"It's all right, Sam."

This time when her eyes met his, she didn't look away. She didn't even look away when he took a step closer and reached out to touch her shoulder.

"I'm not going to let anything happen to you, Ali." He brought his other hand up and lightly wiped the smear of mud from her cheek, not surprised at the silkiness of her skin. "I promise," he said finally, realizing that nothing he'd said before meant as much as those words.

It seemed natural to move even closer to her, to feel her body press against his, to feel her breath whisper along his skin. She didn't turn away. Whatever hesitancy there had been seemed to dissolve, and she brought her hands to his waist as if to steady herself.

He trailed a finger along her jaw to her chin, lifting her mouth to meet his, and when his lips brushed hers, a hot tremor washed over him.

Ali did not pull away. Her own desire seemed to seek out his. She drew herself closer to him and Sam could feel the heat of her skin through his shirt. The longing he'd felt all afternoon, from the moment she'd opened the front door, melted with the exquisite softness of her kiss. Her lips caressed his, embracing his hunger as he traced their silken fullness with his tongue.

After this morning, after what Ali had told him about Duncan, he'd expected apprehension—not this rare sweetness, and certainly not the urgent intimacy that radiated from Ali as their kiss swelled beyond anything Sam was prepared for.

It wasn't as if desire was altogether unfamiliar to him. It was just that he couldn't remember it ever taking his breath away like it did now as Ali lifted a hand to the back of his neck, drawing him closer. He couldn't remember it ever being this immediate, this desperate. He wanted to feel the heat of her body, to feel every curve against his and to feel her desire quenched by his.

If it hadn't been for the distant whine of a car engine, Sam could only guess where their kiss might have taken them. As the sound of the car drew nearer, he pulled away reluctantly. His lips still tingled, and for a moment he felt like a high-school kid caught in the act as the other vehicle passed them and disappeared around the next bend.

He turned and walked to the edge of the embankment. He gazed out at the marshy undergrowth, almost afraid to look at Ali again.

He had to keep his mind on the case. Ali was right to have her own fears, what with today's story in the *Herald*. He and Matt had absolutely no idea what kind of man they were looking for or what possible motives lay behind Jacquie's murder. With the story in the paper, anyone with enough determination and know-how could do some digging. A few inquiries and Ali's name and where she lived could easily be discovered. And until he and Matt closed the case Ali wasn't safe.

Sam looked at her now. She leaned against the car and tilted the water bottle back to drink. Last night somehow Ali had connected with Jacquie's killer. How closely, Sam did not know, but it had been enough for her to direct him to this spot—this secluded stretch of road where Jacquie's killer had stopped that night almost six weeks ago.

"Wait a minute." Sam crossed to her. "What if you're right?"

"About what?"

"What if we *have* been looking in the wrong place?"

Ali shook her head. "This is where he stopped, Sam. I'm sure of it."

"I'm not doubting that, Ali."

He reached past into the glove compartment and pulled out a box of raisins.

"Sam, I'm not hungry," Ali said, giving him a quick smile.

He rattled the box in his hand a couple of times, checking the weight. "Look, Ali, you linked with the killer last night, right?"

She nodded.

"Can you do it again?"

"I don't think so, Sam. It's not that easy. I can't just turn it on and off at will."

He walked away from the car, still bouncing the small red box lightly in his palm. "But can you try? Would it be possible for you to find the exact place where he stood on this road?"

Ali walked over to Sam and shook her head.

"Ali, just try, okay? Walk along the shoulder of the road. Last night, when you linked with him, what did he see when he got out of the car? Where was he looking when he stopped, when he stood with the jeweler's box in his hand?"

Ali paced the gravel shoulder. She closed her eyes, searching her memory of that night, searching *his* memory. She remembered the car, only a few yards from where Sam had parked the Skylark. She'd seen that last night when she'd linked with the killer. He'd pulled over, opened the car door and stepped out into the dark night.

She stopped, turned and moved back toward Sam, her eyes still closed. He'd left the car and walked back this way. Five paces? Six? Maybe more?

No. She stopped now, remembering as if she'd walked from the car to the side of the ditch herself that night.

"Right here." She turned and looked out past the barbed-wire fence. Two massive, rotting willows bracketed her view. She'd seen them last night when she'd been equipped with the killer's memory. But then they'd been only lumbering shadows in the darkness.

"He stood right here." She nodded, affirming her conviction.

"You're sure?"

She nodded again.

"All right, then. Here," he said, resting one hand on her shoulder as he moved up behind her and dropped the box of raisins into her right hand. "I'm guessing that should be about the same weight."

Ali looked back over her shoulder at Sam. His face was close to hers and her longing for his kiss rose within her again.

Sam took a step back as if he, too, felt the desire in her touch.

He cleared his throat. "Throw it," he said finally. "Throw it like he threw the jeweler's box."

Ali looked back at the dying willow trees, balancing the box of raisins in her palm for a moment, and then, in a slow but forceful arc, pitched it into the marsh. She watched with Sam as the small box tumbled through the air. And when it finally met the ground there was nothing more than a light splat.

"See? You were right." Sam moved beside her, his shoulder brushing hers. "We weren't looking in the right place at all. He was angry, right? Pissed off. He didn't just toss the bracelet, he *threw* it. We weren't searching far enough out, Ali."

Sam was already scrambling down the slippery embankment toward the fence. "Wait here. I'll be right back."

She watched him crouch through the wires again and cautiously pick his way from one clump of weeds to the next, cursing softly under his breath whenever his foot sank into soggy ground.

"Can you see it?" she shouted as he came close to where she'd seen the box of raisins land.

He didn't answer. For almost ten minutes, Ali waited at the shoulder of the road, watching Sam weave through the tangle of blooming goldenrod. At one point he picked up the red box that held the raisins, and then, at last, he reached down again.

"I don't believe it!" he shouted back to Ali, and looked at the object in his hand. He held up the dark blue jeweler's box for her to see.

When Sam made his way back to Ali, the smile on his face was like a child's on Christmas morning, she thought as she offered him a hand up the bank.

"I don't believe it," he said again. "You're amazing, Ali."

He took one step closer, wiping his hand on the backside of his jeans before he brought a finger to her chin and lifted her face to meet his kiss. It happened so quickly, in that flurry of excitement, Ali had no chance to give the gesture a second thought. She accepted the warmth of Sam's lips again with the same sense of familiarity that had urged her to kiss him before, the same familiarity that made her wrap one arm around his waist now and pull herself closer to him.

"You're amazing, Ali," he repeated when their lips parted and he took a step back so he could look at her.

"All in a day's work." She shrugged, returning his intoxicating smile.

Sam turned the soiled jeweler's box over in his hand and gingerly popped it open. Inside, on a bed of black velvet that was stained from weeks of resting in muddy water, was the still-glittering diamond bracelet Ali had seen through her reading from the pillow.

"I doubt we'll be able to get any prints at this point," Sam said, heading for the trunk of the car. He pulled out a plastic bag, dropped the soaked velvet box into it and sealed it, then went and retrieved a rag from under the driver's seat. "But there's someone in the lab who owes me a favor. She'll keep this quiet," he assured Ali as he wiped his hands with the rag. "I don't want anyone to know about this."

Ali studied Sam's strong profile as he gazed out at the two drooping willows. The wind had picked up considerably, licking at his dark hair, pulling at the folds of his shirt, and a quick glance skyward was enough to warn Ali of the impending storm. "Not even Matt?" she asked, waiting for Sam to turn to her again.

"Ali, I don't want *anyone* to know about this bracelet. Not yet anyway. Including Matt."

"I thought you said you trusted Matt like a brother. That he wouldn't say anything."

"This isn't a matter of trust anymore, Ali."

He looked back down at his hands and wiped at them some more with the rag. Strong hands, strong fingers, Ali thought, remembering the hot shiver that had raced through her when he'd touched her with those same hands.

But he was silent—too silent. He set down the rag and looked at the jeweler's box in the plastic bag, and for a brief moment the familiarity Ali felt toward Sam slipped away. She didn't know him. She didn't know this man who stood next to her, his dark eyes concealing secrets even she could not read.

Her lips were still warm from their kiss only moments ago, and yet, for all his similarity to Duncan, Ali didn't really know Sam Tremaine at all. Could she put her life in his hands?

"Sam...I...I know you gave Jacquie her high-school ring."

His eyes lifted from the bag, coming up slowly to meet hers, and Ali almost winced at their intensity.

"I know there was something between you and Jacquie."

Sam looked up from the rag and met her gaze. "Listen, Ali, I told you before, that has nothing to do with this case."

"Are you sure, Sam?" Ali challenged, her own doubts sending a rush of adrenaline through her. He looked away. "There's more to this case than what you've told me. You're involved, aren't you, Sam? I know you are. Somehow. I'm just not sure how yet. But there's more than a professional interest in your investigation of Jacquie's murder."

He passed the bag from one hand to the other, as if, like Ali, he was considering its contents.

After another long silence, Ali cleared her throat. When she finally spoke, her voice was hesitant. "Did you give Jacquie the bracelet, too, Sam?"

His eyes shot up to meet hers. Anger, mixed with something Ali could only hope was confusion, flashed through them. "What? What are you suggesting, Ali?"

She didn't answer.

"If there's something you know that you're not telling me..."

"I think there's more that you're not telling me, Sam."

He let out a long breath and shook his head. "So you honestly think I was the one who bought this bracelet for Jacquie?"

"I don't know, Sam. Did you?"

"And you probably think that it was me who drove out here and threw it away, too."

"I didn't say that."

Sam looked squarely at Ali now, his jaw set firmly as he tossed the evidence bag onto the Skylark's front seat. "No, you didn't say it, Ali. But it's what you're thinking, isn't it?"

"I don't know what to think, Sam. Especially since you're not being honest with me. If you're not going to tell me the truth about you and Jacquie, if you're not straight with me now, then there's nothing more I can do to help you with this case."

She stepped back from him, back from the power of his dark eyes. She'd had enough. She *knew* Sam was hiding something. Unless he came clean with her now and told her what had gone on between him and Jacquie, she couldn't trust him. Even though her body ached for him.

Ali struggled to fight back her tears. "I think you'd better find yourself another psychic, Detective Tremaine. Maybe someone who's willing to work with half-truths and cover-ups, because I don't work that way."

Ali headed toward the passenger side of the car.

"Whoa, wait a minute, lady." His hand snatched her wrist with lightning speed and spun her around.

But in that second another car appeared around the bend and the force of Sam's grip slackened. The driver slowed the vehicle at the sight of the couple apparently arguing at the side of the road, and Ali used the opportunity to put distance between herself and Sam. As the vehicle resumed its former speed and drove off, she yanked the passenger door shut behind her and reached for the seat belt.

When Sam caught up with her, he stood at the side of the car, both hands braced on the frame of the open window. She couldn't look at him. He was too close and she knew that if she turned, she would be close enough to kiss those same lips that had led her to believe in him.

His voice was calmer now, but Ali could tell the calm was forced. "Okay, Ali, listen to me. I don't know what it is you're seeing or reading in all this. In fact, I have my own doubts you're telling me everything yourself."

From the corner of her eye she saw him rake a hand through his hair, brushing back the few long strands that strayed across his tanned face.

"I don't know exactly what you've sensed about my relationship with Jacquie, but if we're working together on this case, you have to trust me, Ali. My relationship with Jacquie has nothing to do with this investigation." He waited for her response.

When she turned to meet his stare, her voice was low and firm. "You're wrong there, Sam. On two counts. First, whatever it was you had with Jacquie has everything to do with this case. And second—" Ali tore her gaze from Sam's and looked down the empty road ahead of the car "—I'm *not* working on this case. My involvement ends. Right here."

CHAPTER NINE

ALI TWISTED in her sleep and moaned. She wrestled with the damp sheets even as the dream gripped her.

She'd been here before. She'd felt this suffocating darkness. Fear, hot and familiar, pounded in her chest and coursed through her body, just as it had the last time she'd entered this place. Long shadows receded and the dim blur began to clear.

She knew she was dreaming. But as the thin veil between sleep and the disquieting dream lifted, she was powerless to stop it.

Footsteps, steady and deliberate, echoed hollowly through the empty building. They stopped for a moment, then resumed, louder now.

She searched her surroundings. The shadows offered nothing. Fleeting outlines of stairs glimmered through the darkness. Lines and angles intersected beyond the murky haze that enveloped her, but she could not make out the forms they defined.

And then, as if watching a movie, she saw him—the man who had entered her dream before.

Steadily he walked down the wide corridor, his stride fluid yet wary, through the swirl of fog. She herself moved effortlessly through the darkness, watching him, a silent and unseen observer.

She couldn't see his face, only the breadth of his shoulders and the back of his head. His hair was wet and matted. His shirt clung to the hard lines of his body as he moved forward through the vapor. He stopped again, turning his head and listening, as if searching for someone.

There was a glint of light on metal as he raised his arm and cocked the revolver in his right hand. He looked up, and she followed his gaze. High above the floor where he stood was a large, illuminated circular window. A cross divided the glimmering circle into four neat sections, and in the milky glow, dust particles danced and shimmered.

The man took another step forward, into the light, his revolver raised. As if in slow motion, he turned, and at last she could see his face. Her breath caught in her throat. It was Sam.

He twisted his head around, his eyes squinting into the darkness, until he seemed to look right at her. Panic pulsed through her, mounting with an intensity that threatened to pull her from the dream—but there was no escape.

And then, from the shadows, someone called his name. Sam turned. His left hand joined his right on the grip of the revolver as he looked around, searching the shadows.

There was no warning sound—only the explosion of a bullet. But it was not from Sam's gun.

She heard him cry out as the bullet ripped through his chest, its force throwing him back. In slow motion, his gun tumbled through the air, gleaming in the light from the high window, turning and reeling. It hit the ground moments before Sam did, moments before the scream escaped her throat.

Ali lurched out of bed, a gasp dying on her lips as her eyes flew open and she sucked in a welcome breath of reality. In the slats of moonlight that slipped through the bedroom blinds, she could see Tash. The golden retriever stood at the side of the bed, her head cocked in curiosity, her tail wagging.

Ali took another deep breath and raked a hand through her damp hair. Drawing her knees into the circle of her arms, she glanced over to the red glow of the digital clock—three-fifteen. She wouldn't be able to sleep now, she was certain of that. Two nights ago, when she'd awakened from a similar dream, she'd spent the rest of the night tossing and turning. At that time, the dream hadn't been so vivid, so disturbing. She also hadn't known it was Sam in her dreams.

Even now, with the dream behind her, Ali felt the sinister grip of fear as she thought of Sam. If she closed her eyes, she could still see his body being hurled to the hard floor. She reached for the lamp on the nightstand and welcomed its reassuring light.

There was no explaining the dreams. At first Ali had believed that they were somehow connected with Duncan. That was before she'd known it was Sam. And yet, it would have made more sense if it had been Duncan—he was the one who'd been killed, not Sam.

She'd read about psychics who had premonitions. They had dreams and visions that projected future events, and could actually use these insights to warn people. Others, however, never experienced premonitions.

She'd never had premonitions. In all her years working with Gary and then Duncan, Ali had always been grateful for the limitations of her abilities.

But tonight's dream was strangely different. Even now, she could hear the resonating discharge of the gun. It had been too vivid. Her fear, too immediate. If this was a premonition, it was her first.

Then again, what if it wasn't? A new panic rushed up from her stomach and clutched her throat as Ali thought of Sam. She hadn't spoken to him in almost a week. Not since the day they'd found Jacqueline's bracelet. Maybe her dream wasn't a premonition at all. Maybe something had happened to Sam.

Ali didn't care that it was after three in the morning. She didn't care that she'd vowed not to speak to Sam until he told her the truth about Jacqueline. She reached for the slip of paper on the nightstand and grappled for the phone.

Punching out the number he'd given her, Ali listened to her own racing heart, and then to the empty rings.

After four rings, the phone was answered.

"Yeah, Tremaine here," she heard him say finally, his voice laced with sleep. A wave of relief washed over her.

"Hello?" he said.

She heard the click of a lamp and envisioned him sitting up in bed now.

"Hello?" he asked again.

Ali still didn't answer. Unable to hang up, she held the phone to her ear.

A long silence.

She could hear him breathing, and imagined she could feel the warmth of his breath caress her cheek as if he was there beside her. Her fingers tightened around the phone when she heard him whisper her name.

"Ali? Is that you?"

SAM SWUNG his long legs down from the corner of his desk and tossed the report he'd been reviewing onto the pile of files. His chair rolled back as he stood and crossed the detectives' wing to the water cooler. The smell of Monday afternoon's burned coffee wafted through the room, dispelling all hopes for a last decent cup, so Sam satisfied himself with cold water.

He watched a large bubble gurgle to the top of the cooler before returning to his desk.

"So whatcha working on there, Sammy?" Matt looked up and nodded to the closed folder on Sam's desk.

"Nothing," Sam lied, sliding the folder into his desk along with Jacquie's case file. "Just hoping I'd overlooked something on the Munroe case."

Sam sank back down in his chair and closed the drawer, thinking about the useless report in the manila folder. This was one file no one was going to see—at least not until he had a better idea of what it meant.

After almost six days of waiting, the lab had come up empty on the bracelet he and Ali had found. There'd been only partial prints on the bracelet itself and they'd all been identified as Jacquie's. As for the jeweler's box, Sam had been right when he'd suggested that it had sat for too long in the mud.

Two days ago he'd gone to Marilyn Ballantyne's house alone, hoping she could offer some explanation as to the origin of the bracelet. When she'd opened the door, he'd been greeted by the same cold expression she'd used with him from the day Jacquie married Peter six years ago. She hadn't invited him in, nor offered him a cold drink. Instead, he'd been forced to ask his questions from the front porch, the screen door providing the barrier Marilyn Ballantyne obviously felt she needed.

But she'd only shaken her head, claiming to know nothing about a diamond bracelet, had never seen it on her daughter's wrist.

"I take it our local psychic hasn't come up with anything yet?" Matt asked.

Sam swung his gaze to his partner's and shook his head.

"She's still working with you, isn't she?"

Sam shrugged. "I can only hope so." He'd avoided discussing the case or Ali with Matt all week. He hadn't wanted to tell him about their disagreement. He hadn't wanted to admit he'd let his personal feelings interfere with a case.

"I haven't seen her in a few days," he confessed at last.

"Nothing to do with Charlene's headline, I hope?"

Sam noted Matt's regret and tried to ease it with a shake of his head.

"Because if it is, I can go over there and talk to her, Sammy. I'll apologize myself."

"It's all right, Matt. Really."

"No, listen. If I've jeopardized your working relationship with this woman, then I'll talk to her. It's the least I can do for screwing up."

"That's not necessary." The last thing Sam needed was Matt talking to Ali. Then he'd find out that Sam hadn't told her everything and he'd fill Ali in himself on Jacquie's past. "Honestly, Matt. We just had a misunderstanding . . . about the case, that's all. I can handle it."

His partner studied him for a moment, and Sam hoped Matt didn't notice the personal edge in his last comment.

"Besides, we haven't found anything new lately, anyway," Sam said, leaning back in his chair again. He was pretty sure he'd never lied to Matt in the past and now he realized why he hadn't. It didn't feel right, keeping things from his partner and closest friend. But unless he got somewhere with the bracelet, he wasn't really lying to Matt, anyway—they had nothing new.

"Well, you just let me know if you want me to talk to her for you, Sammy." The tone of Matt's voice alerted Sam to the fact that his partner wasn't speaking strictly professionally now. "I like Ali—I mean, from what I know of her. And I can't tell you how bad I feel about that leak. If there's anything I can do—"

"Really, Matt. We're . . . it's fine."

Matt gave him a nod before turning back to his work. He meant well, Sam thought. But right now, Matt's talking to Ali was not going to be enough to convince her to trust Sam again.

When he'd driven Ali home last week after they'd found Jacquie's bracelet, she hadn't said a word. She'd sat in the passenger seat, staring out the streaked windshield, not once looking at him even when they'd finally pulled into her drive. And when he'd stopped the car, Ali had immediately reached for the door handle.

Her hand had felt cold in his when he'd reached over to stop her.

"Ali, talk to me, please," he'd begged her, his voice sounding desperate in the hush of the car. The whine of a lawn mower and the distant bark of a dog filled the swell of silence.

He waited. "Ali?"

"Look, Sam," she'd said at last, finally meeting his gaze, "there's nothing to talk about."

"Ali, please, trust me on this, okay?" Suddenly Sam had realized he didn't care about the case. At that moment, as he held Ali's gaze, as he saw suspicion shadow the gray depths of her eyes, Sam could think only of Ali. He thought of the kiss they'd shared, of how he wanted to hold her, to be with her, and of how he'd have done anything at that moment to convince her of his feelings for her. Anything but dredge up a past that had nothing to do with the future.

"Please, don't let this come between us, Ali," he'd pleaded, giving her hand a gentle squeeze, hoping she could see past his own confusion.

"It's already between us, Sam." She'd pulled her hand away from his and reached for the door handle again. "And it will be until you're straight with me."

"Ali—"

She'd swung open the car door and stepped out. "Call me when you're ready to tell the truth about Jacqueline, okay, Sam?" Then she'd slammed the door and left him there, sitting in the car, the engine idling.

He'd watched her walk around the car and up the front steps. He'd watched her fumble with her keys, open the door and disappear into the house.

That was the last time he'd seen her. They hadn't spoken in almost a week. He hadn't called because he had no idea of what he could possibly say to her. He hadn't gone to her house, because he wasn't sure what he could tell her. And over the weekend he'd thought about Ali so much he figured he was going mad.

When he'd answered the phone at three the other morning and heard only silence over the line, somehow he'd known it was her. Even after she'd hung up, he'd held the receiver to his ear, his mind stumbling over all the things he'd wanted to say to her.

He'd almost called her back, so certain it was Ali. But what he had to tell her needed to be done in person. He needed to look into her eyes, to be sure she understood what he felt for her, and to know that she, too, felt something for him.

Even now Sam wasn't entirely sure what he could possibly say to close the gap between them, but he knew he had to do something. He couldn't go another day without seeing her.

"HERE'S TO YOU, kid," Jamie said, raising his wine-glass and tipping it toward Ali as they sat at the kitchen table. "You're quite a woman."

"I'll drink to that." She laughed, touching her glass to his with a resounding clink. She took another sip of the dark red wine that had already begun its soothing effect sometime after they'd finished dinner. Lifting her legs onto the seat across from her, she rested her head against the high back of the chair and listened to Billie Holiday's "It's Too Hot for Words" playing on the stereo in the other room.

She hadn't realized how much she missed Jamie's company over the past few weeks.

When he'd called on Saturday afternoon, announcing his imminent arrival, Ali had bustled through the house doing a quick cleanup and then put the final touches on the drawings she planned to send back to New York with him. All week she'd thrown herself into her work, trying desperately to keep her mind off Sam. And even though she'd thought of little else but him, her productivity hadn't suffered.

Jamie was more than pleased with the latest drawings. He'd taken Ali out to dinner to celebrate on Saturday night, and after spending the better part of Sunday reviewing the thumbnail sketches for the last of the series, Jamie and Ali mutually decided they'd done enough work for one weekend.

This morning Jamie's passion for antique shops had at last won out, and they'd set out on a six-hour expedition. Now, with the evidence of Jamie's culinary skills surrounding them, Ali felt exhaustion throbbing in her legs from hours of scouring shops.

"I still can't believe the work you've managed to do here," Jamie went on. "And I can't begin to tell you how impressed Logan is. I told you he was sending more work your way, didn't I?"

Ali nodded. A manuscript had come in the mail three days ago, but she hadn't found the energy to look at it yet.

"You ready for another glass?" Jamie asked as he reached for the second bottle of the evening and swished the last of the wine in the bottom.

"Not for me." Ali gave him a smile and swirled the wine in her glass, watching the play of light through the crimson liquid. "I'm definitely for coffee after this one," she admitted, feeling the warm tingle of the wine travel through her body as she took another sip. "Besides, the last of the bottle..."

"...always goes to the cook," Jamie finished for her as he filled his glass and looked across the table in time to see her glowing smile falter.

She hadn't heard those words in a long time, yet it was as if Duncan had said them only yesterday. Perhaps it was the familiarity of Jamie's company or Billie Holiday's lilting voice in the background that had brought the memories flooding back. How many times had Duncan cooked for her and Jamie in their loft apartment? And how many times had Duncan used the same remark to appropriate the last glass of wine for himself?

Ali could tell by the flicker of concern in Jamie's expression that he regretted having finished the statement that had become Duncan's trademark. She gave him a smile to ease his concern.

"You still miss him, don't you, Al?"

She nodded and looked down at the thin gold wedding band on her left hand, rubbing it with her thumb. "Sometimes," she said at last, not sure how to tell Jamie that not a day went by when she didn't think of Duncan at least a dozen times, where she didn't imagine she'd heard his voice or the gentle roll of his laughter.

"Have the nightmares stopped?" Jamie asked, brushing aside a shock of red hair as he leaned back and cradled his wineglass.

"The ones about Duncan have."

"You mean there are others?"

Ali shrugged. "Just one. It's probably nothing."

"It's this case you're working on, isn't it?"

"I don't know that for sure, Jamie." Over dinner on Saturday, Ali had given into Jamie's pressuring and briefly discussed her limited involvement in the Munroe case. At the time she'd been able to divert the conversation, but now she knew Jamie's concern would draw it out of her.

"Have you talked to Sam about these dreams?"

She shook her head.

"Well, if they're related to the case, maybe you should. I mean, if it's going to speed up the investigation at all and put an end to your involvement with it..."

"I haven't spoken to Sam in days."

"Why not?"

"I told him I wouldn't talk to him until he was straight with me."

"Straight about what?"

"About this case and his personal involvement with it."

Jamie looked confused.

Ali let out a long breath. There was no sense hiding it any longer. She had to tell someone, and she could trust Jamie. When she looked at him, she knew he sensed her personal commitment to the investigation. Through their years of friendship, Jamie had come to know Ali almost better than anyone.

"Listen, Jamie, there's a lot more to this case than I've told you."

"And obviously a lot more to Sam Tremaine than you've let on, as well. Is there something going on between the two of you?"

"I wouldn't exactly call it that. Not yet, anyway," Ali confessed. "We haven't spent that much time together."

Ali remembered their dinner at Morty's, how Sam had made her laugh for the first time in months, how his touch had made her feel alive again. No, they hadn't spent much time together, but somehow that didn't seem to matter.

"I'm not sure what it is about Sam, Jamie. There's something between us. Maybe it's me, you know? Maybe it's just working a case again after so long." She picked up her glass and stared into the wine. "I don't know. It's as if I *know* this guy. I feel comfortable around him. Like there's this kind of familiarity between us.''

''He's a cop, Al.''

''Trust me, I've more than considered that.''

''So you feel something for him. Is that such a crime? Come on, Al, you know what I'm going to say.''

She nodded. Of course she knew what he was going to say. ''It's about time.'' That was Jamie—Mr. Practical. She could always count on him to bring her back to earth.

''It was bound to happen sooner or later, Al. I warned you.''

Months after Duncan had died, even after Gary had practically given up on her ever leaving the apartment, Jamie had been there for her. They'd talked about this day—when she would meet someone who would make her forget about Duncan. Or at least forget the pain and the loss. And even though she'd appreciated Jamie's realistic outlook at the time, she'd never really believed him—not until she'd looked into Sam's eyes.

''So how does it feel?''

''How does what feel?'' she asked.

''Falling in love.''

''Come on, Jamie. I never said it was anything like that. I hardly know the guy.''

''You just told me you felt like you know him pretty well.''

Ali tossed back the last of her wine, wishing for an easy exit from the conversation.

''Ali, this is Jamie here, remember? You can talk to me.''

''I know. It's just that there's nothing to talk about.'' Why was this so difficult? Why had voicing her feelings to her best friend suddenly become so impossible?

"You know what it is, don't you? You can't bring yourself to talk about this guy, to admit you feel something for him, because that might in some way deny everything you had with Duncan."

"Don't be ridiculous."

"It's true. Whether you believe it or not, it's true," he said, and turned his attention back to his wine.

Ali watched him for a moment, letting Billie Holiday's music wash over her. He was right of course. That was why she'd been so tense when she'd kissed Sam, why it had been so difficult to open up to him about Duncan. And that was why she'd used the excuse of the bracelet to break off whatever it was she'd seen developing between her and Sam—break it off before it had gotten to a point where she'd be forced to face the imminent changes in her life. It wasn't just that there had been something between Sam and Jacqueline; she couldn't bear the thought of letting go of Duncan.

"So how do you think Sam feels about you?" Ali knew he felt the same way. She'd seen it in his eyes when she'd turned to him in the car the last time they'd spoken. She'd seen his sense of helplessness when she'd given him her ultimatum and left him sitting in her driveway.

"I'm pretty sure the feelings are mutual," she admitted finally, remembering the intensity and desire in their last kiss.

"So what's the problem?"

"He's not telling me everything, Jamie."

"Oh, and this should bother you? Ali, you've got to be one of the most private people I know. I mean, there isn't anything you don't play close to the chest until you're damned good and ready. And you're pissed off at this guy because he doesn't tell you everything?''

"It's not like that, Jamie. I don't need to know everything about a person. It's just that when that person is directly linked to a murder investigation—''

"And how is Sam related?''

"I don't know exactly how. Not yet, anyway. But there was something between Sam and Jacqueline Munroe.''

"What do you mean by 'something'?''

It wouldn't be the first time Ali had used Jamie as a sounding board for the cases she'd worked on. Before she and Duncan had started working together, she'd always gone to Jamie to try to sort out her feelings on an investigation. Often bouncing them off a neutral person like Jamie was far more constructive than talking to Duncan or Gary, who were always wrapped up in the investigation.

"All I know is that Jacqueline's murder was not premeditated. It was too intense, too angry. The police still think it was Peter Munroe, the husband, since he's the only one who gained from his wife's death— through the insurance money. But if it was the husband and if he had gone over there with the intent to kill his wife, I think he would have been calmer, more collected. This guy—'' she shook her head, remembering the intensity of the reading she'd taken from the pillow ''—whoever it was, was driven by rage. When he held that pillow over Jacqueline's face, he hated her. He hated her so much he didn't think twice when he felt her weakening beneath him.''

"And afterward, when he was looking down at her, lying there on the bed, I can't describe it, but...there was this tenderness. At first, after the reading, I couldn't figure it out. I mean here's this guy, absolutely livid with rage, who's just smothered the life out of this woman, and then he takes the time to straighten her nightgown, to touch her face and brush her hair back as if..."

"...as if he loved her," Jamie finished, and Ali felt the same chill that had swept through her the first time she'd considered the possibility.

"I think Jacqueline Munroe was having an affair. Possibly even before she left her husband. When her lover found out that she was going back to her husband, he went over there to confront her—perhaps only to convince her she was making a mistake. I don't know. But I don't think he went over there with the intent to kill her.

"They probably got into an argument or something. Jacqueline couldn't be persuaded to change her mind, and insane with jealousy, he became violent."

Jamie cleared his throat before he spoke, his voice low and calm. "And you think that Jacqueline Munroe's jealous lover was your detective?"

Sam's eyes flashed through Ali's mind—dark, guarded eyes that held secrets she hadn't wanted to know at first but now wished she did.

"I don't know," she answered, hearing her own voice cool and distant.

"Wait a minute, Al." Jamie pulled himself to the edge of his chair and leaned across the long-forgotten remains of dinner. "Do you realize what you're saying? You're talking about the same guy you just said you might be falling in love with—"

"I never said that, Jamie."

"Whatever." He waved his hand as if her true feelings for Sam were a mere technicality. "The point is, you said you knew this guy. Surely you know him well enough to judge his character. I mean, does he fit the profile of a killer?"

Ali shook her head, recalling the tenderness Sam had displayed the night she'd told him about Duncan.

"No, I don't think so. But he did give Jacqueline that school ring."

"Ali, even if your reading was correct, which I'm not doubting, that must have been years ago."

"And the bracelet?"

Jamie polished off the last of his wine and shook his head. "You're only guessing, Al. And, yes—" he pointed at her "—even *you* can guess wrong. Besides which," he continued, "doesn't it strike you as odd, if your assumption that Sam might have something to do with this woman's death is correct, that he would be so determined to find this bracelet? I mean, it would most certainly lead right back to him."

Maybe Jamie was right. Maybe she was jumping to conclusions. And maybe she was grasping for any reason to push Sam away because she couldn't face the fact she might actually feel something for someone other than Duncan. The bracelet and Sam's secrecy were the only excuses she'd been able to come up with to drive him away.

"So have you talked to Sam about this jealous-lover theory of yours?"

"No. I wanted to be sure first."

"Well, as far as I can see it, there's only one way you're going to know for sure, and that's by talking to him." Jamie stood up from the table and began gathering up the cutlery and plates. "Listen to me, Ali. No,

wait, on second thought, listen to yourself, to your instincts. You feel something for this guy, so he can't be
all that bad. Go with your gut feelings on this, Ali, not
your visions."

Just as Jamie started across the kitchen to the sink
the doorbell rang. Exploding from her slumber, Tash
raced to the front door with an excited bark.

"You expecting someone?"

Ali stood up from the table and checked her watch.
It was after ten. "Not at this hour."

She left the kitchen, shouting once for Tash to calm
down, then switched on the front-hall light.

"Hey," Jamie shouted above the clatter of dishes,
"maybe it's the neighbors come to complain about
your Billie Holiday records."

Ali laughed and unfastened the chain. But her smile
vanished when she opened the door.

CHAPTER TEN

IN THE FLOOD of light that spilled through the front door into the dark night, Ali looked at Sam. His hands were buried in the pockets of his leather jacket, and when his gaze lifted, his dark eyes held hers, pinning her, speechless, in the doorway.

The corners of his mouth curled slightly as a smile struggled to cover his apparent uneasiness. "I know it's late," he said, shifting his weight. "But I saw your lights and figured you were still up."

Ali nodded. Why was it she felt the sudden urge to step into his arms and let their embrace dispel the awkwardness between them?

Beyond the bluesy sound of Billie Holiday, Ali heard the clatter of dishes from the kitchen. Sam heard it, as well.

"I'm sorry, Ali. You've got company. Look, maybe I should come back."

"No." She swung the door open. "No, Sam, really. Please come in."

He gave her another half smile, and when he stepped past her into the front hall, Ali caught the now familiar combination of leather and subtle cologne.

She felt the need to explain. "It's my friend Jamie. He's up from New York for a few days. We're just finishing a late dinner. Would you like to have a drink?"

Sam paused, his eyes never leaving hers as he seemed to weigh his options. Eventually he shook his head and lowered his voice, afraid that Jamie might hear from the other room. "I...I wanted to talk to you, Ali. There's something I think you should know."

Ali nodded.

"About me and Jacquie." He looked down to the floor, tucking his hands into his pockets again. "And about you and me."

"Is everything all right, Al?"

Sam turned at the sound of Jamie's voice, and when Ali followed his gaze, she saw Jamie walk through the entrance into the front hall, a dish towel over one shoulder. He stopped when he saw Sam.

"Yes, everything's fine," she said, closing the front door. "Jamie, this is Detective Sam Tremaine. Sam, my friend Jamie Ackerman."

"Ah, Sam. Al's told me a lot about you," Jamie said, shaking the detective's hand and ignoring Ali's warning look.

"Well, you should probably hear my side of the story sometime." Sam glanced at Ali, and she could see the tension easing from the hard lines of his face.

"Fine, then. I'll just go to the kitchen and open another bottle of the ol' cabernet. You can tell me all about it." Jamie gave Ali a wink and headed back to the kitchen before Sam had any opportunity to decline the offer.

"I really shouldn't stay, Ali," he said. "This isn't a good time. We really have to talk."

"I'd like you to stay, Sam," she told him, putting her hand on his arm and feeling a surge go through her. She wanted to tell him how much she'd missed him over the past week, how many times she'd wanted to call him and apologize for being short-tempered. She wanted to tell him how much, when she'd heard his voice over the phone the other night whisper her name, she'd wanted to be with him.

"Besides, we can talk later."

Sam studied her for a long moment before nodding. "Are you free tomorrow evening?"

"Sure. Now, come on," she urged, hearing the clink of wineglasses from the kitchen. "Why don't we have a drink and relax a little?"

ALI HAD PUT coffee on around eleven-thirty, but the pot remained untouched as Sam and Jamie showed no signs of being affected by the wine. By midnight they were still discussing everything from politics to sports, and Ali had spent the past two hours wondering how it was that this scene, Jamie and Sam talking to each other as if they'd been friends for years, seemed so familiar.

With dinner's dishes piled on the counter and another empty wine bottle in the middle of the table, Ali looked at the two men. This was not unlike the evenings she and Jamie had shared in the past—evenings with Duncan. And yet it was different, too. Her memory of those hours when the three of them had sat around the kitchen table were flat somehow, fixed in time and inanimate. But this now, Jamie and Sam . . . this was real.

Sam's laughter rolled into her thoughts, bringing a smile to her lips even though she'd missed the joke. And when Sam looked over at her, he seemed to recognize the exhaustion behind the smile.

"Well," he announced, setting down his wineglass, "I'm afraid I have to get going. I have a full day tomorrow." He stood up and extended a hand across the table to Jamie. "It was a pleasure meeting you, Jamie. I'm sorry to hear you're heading back to New York tomorrow. Maybe I'll see you again sometime."

"I don't doubt that," he said, shaking Sam's hand and giving Ali a quick wink before starting to clear the glasses and empty bottles.

Ali followed Sam to the front door and then down the steps to the driveway where the Bronco sat under a clear, dark sky, the three-quarter moon reflecting off its hood. Their footsteps on the fine gravel of the drive brought a pause in the constant hum of crickets, and only when they'd reached the car and Sam turned to Ali did the crickets resume their chirping.

When he looked at Ali, seeing the soft glow of the moon whispering along her skin, he again felt the urge to talk to her. It didn't matter that it was late or that they were standing in the middle of her driveway. He wanted to tell her everything, including how much he'd thought of her during the past week.

"So, I'll see you tomorrow night, then?"

Ali nodded, taking a step closer to him as he leaned back against the Bronco.

"I have a couple of meetings in the afternoon. Is eight-thirty all right?"

"That'd be fine, Sam."

He watched her lips curve into a gentle smile. She stuck her hands into the back pockets of her shorts as if unsure of what to do with them now that she stood only at arm's length away. He could smell her perfume as he took in a deep breath of air.

"I've missed you, Ali," he said suddenly, hoping he didn't sound too forward. "I . . . I know I should have called sooner. I can't tell you how sorry I am for waiting so long."

"I've missed you, too, Sam," she admitted, her soft voice reaching out through the dark silence with a bare honesty that touched Sam. Closing the gap between them, Ali took her hands from her pockets and placed them on his hips.

Sam followed suit, feeling the play of muscles along her back through her thin cotton shirt when she lifted her hands to his shoulders. He felt the softness of her fingertips caress his cheek, his chin and then his lips, before trailing to the back of his neck and guiding his mouth to hers. A tremor ran through him as she drew nearer, bringing herself even closer by stepping into the triangle of his legs. And when her lips brushed his with all the tenderness of their first kiss, Sam felt her hips press against his, pinning him against the Bronco. He felt his own desire straining against the thick denim as Ali's kiss deepened.

Gone was the hesitancy of their first kiss. Gone was the wariness he knew Ali had felt. And gone were his own doubts now, as Ali's body moved against his, as every fibre of his being cried out to be with her.

He tasted the lingering hint of wine on her lips. Even after she'd pulled back, Sam savored the sweetness of her kiss tingling on his lips. And then, as Ali gently eased away, he stared down into her sparkling eyes. He considered telling her how much he wanted to be with her, how he'd imagined the feel of her body next to his.

But he couldn't—not yet. Instead, he whispered a regretful good-night, promising to see her tomorrow, and got into the Bronco.

Even after he'd backed down the drive and headed along Blucher Street, Sam could smell Ali's perfume on his shirt. He could still feel the desire that had raged through him when her body had pressed so longingly against his.

HARRINGTON'S MONTHLY staff meeting had gone far later than any of the detectives on the force had counted on. At seven-thirty, most of them had rushed out of the assembly room, late for their kids' piano lesson or Little League game.

Sam hadn't stuck around, either. He was rarely one of the first out the door. But then, it wasn't often he had anywhere to go.

When he got home fifteen minutes later, Ziggy was waiting for him at the door, eager for his evening run. When Sam bypassed the dog and headed upstairs, he heard the disgruntled Great Dane go out through the specially built flap on the kitchen door to the back yard.

Twenty minutes later, after Sam had showered and shaved, the dog wandered through the house, following him as he searched for a fresh shirt and jeans. Sam couldn't help but feel a pang of guilt for deserting his best friend, but then again, it wasn't like he had a date every night.

He was pouring kibble and filling a bowl with fresh water when he heard the front screen door bang shut, followed by Ziggy's bark.

"Hey, Sammy," Matt called from the hall. "Hope you haven't had dinner yet. I brought a..." He paused when he saw Sam, freshly shaved and dressed, come down the hall. "I brought a pizza."

Matt stood with the pizza box in one hand and a six-pack in the other, disappointment clouding his tanned face.

"Great," Sam said, stopping long enough to button his cuffs. "You can share it with Zig. He hasn't eaten yet."

"Aw, come on, Sammy. What is this? You take off like a bat outta hell after Harrington's finally finished blowing off his hot air for the month, and now you're deserting me? Come on, there's a game tonight. We've already missed the first inning. What, you got a heavy date or something?"

"In a manner of speaking."

"Shit, I don't believe it." Matt tossed the pizza box onto the sheet-covered couch and Ziggy sniffed at it, a long string of drool dangling to the hardwood floor before Matt pushed him away. "You actually got a date?" he asked as Sam checked himself in the hall mirror.

"Is that so hard to believe?" Sam turned to face him. "It's not like I've never dated before, you know."

"Well, I know, but . . ."

"But what?"

"But not on the night of a game."

Sam shook his head and squatted down to tie the laces of his white sneakers. "Trust me, Matt. There are more important things than a Mets' game."

"All right, all right. So tell me one thing—does this distraction have a name?"

"Come to think of it, I believe she does."

"Anyone I know?"

"Does it matter?"

Matt shrugged. "Well, yeah, of course it matters. I have to look out for my buddy, right?"

"I think I can manage," Sam assured him, and stood up.

"Wait a minute, wait a minute." Matt followed Sam to the front door as he gathered his jacket and car keys. "It's not who I think it is, is it?"

"I don't know, Matt. I don't know what you're thinking."

"It's not Van Horn, is it?"

"Maybe," Sam answered quickly, careful not to meet his partner's eyes. He knew what was coming, and he didn't have the time for it right now. He was already running late.

"Whoa. Wait a second, Sammy. Do you think this is very professional?"

"What the hell are you talking about, Matt?"

"Well, she's working on this investigation with you, isn't she? I mean, it might jeopardize the case if you're..."

"If I'm what?"

He didn't have to say it.

"Listen, Matt, it's not like she's on the force or anything, all right? And it's not like you're going to tell Harrington about this, right? Now just relax. It's under control." He reached for Ziggy's leash and the dog perked up when Sam slapped the nylon cord into Matt's hand. "Since you're not doing anything, anyway, you wanna take Zig for his walk? He'll love you for it." Sam flashed him a smile.

He didn't wait for Matt's response. He pushed open the screen door and headed for his Bronco. "And lock up on your way out, will you?" he shouted back.

JAMIE HAD LEFT Danby sometime after three that afternoon. Ali had walked him to his car, stood in the driveway as he started the engine and gave him a quick kiss through the open window before he pulled out.

Now, as she recapped her drafting pen and straightened the drawings on her table in the living room, Ali felt a strange emptiness in the house. For three days it had been filled with the lilt of Jamie's laughter. Now there was only silence.

She looked around the room. It was strange how, even though this was her sister's house, Ali felt more at home here than she had in the apartment in New York. She felt more alive here, freer in a sense, as if removing herself from all the memories of her life with Duncan had somehow made her into a different person—someone who could see beyond the past and once again hope for the future.

On her way to the stereo, Ali paused at the fireplace. From the framed picture on the mantelpiece, Duncan looked back at her. That week had been the happiest time in her life, and for the few short months after that, her life had come together. It had been complete.

She often thought of the child she'd lost the night of Duncan's death. Still wondered, on occasion, if she might have been happier and better equipped to handle her loss if she'd had a part of Duncan to cherish. Yet at the same time, she'd often wondered if she would have been strong enough to raise a child on her own, if she could have gone on with her life seeing Duncan's face reflected back at her every day. The doctor had told her it was a boy.

Ali looked down at her hands where she was unconsciously rubbing her wedding band. Somehow, with Sam around, she'd begun to think less and less of the little boy who might have possessed Duncan's shining smile. And she'd begun to recall less and less of the dreams she'd once shared with his father.

The shrill chime of the doorbell interrupted her thoughts, and she turned from the picture on the mantelpiece. Checking herself once in the hall mirror, she swallowed the fleeting sensation of butterflies as she opened the front door.

"Hi, Sam." She held the door for him, returning his beaming smile.

"Seems I'm always showing up late," he apologized. "The chief kept us overtime for this meeting, and I'm—"

"You don't have to apologize, Sam. I'm more than familiar with precinct politics. So, are you hungry?"

Ali headed for the kitchen and Sam followed. "Actually I'm not. I had a late lunch with Matt."

"Good," she shot him a smile as she pulled a chilled bottle of wine from the fridge. "Cuz I didn't cook for you." She handed him a bottle of chardonnay and turned to one of the drawers.

"So, Jamie got off all right?"

"He headed out this afternoon."

Sam watched Ali as she rummaged through the drawer. He couldn't remember if he'd seen her in a skirt before. Its thin fabric moved with her, hinting at the gentle curves beneath. "You two seem very close."

"Well, it's just your typical platonic relationship. We met in college years ago. He dated my roommate for a while," she explained, still intent on her search. "We stayed in touch after graduation, and shortly after that, we started working on a few books together. Ah..." She turned, smiling at her find as she presented the corkscrew.

"It's always been my mother's undying belief that if only Jamie and I could *learn* to be attracted to each other, we might actually have something." She laughed, the sound bringing a smile to Sam's face.

Even her eyes laughed, he noticed as she handed him the corkscrew. When he took it, her fingers brushed his palm, and her touch made Sam want to take her into his arms and feel her embrace.

He cleared his throat, breaking the stare that held them in that suspended moment, and turned his attention to the bottle.

"So what about you?" she asked.

Sam looked from the wine bottle to Ali. She leaned back against the kitchen counter, her arms crossed over her chest.

"What about me?"

"Any friends?"

"Platonic?"

"Or otherwise."

"Women friends, you mean?"

"Well, I never exactly pictured you and Matt..."

He caught her smile and turned back to the task of uncorking the bottle. "No," he answered, aware that at this point Ali needed to know his current status. "There's no one."

He popped the cork and followed Ali as she carried two glasses to the living room. He sank onto the couch, watched her choose a CD and adjust the volume on the stereo.

"I don't get it," Ali said when she joined him on the couch and picked up her glass of wine.

"What don't you get?"

"That there isn't someone in your life."

"I guess I could never make the time."

"Never *could* or never *would?*"

Sam shrugged. "I don't know. For the past few years there hasn't exactly been anyone who made me want to make the time."

"And Jacquie?"

Sam let out a long breath. Ali certainly wasn't wasting any time. Then again, it was better to get this over with. If he and Ali were to have a chance of being together, he had to put an end to this ghost from his past.

"No," he admitted at last. "Jacquie was different. I was able to make the time for her—at one point in my life...."

And then Ali listened. For close to an hour, she didn't interrupt. Sam told her about his high-school romance with Jacquie, how they'd been first-time lovers and how they'd even made vows to one another in a mock wedding ceremony only months before they'd graduated. He told Ali about the school ring he'd given Jacquie, that he'd asked her to marry him and that they'd decided to wait. And then he told her about those first few months at college, how he'd thought he would die without Jacquie.

"But surely you saw her during your training?" Ali prompted him gently when he'd paused to refill their glasses.

"Off and on. But once I'd started with the academy, the demands they put on us became heavier and heavier. I wasn't able to get home as often, and I hadn't even seen Jacquie for a couple of months until my father died.

"When I came back for the funeral, Jacquie was there for me. It was hard at first, dealing with my father's death. He'd had a heart attack. None of us were prepared for it—if you *could* be prepared for something like that. But it was just so unexpected. He was a cop, too, on the Danby force. Healthy, energetic, maybe a little too committed to his work but not your average heart-attack victim.

"Jacquie, though—" Sam shook his head and looked past Ali to the soft glow of the lamp she had turned on when the living room had begun to darken some time ago "—she was so supportive. She was all I had then. I had to be strong for my mother. I couldn't let her see how Dad's death had affected me."

Sam took a sip of wine. "I stayed in Danby for a couple of weeks after Dad died. I helped my mother make the arrangements to sell the house. They'd just put a big down payment on a place in Florida and she decided that was where she wanted to be. I knew I had to get back to the academy if I wanted to finish my training so, once everything was settled as much as possible, I went.

"Actually, if it hadn't been for Jacquie, I wouldn't have gone back." He could still remember every word of their argument the day he'd told her he wanted to quit the academy to be with her.

"I didn't want to go back, not after being with Jacquie for two weeks and realizing what I'd been missing. Maybe burying my father scared me a bit, too. I mean, a man that age, with his health, well, he shouldn't have just keeled over and died on a routine beat. So I blamed the force and his commitment to it. And I started to doubt my own future in law enforcement.

"I panicked. I didn't want to be to Jacquie what my father had been to my mother all those years. I didn't want the woman in my life to come second to my job the way my father had lived his life. So I asked Jacquie to marry me. I had all kinds of plans, and none of them involved the academy. It was Jacquie who pointed out that my desperation to be with her was not the right reason for us to get married. So I went back.''

Sam let the cool wine wet his throat and looked at Ali. She faced him, her legs drawn up beneath her as she twisted a curl of hair around one finger.

"Anyway, that last year at the academy was the toughest. I think I saw Jacquie twice in eight months. We wrote, but the letters were infrequent. Then I landed the position in Danby and packed my bags. Even then, I wasn't sure what I was coming home to or if I was coming *home* at all. My mother was living in Florida, and I hadn't heard from Jacquie in months.

"I'd called her the day before I was due to leave for Danby, and she'd sounded strange on the phone. I should have sensed that something was wrong. When I went over to her house unannounced, Jacquie was really nervous and I guess it was only then that I realized it was over between us.''

Sam would never forget the blank expression on Jacquie's face when she had crossed the lawn to meet him. He'd swept her into his arms and kissed her, but her expression had said it all. When her mother and Peter Munroe had walked toward them from the house, Sam had begun to understand. That was when Jacquie told him, in front of Peter and in front of her mother, that she and Peter were getting married in a month. She'd even told him about the unplanned pregnancy, right there in the middle of her family's lawn.

"I'll never forget the way she looked at me," Sam said, feeling a trace of the old bitterness. "Like everything we'd been promising each other for six years meant nothing.''

"Anyway, we didn't speak for a few years. Cassie was born. I read it in the paper. We'd run into each other once in a while and there was still a strong attraction between us. I knew it was mutual, and I could tell she wasn't entirely happy in her marriage to Peter. He worked long hours as an accountant, and she even told me, once we started having coffee together on occasion, that he was always exhausted from work and was never really there for her."

"Did you have an affair with her, Sam?"

He met Ali's calm gaze. This wasn't just about the investigation or their partnership on this case. Sam could see that in Ali's cool expression. She'd known all along, and she knew he needed to get it off his chest once and for all if there was to be anything between them.

"I suppose you might call it that." He took another swallow of wine, wishing it could wash away the numbing guilt he still felt. "The first time was a mistake. I was at Morty's with some of the guys on the force when she and a couple of her friends came in. She'd had a bit too much to drink and wanted me to drive her home. On the way she persuaded me to take her to our old spot at the lake. One thing led to another. It was the dumbest thing I'd ever done... well, one of the dumbest things."

"What was the other?"

Sam looked at Ali, aware that his confessions would affect the way she viewed him. But at this point there was no sense in being anything but honest.

"The other was the next time I slept with Jacquie. It was some sleazy hotel outside of Danby. I think both of us were feeling too guilty to enjoy anything at the time. We never really talked about it after that, but I

knew I wasn't capable of having an affair. I can't say
if that's what Jacquie wanted, though. But after she
left Peter, we continued to see each other as friends.
And I knew she wasn't happy."

"So did Peter ever find out? About you and Jacquie?"

"I don't think so."

"Was there any possibility that Jacquie was having
an affair with someone else?"

"After the breakup?"

"Or before."

Ali watched Sam shake his head. She hadn't intended to discuss the case tonight. After their kiss last
night, she'd had other things in mind—the same things
she'd seen in Sam's eyes when she caught him staring
at her in the kitchen a couple of hours ago.

"I don't think so, Ali. Somehow I think she would
have told me. Why? Is that what you think?"

She spent the next fifteen minutes telling Sam everything she'd told Jamie the other evening—everything except that she'd suspected the jealous lover was
Sam himself. And when she'd finished, Sam was nodding.

"You know, you're probably right, Ali. I did consider that possibility, but I guess I just didn't want to
believe it. I mean, Jacquie was so...she was a good
person, you know?"

Ali could see the sense of loss flicker behind Sam's
eyes then as he held her gaze, and she imagined he was
remembering the night he'd looked at Jacquie for the
last time—lying lifeless in a bed in her mother's house,
surrounded by other cops so that Sam could not even
touch her or say goodbye.

At least Ali had had that. At least she'd been able to hold Duncan when he died. She'd been able to say goodbye and tell him she loved him.

"We'll get the guy, Sam," she promised, taking his hand in hers briefly. "Don't worry. Whatever it takes, we'll get him."

When she slipped her hand from his grasp, Sam felt its absence immediately. And when Ali stood up from the couch to gather their glasses and the empty wine bottle, he joined her.

"I know we've talked enough about the case tonight," Ali said as he followed her into the kitchen, "but I think you should speak with Peter Munroe. Maybe he knows something."

Sam watched her as she rinsed the wineglasses in the sink. The only light in the kitchen was the pale yellow glow of the range lamp, and as he saw it glimmer softly along Ali's skin, Sam knew he had to touch her.

She didn't hear him come up behind her—he could tell by the way she almost dropped one of the glasses.

"He might even know something about the bracelet," she added, turning off the taps.

"Who?"

"Peter Munroe."

"I'll talk to him." Sam could feel her muscles ease beneath his touch when he lifted his hands to her shoulders. He slid them down her arms until his hands were holding hers again. "You know something?" he asked, whispering in her ear.

"What?" Her own voice was little more than a ragged whisper.

"I think you were right."

"About what?"

He kissed her ear and then moved down to her neck, entwining his fingers in hers as he shifted closer behind her, longing to feel the caress of her body again.

"About having discussed the case enough tonight."

Ali didn't respond. She drew her hands from his and turned within the circle of his arms to look up at him. What Sam saw in her eyes was all he needed. When he held her face in his hands and lowered his lips to hers, he knew that Ali wanted to be with him as much as he'd ached to be with her. He knew, as he'd known from the first moment he'd seen her through the screen door, that there was something between them, something that could no longer be denied.

Ali responded to his kiss; her breathing quickened, her tongue met his and her fingers feathered back through his hair to pull him closer. He swayed for a moment, drowning in her sweetness. His hands traveled to her waist, and when he heard her moan as he pulled her hips against his, he thought he would shatter from desire.

"God, I want to be with you so much," he murmured. "I want to make love to you, Ali." And in that moment, Sam couldn't remember if there'd been anything he'd ever wanted as much as he wanted Ali right now.

Silently she took his hand, steadying herself for a moment against the counter, and led him from the kitchen. She didn't say anything as she guided him up the stairs and down the hall to the bedroom. She didn't speak as she carefully lit several candles on the dresser and nightstand. Only when she finally joined him in the middle of the room did Sam see a flicker of hesitation in her face.

He stared at her for a moment, wondering if he'd imagined it. He kissed her silken lips again, amazed at her response. But when he looked down into the face he cradled in his hands, he knew he hadn't imagined the apprehension there.

"Ali, what is it?"

She gave a tremulous smile. "Nothing, Sam. It's okay."

"No, it's not. Something's the matter." He felt her hand flutter against his chest. He waited, hoping for a response, but none came. Finally he asked, "It's Duncan, isn't it?"

She looked down, unable to meet his stare, and Sam watched her struggle for an answer.

"Ali?"

She shook her head. "I'm sorry, Sam. It's...it's been a long time. I haven't been with anyone since..." Her hand balled into a fist against his chest, and he reached up to smooth it out, holding it down to stop its trembling. "I mean, until I met you...I never felt anything for anyone but Duncan. Until you..."

"Listen, Ali—" he lifted her chin with one finger so that he could see her face again "—maybe this is too soon. Maybe we should wait awhile."

Ali held his gaze, and for a moment Sam wondered again if Ali could read his thoughts—rampant thoughts of desire that raged through his mind as he swayed in her nearness. Then she shook her head.

"No." She lifted a hand to caress his cheek, and this time it did not tremble. "I want to be with you, Sam."

His eyes never left hers. In the hush of the bedroom, he studied her face, waiting, giving her time to change her mind. But Ali had decided.

Her fingers unfastened the buttons of his shirt one by one, and then she brushed it open, revealing the tanned ripple of muscles. As she slid her fingers across the contours of his chest and then over his shoulders to his back, Ali felt his body quiver with the same hunger her own had. His shirt fell to the floor, and anticipating the searing touch of his skin against hers, Ali felt her breath catch.

Sam guided her hands to his hips and left them there as he undid her shirt. Deft fingers worked the buttons, and when the last one had been freed, he gently pulled the shirt back over her shoulders. She thought she heard a strangled moan as Sam gazed at her, a look of adoration warming his face. He moved closer to her, trailing kisses down her neck, past her shoulder and finally to her breasts.

When he reached the delicate lace of her bra, he gently pulled it back with one finger, cupping her breast in his hand as the excruciating heat of his lips sought out her already erect nipple. This time it was Ali's turn to stifle a whimper.

His kisses burned downward, dammed by the top of her skirt, and Ali could no longer keep her own hands still. She wrapped her fingers around his belt and pulled him closer, seeking his lips again. He moved against her, his mouth devouring hers, and she felt the immediacy of his desire through the barrier of his jeans.

In one fluid motion, their lips barely parting, Sam swept her up into his arms and lowered her to the bed. His hands trailed down her body, followed by a searing path of kisses. This time when he met the top of her skirt, he did not stop and the cry Ali had suppressed earlier erupted from her throat.

She entwined her fingers in his hair as his lips sought the rising heat of her desire, and she pulled him to her. Tears welled in her eyes at the tenderness of Sam's touch, and when she could take no more, Ali guided him back. Each kiss brought with it an explosion more immediate than the one before it, more urgent than the last. And when he finally reached her throat, Ali rolled him over onto his back.

Muscles quivered beneath her feathery touch, and fervent kisses sent waves of desire trembling through her, as well as Sam. Her fingers fanned, migrating down his firm stomach, sliding along skin slick with the sweat of their passion until, at last, she reached the denim barrier. Eagerly she unbuckled his belt.

With her heart racing, Ali embraced the straining hardness there, caressing it with trembling fingers, marveling at his readiness. She heard Sam moan as she tugged his jeans free of his waist, running her fingers along his thighs and up his body. Time became endless as they swayed between unbridled yearning and lingering, exploratory caresses, until finally Ali straddled him.

When her mouth found his again, even more ardent than before, Sam responded with a hunger all his own. Each hand cupped a breast, kneading them gently as he drank in her kiss. Then he slid his hands slowly down, over her rib cage to her hips. It was there that his hands stopped, and gently he lifted her, guiding her onto him.

This time, Ali couldn't tell if the guttural moan she heard had risen from her own throat or from Sam's as she lowered herself and felt him move inside her. She rocked above him, savoring his avid thrusts, feeling him strain beneath her until he could wait no longer. In one movement, he rolled her over and drew himself up on his elbows so that he could look down into her face.

Affectionately he brushed away a stray curl and lowered his lips to her throat as she arched against him, raising her hips to meet his slow, steady thrusts. Her fingers found the flex of tight muscles along his back as his motion quickened, and instinctively her legs encircled him. She slid her hands from his back to the tautness of his buttocks, pulling him into her, drawing him deeper until she knew that neither of them could hold back any longer.

When Sam took her mouth again, he carried her to a plateau she'd long forgotten. And there, as she heard him cry out her name, Ali was one with Sam.

EVEN WITH the bedroom blinds drawn, he could see a dim flickering of what he guessed were candles. They were having some night, he thought, easing his weight onto his right hip to alleviate the pins and needles that prickled along his leg.

Through the patio doors, he'd seen them in the kitchen some time ago, an empty wine bottle and a couple of glasses in their hands. Then he'd watched as Tremaine had come up behind her at the sink, bringing his body close to hers, wrapping his arms around her and nuzzling her neck. Through the binoculars, he'd seen her eyes close when she'd tilted back her head, welcoming his kisses.

For close to three hours now he'd sat here, wedged in the branches of one of the maples that bordered the back of the Nolan property. He had a cramp in his right leg, and his left had fallen asleep almost an hour ago. He'd scraped his elbow on the rough bark when he'd climbed up to his vantage point and had almost cracked his skull on a branch he hadn't seen. And for what? To watch a grope session?

But he couldn't ignore the real reason Sam Tremaine was with Van Horn tonight. And he couldn't overlook the fact that she might find a lead in the investigation that had shuddered to a dead end.

If this woman was for real, if she actually saw something, Sam Tremaine would be the first person she'd go to—especially after what he'd witnessed in the kitchen. He'd have to keep a closer eye on her—and on Sam Tremaine.

In the meantime, they weren't going anywhere, he guessed as he looked again to the warm glow that flickered behind the closed blinds. No sense in hanging around. He needed to stretch.

Moving slowly so as not to lose his balance in the darkness, he lowered himself from the rough branches to the top of the wooden fence that enclosed the backyard. From there he dropped to the ground, his legs slow to respond as he slipped through the back gate and followed the fence to the street.

He'd be back. He'd watch Van Horn. And he'd do whatever else was necessary, he thought as he brushed himself off and strode calmly to where he'd parked his car at the end of the street. Yes, he *would* do whatever was necessary.

CHAPTER ELEVEN

SHE RECOGNIZED the darkness. She'd felt its closeness before.

She saw Sam again, stepping into the circle of light from the round window high above him. He stopped, looked into the shadows and cocked his revolver.

Ali felt panic rising in her throat—the same panic she'd felt the last time she'd been here. But somehow it was different this time.

She watched Sam from a platform, looking down from above, cloaked in darkness. And she felt the cool grip of a revolver in her own hand.

He had stopped in the light—an easy target. Her hand came up, raising the weapon.

Then, in a flash, she saw Jacquie's face—the pillow pulled to one side, her lifeless eyes gazing upward. In another instant she saw the bracelet, glittering in the jeweler's box, and the slouching silhouettes of the rotting willows in the swamp.

One image after another snapped before her eyes, shuttering like a rapid slide show. And then she found Sam again, poised in the long shaft of light.

The revolver in her hand was cocked and ready. She felt its weight. Down the sight of the gun, she saw Sam. The gentle curve of the trigger hugged her finger.

Only when he looked up to where the shadows concealed her did she tighten her grip. Only when she saw

Sam bring his own weapon around, training it on her, did she squeeze that gentle curve back in one easy pull.

It wasn't the explosion of the bullet that yanked her from the nightmare this time. The blast rang in her ears, echoed through the empty building, and still she was there.

She felt the kick of the gun. And when she looked down into the circle of light, she saw Sam stagger.

It wasn't until she felt the searing pain of Sam's wound deep in her own chest, that Ali lurched up in bed with a gasp.

Arms reached for her. Alarmed, she jerked away.

"Ali, it's me." Sam tried to touch her, but again she pulled back. "It's all right. I'm here. Ali?"

He fumbled for the bedside lamp, and in its soft glow, he watched her horrified expression slacken. When he reached for her this time, she sank into his embrace, and Sam felt her body tremble as she drew herself closer to him.

"It's all right, Ali. It was just a dream," he whispered, rocking her slowly, stroking her hair as he felt another shudder go through her. "It's okay. I'm here."

He waited, feeling her fear ebb as her body gradually relaxed in his arms.

"Are you okay?" He brushed a damp curl of hair back from her face when she looked up at him.

"Yeah, I'm okay, Sam." She struggled to give him a reassuring smile. "Thanks for being here."

"Do you want to talk about it?"

She shook her head. "Not really."

"Is it something to do with the case?"

"I don't know. These dreams don't make any sense."

"You've had them before?"

Ali nodded. "For the past week now," she confessed, placing a hand on Sam's chest to push herself out of his embrace. "But this one was different."

"How?"

Ali looked straight at him now, studying him as if searching for an answer to ease the concern that creased his brow.

"How was this one different from the rest, Ali?" he prompted.

When she finally answered him, her words sent a chill through him. "I shot you, Sam."

"You . . . you shot me?"

Ali nodded, and when she looked away, Sam felt the need to touch her. He took her hand in his, its warmth easing the chill he'd just felt.

"You don't think it means anything, do you?"

"I'm not sure, Sam. I've never had a dream like this before. I've never had my abilities work on any subconscious level. And I don't have premonitions."

"Well, maybe your abilities are changing."

"Oh, really? So you're telling me I'm going to end up shooting you?"

"I don't know." Sam shrugged. Then, seeing the apprehension in her eyes, he said, "I'm sorry, Ali."

She shoved her pillow against the headboard and sat back, drawing her legs up and resting her chin on her knees.

"Maybe if you tell me what you saw in your dreams, we can sort through them and find some answers."

Ali looked over at Sam. In the soft glow of the lamp, he looked different than he had standing in the shimmering circle of light in her dream. She reached out to place her hand over the very spot she'd felt the bullet rip through him. Beneath her palm, she felt the steady rhythm of his heart.

He put his hand over hers. "Ali?"

Eventually she nodded, letting Sam hold her hand while she told him every detail she could remember of the dream that had haunted her sleep. When she told him about her gunning him down, Sam squeezed her hand more tightly, but he did not interrupt until she'd finished.

"Do *you* think this dream has any bearing on the case?" Sam asked. "Do you believe it's a premonition?"

Ali shook her head. "I don't know. Maybe it's just that I haven't used my abilities in so long that everything's getting all jumbled up in my head."

Sam leaned back against the headboard, too. Slipping an arm around her shoulder, he brought her closer and put both arms around her. She leaned against his chest, feeling at peace.

"Try to forget it, Ali. They're only dreams."

"How do you know that?"

"First of all, I don't think you'd shoot me." He drew her closer and nuzzled her ear. "And second, that church window you said you'd seen several times? There aren't any churches in Danby with windows like that."

"But that doesn't rule out the possibility that these dreams might mean something, Sam. My having premonitions isn't entirely impossible. I mean, no one really knows how these things work. Sometimes I don't even have any control over what I receive. It just happens." She took his hand and squeezed it. "I hadn't had any ability to link in the present with another person—not until the night Duncan was shot."

"Wait a minute. Is that what this is about, Ali? Is that why this dream's upset you so much? Because of what happened to Duncan?"

She shrugged. "I don't know, Sam. I'm just worried that—"

"Ali, listen to me." He leaned over, turning her slightly so that he could look into her eyes. "They're just dreams. You can't let them rule your life. There isn't some great thing called Fate. We shape our own futures."

"I believe that, too, Sam, but...how can you be so sure?" she asked, searching his eyes, wishing she could believe him.

"Because I just know, Ali. I feel it. Besides, I can take care of myself."

In a flash, she twisted away from Sam and grabbed her robe. She didn't need to hear those empty words again. She'd heard them before. She'd allowed herself to believe them even after Duncan had been shot one night on a routine call. She'd taken false comfort in his promise to be careful. She wouldn't let it happen to her again; she'd made that vow to herself the night Duncan had died in her arms. Promises meant nothing, she thought as she pulled the robe around her and swung her legs over the edge of the bed.

"Ali, wait." Sam scrambled off the bed and knelt before her. "Listen to me." He took her hands and looked up at her. "I *can* take care of myself."

"That's what Duncan told me."

She wrenched her hands from his and tried to brush past him, but Sam was too quick. He took hold of her arm, turning her around to face him. As he lifted her chin, he held her eyes with his hard stare.

"Is that what you're afraid of, Ali? Do you think I'm going to leave you the way Duncan did?" Ali clenched her jaw, fighting back the tears, and took a ragged breath. "Yes."

"Ali—" he shook his head "—I'm not Duncan. I promise you, I won't let anything happen."

When Sam pulled her into his arms, Ali tried to find comfort in the embrace. But the uneasiness of the dream still clung to her, clouding her heart. She knew she couldn't live through that kind of loss again.

"I won't leave you, Ali," Sam whispered as he held her close. "Believe me, I won't."

FOR FIVE DAYS Sam had called Peter Munroe's office. And for five days he'd heard the same story—Mr. Munroe was with a client and a message would be forwarded to him. By Friday, Sam had started phoning Peter's home number and now he could recite the entire outgoing message of the Munroe's answering machine by heart. Ali had even suggested that Sam drive over to the man's house, but Sam suspected that, given enough time, Peter would eventually agree to see him.

His hunch had been correct. It had taken Peter Munroe the weekend to realize that Sam was his only hope. With enough deliberation, he must have recognized that Sam was the one person who could possibly uncover the truth behind Jacquie's murder and thus free him of suspicion. So, Peter had finally called the precinct at ten Monday morning. And he'd made his terms quite clear—their meeting was to be kept confidential and completely off-the-record.

Now, as Peter Munroe shifted uneasily in his chair at Water Street Café, he took a long drag on his cigarette. Sam had figured that Peter would find the new café less threatening than the precinct, but Peter still seemed nervous.

He had come to the café straight from the office, his blond hair windblown and his suit looking almost as tired as he did. The first thing he'd done when he sat down was loosen his tie. Now the knot hung lopsided below his unbuttoned collar.

Sam watched him clumsily butt out the cigarette, then reach for another. It didn't take much to recognize the man's shattered nerves, and Sam now understood why Peter had agreed to the meeting. It wasn't just the fact that he knew he had to help Sam in order to clear his name.

Peter Munroe desperately wanted somebody to talk to. Someone who'd known Jacquie. Someone who could understand the genuine loss he'd suffered—even if it was her old boyfriend.

"Well, at least the damned surveillance has stopped," Peter mumbled, flicking the ash from the cigarette and staring into his coffee. "I don't think I could have taken much more of it."

"I'm sorry about that, Peter."

"Yeah, well, I guess there wasn't much you could have done about it, right?" he asked as if testing Sam's position.

Sam shook his head.

"So how are you holding up, Peter?"

The sound he made was somewhere between a grunt and a cough. "How do you think?"

Sam shrugged.

"It isn't easy at work. I'm losing clients left and right. People talk, you know. 'Innocent until proven guilty,' my foot." He took another drag from the cigarette. "And the irony of it is, I go to the office to get away from it all."

Sam motioned to the waitress for another coffee and Peter waited until she'd filled their cups and left.

"I can't even see Cassie."

"But she's—"

Peter waved a hand. "It's Jacquie's parents. They've got Cassie all worked up. They think it'll be easier if she just stays there until this whole mess is sorted out." He shrugged. "Hell, they're probably right. Cassie's a bright kid. She's knows what's going on. Besides, she should stay with someone who can be there for her all day. At least until this is all over." He tipped his cigarette toward Sam. "You haven't seen her, have you?"

"Cassie, you mean?"

He nodded.

"Yeah, I have. A couple of weeks ago."

"How's she doing?"

Sam couldn't suppress the small smile that crept to his lips when he thought of the reception he'd received from the little girl. "She's holding up."

Peter stared out the window for a moment, probably remembering happier days. "I've been thinking of selling the house. It's just too much to face those memories every day, you know. I don't know. Maybe once Cassie's with me again, we'll be able to get our lives back on track. Things are just so screwed up right now."

"I'm sorry, Peter. I know you must miss Jacquie. And then not to have Cassie around, too..." Sam shook his head when Peter's vacant eyes met his. What else could he say? What could he possibly tell the man when he, too, felt the void Jacquie's death had left in his own life?

"Well, you didn't try reaching me for five days just so you could sit here and listen to me moan about my miserable life. You said you had some questions. I presume it's about the investigation."

Sam nodded. "I'm afraid that what I have to ask might not be easy for you to hear," he explained as his hand checked for the jeweler's box in his jacket pocket.

"Sam, I don't understand the word 'easy' anymore."

Sam took a deep breath. Even though three years had passed since he'd had that brief fling with Jacquie, Sam still felt strange asking Peter Munroe about his wife's infidelity. "Peter, do you think there was any possibility that Jacquie was having an affair?"

"When?"

"After or even before the separation?"

Peter butted out his cigarette and squinted at Sam. "Maybe. Maybe she was. I guess a few months before the separation, I figured there might be someone else. Her little trips out of town were becoming more frequent. When I asked her about them, she said she had a couple of clients over in Jefferson and another in Newport. Big clients, she said. She was redesigning their entire house. She'd stay overnight sometimes when she was decorating there."

"Did you ever check her daybook or anything? Were there ever any discrepancies in dates or receipts? Anything?"

"I never went into her office at home. That's where she did all her interior-design work. She set up the business all on her own, and I respected her privacy."

"Have you been in there since?"

Peter nodded. "Yeah, but there was nothing that made me suspect she was having an affair."

"But for a while you thought she might be seeing someone, right?"

Peter nodded, reached for the cigarette pack and then changed his mind. "Yeah, I thought she was seeing someone, Sam. I thought she was seeing you."

"Me?" Sam almost choked.

"Sure. Why not? If Jacquie was going to have an affair with anyone, who else would it be but you? You were the man she'd always been in love with."

"Peter, I—"

He waved his hand at Sam. "Hey, forget it, Sam. It's over now, anyway, right?"

"Well, yeah, but you don't think that—"

"No. At first I did, but then details didn't really correspond."

"What kind of details?"

"Just little things. Like she'd be away for a couple of days, telling me it was business, and I'd be driving down your street and see you working on your roof. Or she'd claim to be at a client's house, and I'd go to Morty's and see you there with some of the other cops. Little things like that."

The waitress came over to top up their cups, and he waited until she was gone. "Anyway, after that I knew it couldn't be you, and then I just figured I'd been wrong. She really was away on business. I chalked it up to paranoia. I was afraid, since things weren't going so well in our marriage, that maybe she'd start seeing someone else. Someone who could give her more time, more attention, you know? It was hard keeping up with Jacquie, if you know what I mean."

Peter gave in to his urge to smoke and lit up again.

"So, now you're asking me if she was having an affair? Well, if it wasn't with you, then I don't know."

"And you don't think there was any possibility that she might have been seeing someone else? Even after the separation?"

Peter shook his head. "I can't tell you that, Sam. Sure, it's possible, as much as I don't want to believe it. I wouldn't blame her if she had."

Sam rubbed the velvety surface of the jeweler's box in his pocket. It was inevitable. He had to ask.

He drew out the box and slid it across the table.

"What's this?" Peter asked.

"I was hoping you could tell me."

Peter let the cigarette dangle from the corner of his lips as he reached for the box. He opened it slowly, and Sam studied his face for a reaction. There was none.

"Am I supposed to recognize this?"

"I was hoping you would. You didn't give it to Jacquie? As an anniversary present or perhaps as a gesture of reconciliation?"

"No." Peter looked at the glittering bracelet one more time before snapping the box shut and pushing it back to Sam. "I've never seen it before. Where did you get it?"

"I think it was Jacquie's."

"But she's never worn it. I would have noticed. Where did you find it?"

Sam tucked the box in his pocket again. "On her nightstand at her mother's," he lied.

"You think it might lead to her killer?"

"I hope so. But I need you to keep it quiet."

"Hey, I'm not talking to anyone. I shouldn't even be talking to you. If my lawyer finds out . . ."

"Well, I do appreciate it, Peter. I know this isn't easy for you. But believe me, we want the same thing. I want the guy who killed Jacquie. And I want you and Cassie to be a family again. She needs her father.''

''Yeah, well, all in good time, right?''

Sam nodded.

''So you wanna tell *me* something?'' Peter asked, leaning back in his chair.

''What?''

''Tell me about this Van Horn woman,'' he said, placing a biting emphasis on Ali's name.

''What do you know about her?''

''Just what I read in the paper. But that's all I need to know.''

''Look, Peter—'' Sam shook his head ''—I can't discuss that with you. I'm sorry.''

''Damn it, Sam, this is my wife's murder you're investigating for God's sake. Don't you think I should become concerned when the investigation starts looking like some three-ring circus? What's next? A séance? Hey, now there's an idea. We can just ask *Jacquie* who killed her.''

''You've got the wrong impression, Peter.''

''Do I?''

''Van Horn is a reputable psychic. She's worked with—''

''And you believe that shit? Come on, Sam. I thought you were smarter than that.''

Sam looked at the coffee mug in his hands. There was no convincing a skeptic. He knew that. He'd had to see Ali's abilities for himself before he'd believed any of it. And even now, he still had occasional doubts.

''I'm sorry you feel that way, Peter.''

''Look, Sam.'' He leaned across the table. ''I want Jacquie's killer, too. More than you do, I bet. But this isn't the way.''

"Peter, she's helping us. It's only because of her that I have the few leads I do right now. I can't believe you're suggesting—"

"I'm not suggesting anything, Sam. I'm *telling* you. This is *not* the way. This is just a bunch of sensationalistic crap that Ballantyne's stirred up. Can't you see that?"

Sam looked away, unable to match the intensity of Peter's stare. Hadn't he said the same thing to Matt weeks ago when Harrington had sent them to Ali's house? Maybe Peter was right. Maybe Ali's involvement did have the potential for sensationalism. And maybe he had conveniently forgotten that when he realized she might actually help his investigation. Or maybe there were other reasons he'd been able to overlook that possibility—such as the fact that he was falling in love with her.

"Damn, I wish there were laws against this sort of thing," Peter said. "Something to protect a victim's rights, for crying out loud. Next thing you know, there'll be some story in the tabloids." He squashed the rest of his cigarette in the ashtray. "Even if this woman does give you answers, Sam, is it worth the hype you're creating? I don't know about you, but that's not the way I want Jacquie remembered."

Peter pulled out his wallet and tossed down a couple of bills. He shoved his chair back.

"Peter, please—"

"Don't bother apologizing, Sam. I'm sick of hearing it." His chair scraped against the floor. "I'll see you around."

Sam didn't have a chance to reply. Peter turned from the table and headed for the door, nearly bowling over another customer on his way out.

Raking a hand through his hair in frustration, Sam watched Peter cross the street. Even through the glass, he heard the warbled chirp of the car-alarm release and saw Peter climb into his red BMW.

Whatever personal hell Peter Munroe was going through, Sam could only imagine.

ALI CHECKED her watch again—it was almost nine.

Sam had told her this morning that he'd be finished work around seven and that he would try his best to be out even earlier.

By eight, Ali had given up any hope of accomplishing more drawing and made herself a cup of tea to calm her nerves. She sat on the couch, the television remote control in her hand, and clicked through the channels. How many times had she sat in her apartment in New York just like this—worrying about Duncan because he was an hour late? How many times had she flipped from station to station on the television, hoping to find anything to take her mind off the possibility that something might have happened to Duncan?

At least in New York, the guys at the twenty-first precinct knew about her and Duncan. She'd known they'd call her if anything happened. With Sam she had no way of knowing.

Then again, this wasn't the city, she reminded herself. Sam was all right. He just hadn't been able to get to a phone.

She had to relax. He'd be at the front door any second now with the same apologetic look in his eyes she'd seen numerous times already. Even on Friday, when he'd been twenty minutes late picking her up for dinner, Ali had only smiled and planted a kiss on his lips before he could begin to utter his apology.

But Sam had made it up to her. They'd slept in on Saturday at her place, and he'd left for the station after one. When he'd called her at the end of his shift, she had expected another dinner out, but instead, Sam had driven her to his house where he'd prepared a romantic meal, complete with candles and champagne.

After spending most of Sunday in Sam's bed, Ali had finally demanded a full tour of his home. As they'd wandered from room to room, Ali realized that for the past few years Sam had had little else in his life but his work and his house. She'd admired his commitment to the house and how much he'd put into it, and by late afternoon, donning an old T-shirt of his, Ali had helped him paint the upstairs bathroom. There were still traces of the apricot-colored paint on her hands, she noticed as she clicked the remote again.

Even though she'd been expecting it, Ali jumped when the phone on the table behind her rang. But when her hand reached the receiver, she paused, reluctant to answer it, imagining the worst.

"Hello?"

"Yes, good evening," a nasal voice droned. "I'm calling from *Women's World* magazine and I was wondering if you were aware of our—"

"I'm sorry. I'm not interested, thank you," Ali replied, feeling her heart rate slowly return to normal as she hung up. She pulled herself from the couch and started pacing. How could she ever learn to live this way again? Always afraid to answer the phone, always wondering if it was the hospital calling. And constantly worried, when the doorbell rang, if she'd find a couple of officers with downcast faces, bearing bad news.

Had it been this way when she'd lived with Duncan? Or was it only worse now that she'd experienced the reality of it firsthand?

She was about to sit down again when Tash jolted from her slumber. A low growl rose from the retriever's throat, and Ali noted the dog's unbroken stare in the direction of the kitchen.

"What is it, Tash?" Ali muted the television and listened to the silence of the house. Nothing. She looked around for Hector, but the old cat was fast asleep in the wing chair.

Ali chose to adopt Hector's attitude. "It's nothing, Tash. Just relax," she suggested, patting the dog's head. Ali crossed the living room and pulled back the blinds. The sky was already getting dark, and the lamps washed the empty street with a warm glow.

When Tash growled a second time, Ali jumped.

"All right, then," Ali told the dog after she took a calming breath. "If there's something there, then go get it."

As though understanding Ali's words, the retriever got up and trotted to the kitchen. When Ali caught up with her, Tash was at the back door, sniffing and wagging her tail.

"So you want out. Is that what this is all about?"

Tash looked up at her and then sniffed the door again.

"Fine, then. But I'm not coming out with you this time, you hear? You're on your own."

Ali reached for the doorknob. Even as her fingers touched the cool brass, she looked at the dog, thinking it strange that she wanted out again so soon. It had only been an hour since the last time. And then, as her fingers wrapped around the doorknob, Ali gasped.

Like a burning rod behind her left eye, a sharp pain pierced through her head. She gripped the doorknob more tightly, using it for balance, as she brought her other hand to her temple, where the pain racked her again, sharper this time.

And before she saw anything, Ali knew the vision was hurtling toward her.

It was just a bright flash at first, elusive and undefined. Ali pressed her hand to her head, trying to see through the blur of pain.

And when the vision struck again, she held on to it as desperately as she clutched the doorknob.

With fear coursing through her, it took her a mere second to recognize the black leather glove. And it took only one more second for Ali to recognize what it was reaching for—the brass knob on the other side of the door.

CHAPTER TWELVE

"THANKS FOR COMING ALONG with me on this one, Sam. I know your own caseload's piling up these days."

Nancy sat on the other side of the Skylark's bench seat. She had wedged one foot up against the faded dash and rested her elbow on her knee.

"I told you before, Nance, it's not a problem."

"Yeah, well, it is if you're Coleman," she said tucking a strand of hair behind her ear and staring past the dash. She frowned and shifted in her seat, shoving the holster beneath her jacket to one side. "I tell you, Sam, if Coleman isn't the primary on a case, he's absolutely impossible to budge when it comes to getting even the smallest bit of help."

"Well, maybe you have to start working more on your own. Let Coleman handle his own cases."

"That's what I've been doing. But you know, I don't think I would've had the same effect tonight if I'd had to question those punks by myself."

"You don't know that, Nance. You handled them fine," Sam said as he pulled up in front of her apartment building. "I think you'd be surprised at yourself."

"Well, that's your opinion, Sam. I hate to be the one to say this, but the fact remains that, when faced with a bunch of thugs who'd rather go down than finger one of their buddies, the best authority is still a man."

She had a point, Sam thought. The four high-school kids they'd just spent the past hour questioning were not only bigger than anything Sam remembered in high school, but they'd almost managed to intimidate him.

"Listen, Sam, I know it's getting late, but do you want to grab a bite? Maybe a beer at Morty's?"

"Sorry, Nance. I gotta meet somebody."

She reached for the door handle. "Sure. I get the picture. Some other time, then." She opened the door and then glanced at him again. "So is this something serious?"

"What?"

"Between you and Van Horn."

Sam let out a short laugh. There was no sense in asking how she'd found out about him and Ali. He knew nothing got by Nancy Peterson.

"Could be," he answered.

He stared at her for a moment, wondering if Nancy'd had her own ideas about the friendship that had developed between them in the six months she'd been with the department. He dismissed it with a quick smile and a wink. "I'll see you tomorrow, Nance."

"Yeah, have a good night, Tremaine. And don't do anything I wouldn't do," she warned, flashing him one of her characteristic grins as she shoved the door shut and fumbled for her keys.

Sam pulled away from the curb. In the rearview mirror, he saw her step into the building. They'd taken a lot longer than he'd anticipated and he wished he'd phoned Ali from the precinct after the meeting. When Nancy had asked for his assistance with questioning a couple of kids that had been involved in a shooting at their high school last week, Sam had figured it wouldn't take them more than an hour to extract the few details they had from the boys.

In the back of his mind, Sam was still trying to figure out what went through kids' heads these days. But it was Ali who was on the forefront of his thoughts.

He checked his watch again. It was already past nine, and he still had to drop the car off at the station.

ALI JERKED her hand from the doorknob as if it were molten lead. She stared at the back door, her heart hammering in her ears as she listened for movement on the other side.

There was none. But that didn't mean he wasn't standing there just inches away, listening for her, as well.

She had to move. In those long seconds, Ali considered racing upstairs to get her gun. She thought of phoning the precinct, of trying to reach Sam. But if Jacquie's killer was really just beyond this door, she wouldn't have time for any of that.

No, she had to run. She threw a panicked glance over to the side door leading to the garage. On the wall next to the door, the car keys dangled from a hook.

With a rush of adrenaline, Ali grabbed Tash's collar and scrambled to the side door. The keys almost slipped from her grasp as she struggled with the handle. And when she paused for a split second to glance behind her, Ali thought she saw the knob on the back door turn.

She needed no further prompting. Ali slammed the side door behind her and yanked open the door of the Cherokee. Tash clambered in ahead of her, and Ali locked the car. Only then did she release the garage door.

In the confinement of the garage, the Cherokee roared to life. Ali didn't look behind her as she shot out the drive, and she didn't even think to put on the lights until she was halfway down the block.

Fifteen minutes later she pulled into the potholed parking lot of the Danby Police Department, still clutching the steering wheel in a white-knuckled grip. She wrenched the wheel sharply to the left, slammed on the brake and cut the engine. Tash was still dragging herself back up from the floor to the passenger seat as Ali flew out of the car.

She sprinted up the front steps and swung open the heavy glass door. The harsh light of the precinct washed over her, the sterile odor sending a wave of nausea through her. As she turned down the corridor that led to the detectives' wing, she felt the gray walls close in on her.

"Excuse me, miss?" someone called after her from the front counter. "Miss, can I help you?"

Ali waved a hand, dismissing his offer. "I'm here to see Detective Tremaine," she shouted back to him, her voice echoing down the hall above the clatter of printers and the ringing of phones.

"I don't think he's back yet, miss, but—"

The rest of his words were lost as she exploded through the swinging door that led to the detectives' wing. Ali stopped. Frantically she scanned the array of cluttered desks and file cabinets searching for Sam, but she was only met by the puzzled gazes of two detectives at their desks.

"I'm looking for Detective Tremaine," she announced.

The shorter of the two stood up and took a step toward her. "I'm sorry, miss. He's still out on a call. He should be back soon, though, if you'd like to wait for him. Is there anything I can help you with?"

With the scare she'd had back at the house, coupled with the flood of memories that clung to her now like a cold sweat as she stood in the familiar environment of the station, Ali had no doubt she probably looked like she needed help.

"No, that's all right, thanks," she said as she felt another wave of nausea swell inside of her. She reached out to support herself on the corner of the nearest desk.

"Would you like to sit down?" The detective crossed the room, concern creasing his freckled face as he extended a hand to lend her support.

"I'm fine, thank you." Ali drew in a breath and straightened up. "Which is his desk? I'll leave him a note if that's okay."

"It's the one with the light on." He nodded to the far wall and Ali wove her way through the maze of desks.

Under the glare of the fluorescent bulb, Ali saw the files marked Munroe. She felt the urge to open one, to finger through the notes, but she knew the two detectives across the room were still watching her. Instead, she dropped her purse onto the desk and rummaged for a notepad. She scanned Sam's desk for a pen, and sliding a file to one side, she picked up a ballpoint.

Her hand shook as she wrote Sam's name at the top of the paper, and when the pen stuttered dryly across the page, out of ink, Ali tossed it back down on the desk with an inaudible curse. She was about to ask one of the detectives for a pen when she spotted the chipped pen holder under the lamp and reached for another ballpoint. She shook it twice and was about to write when the door of the wing swung open.

"Hey, guys."

Ali started at the familiar voice. She looked up to see Matt enter the wing.

"Ms. Van Horn." He gave her a dazzling smile as he came toward her. "This is a pleasant surprise."

Ali lowered the pen. "Good evening, Detective Dobson."

"Please—" he held out his hand "—it's Matt."

She slipped the pad and pen into her purse and took his hand in greeting. "All right, Matt. Call me Ali."

"So what brings you to the precinct?"

"I was looking for Sam," she told him, hoping her voice sounded calm.

Matt loosened his tie. "I think he went out with one of the other detectives. He should be back any second. If you're not in a rush, why don't you wait here for him?"

Matt's warm smile was beginning to ease Ali's frayed nerves. Besides, where else could she go? She couldn't go back to the house—Jacquie's killer might still be there. "Sure." She nodded. "I suppose I can wait."

"Great. Would you like some water or a coffee maybe?"

"No, I'm fine, thank you."

"Well, then—" he motioned toward the back of the detectives' wing "—why don't we go to the lounge? It's a little more comfortable."

Ali followed him into a small gray room that smelled of the ubiquitous burned coffee and stale sandwiches. A sagging couch had been pushed up along one wall, and deciding this looked more comfortable than the hard vinyl chairs, Ali lowered herself onto it.

"Listen—" Matt filled a glass of water for himself from the tap in the corner "—I've been meaning to call you." He picked up one of the vinyl chairs, turned it around and straddled it, propping his forearms along the stained back.

"About what?"

"About my blunder. You know, the story in the *Herald?*"

Ali nodded.

"I'm sure Sam explained how it happened and he obviously apologized, or you wouldn't be here now. But I really wanted you to know how sorry I am that it happened, Ali. I never meant—"

"It's all right, Matt. It was bound to happen sooner or later." If he hadn't been sitting out of reach, Ali might have reached out to touch him to try to ease the guilt she saw in his eyes. "I shouldn't have made Sam promise something like that in the first place."

Matt stared at her for so long that Ali grew uncomfortable.

"I can't believe how understanding you are, Ali," he said finally. "No wonder Sam has this thing for you."

She looked up in time to catch his wink.

"Let me tell you, it takes a damned special person to put up with a cop."

"Well, I guess you could say I've had a little experience in the area," Ali said, wondering if Matt understood just how much truth there was in his statement.

She found herself under close observation again and was about to look away when Matt shook his head.

"Well, I just hope Sammy realizes what a good thing he's got with you."

"ANY CALLS, John?" Sam asked, sliding the keys to the Skylark across the front counter.

The officer on the other side checked the slots for messages and then shook his head as he hung the keys on the rack under the counter. "Nope, nothing. Guess that means you can go home early, huh?"

"Yeah, right." There was no accounting for precinct humor, Sam thought as he turned back toward the front doors. He was already almost two hours late—he'd really have to make it up to Ali this time.

"Hey, wait a second, Tremaine," the front-desk officer called. "Did that lady find you?"

"What lady?"

"A real looker. She came stormin' in here lookin' real rattled. I think she went back to look for you about fifteen minutes ago. I tried to—"

But Sam was already sprinting down the corridor to the detectives' wing.

When he barged through the door, Bobby Groff looked up from his desk with a bleary-eyed gaze, which reflected the long hours he'd been working.

"She's in the lounge with Dobson," he said, shoving a thumb toward the back of the wing and returning to his paperwork.

Sam could hear the delicate lilt of Ali's laughter, but even that didn't ease his alarm. What could possibly have happened to make Ali come to the precinct?

She stood up from the old couch the second she saw Sam in the doorway, and he could tell immediately that the smile wavering on her lips was only a facade.

"Sammy." Matt stood, as well. "It's about time you dragged your sorry butt in here."

"What's the matter, Ali?" He looked past Matt, his eyes locked on Ali. She shook her head, her smile faltering.

"Seems she had a bit of a scare at the house, that's all," Matt explained for her.

"Ali?"

"I'm all right, Sam. Matt figures it was probably just a raccoon or something."

"Listen—" Matt slapped Sam's shoulder "—I gotta be going. Ali, it was nice seeing you again. Take care of yourself. We'll have to get together for dinner some time soon, okay?" He waited for Ali's nod. "Sammy, you take care of her now, hmm?" he murmured as he brushed past Sam. "She's one helluva woman."

Sam waited for the door to swing shut before he crossed the room and stood in front of her. He said nothing at first, only took her hands in his and looked at her.

"What happened, Ali?"

She shook her head. "I'm not really sure, Sam. Like Matt said, it was probably just a raccoon on the back porch."

"Ali?" He knew there was more to it than that. He could tell by the way her hands trembled.

"I'm not sure what I saw, Sam. Maybe I was just worked up because you were late. I don't know."

"What happened?"

"Tash got excited about something at the back door, so I went to let her out. When I grabbed the door handle...I had a vision."

"What kind of a vision?"

"Just a flash, really. A brief connection. I saw the black leather glove." She looked up at him, and Sam could still see the fear flicker in her eyes. She may have been laughing with Matt a moment ago, but she hadn't been able to shake whatever had happened at the house. "I . . . I thought I saw him reaching for the handle on the other side of the door."

"Jacquie's killer?"

Ali shrugged and stepped into Sam's embrace, wrapping her arms around his waist, needing to feel his strength surround her. "I think it was him," she said at last, her voice muffled against his chest.

After a long silence she pulled back and looked up at him. He could see her confusion. "I don't know what's happening, Sam. I don't understand these images. The visions, the dreams."

"I'm going to talk to Harrington tomorrow," Sam told her, reaching for her purse and handing it to her. "We'll arrange for some protection."

"Sam, no. I don't think—"

"Ali, what you think doesn't matter right now, okay? We should have had you under protection from the second that story ran in the *Herald*."

"Really, Sam, I'm not even sure that what I saw tonight was real."

"I don't care, Ali. I told you before I wasn't going to let anything happen to you, and that's a promise I intend to keep. Now come on. I'm taking you home."

ALI HADN'T SEEN this side of Sam before. At first it had reminded her of Duncan—the way he'd get concerned about her if a case was getting too risky. But after Ali had watched Sam go through her house, his revolver drawn as he walked from room to room, and then had practically demanded she pack a few essentials and move into his place, Ali realized that Sam could not cope with the fact that her life might be at risk.

Duncan had come to understand those risks after the first couple of cases. But he had never let her forget the day they'd brought in Martin Burack, the man responsible for the slaughter of twelve people over a period of only eight weeks. The madman had been thoroughly restrained when three officers had dragged him into the twenty-first precinct, yet he'd still managed to tear free of them and attack Ali when she'd stepped out of Gary's office. Even though she'd sustained only a minor gash to the head and one bruised rib, Duncan had used that incident countless times as a reminder of the risks she ran—and the fear they instilled in him.

And as Ali had watched Sam during the drive to his house, she had recognized that same fear in his silence. Now she sat on his couch and listened to him rummage through the kitchen in search of a bottle of whiskey he had stashed away.

In the middle of the living-room floor, Ziggy was flaked out in a lanky, black heap while Tash kept a careful eye from her position beside the couch. Ali lowered a hand to stroke the dog's head, aware that the retriever was not entirely pleased with the new arrangements. Even Hector had snarled a mild protest earlier when she'd put him out for the night and filled his food bowl on the back porch before she and Sam had left her sister's house.

"Are you sure I can't give you a hand, Sam?"

"I'll be there in just a minute," he called back, and she heard the clatter of more dishes being shoved aside.

"Do you realize these library books are overdue?" she asked loudly as she lifted the cover of one of the books on psychic phenomena she'd picked up off the coffee table.

"Yeah," Sam called. "So what are they going to do? Call the cops?"

There wasn't much humor in his voice and Ali let it go. She closed her eyes and eased her head back against the couch. She might have even dozed off if it hadn't been for the sudden shatter of glass against the ceramic tiles of the kitchen floor.

Ziggy bolted up out of his sleep, but stayed put when he heard his owner curse vehemently from the other room. And by the time Ali reached the doorway of the kitchen, Sam was already fetching the broom.

"I sure hope that wasn't the whiskey," Ali joked, but her smile fell when she saw the dark expression on Sam's face.

"No, I found the damned whiskey. I was trying to find a couple of glasses in this dump." He dragged the broom across the floor, sweeping the scattered shards into a neat pile. "Watch yourself—there's glass everywhere." He nodded at her stocking feet.

Ali handed him a dustpan and boosted herself onto the edge of the counter. Silently Sam swept the shards into the pan.

Ali looked around, and finding one glass, poured him a shot of the whiskey.

"Here, Sam," she said, holding out the glass. "I think you need this more than I do."

He put the broom away and took the glass. Mumbling a thanks, he tossed back the amber liquid. Ali poured a second shot.

"Have another."

When Sam looked at her this time, Ali recognized that his anger had nothing to do with the broken glass or the misplaced bottle of whiskey.

"I'm sorry, Ali." He started pacing. "I just don't know how to handle this."

"Handle what, Sam?" She poured herself a shot and let the whiskey warm her throat and soothe her nerves.

"The fact that Jacquie's killer is coming after you."

"We don't know that for sure."

"But you saw—"

"I don't know what I saw! Listen Sam, I can't believe I'm suggesting that my visions might be wrong on this, but I have to admit that it *has* been a long time. I seem to be getting all kinds of signals crossed here. There is the possibility that I could be wrong, you know."

"Do you really believe that?"

Ali shrugged. What could she tell him? The truth? Even *she* couldn't handle the truth right now. Nor could she face the fact that Jacquie's killer was, in all likelihood, coming after her. Who was next? Sam?

"See?" he shot back at her. "Even you aren't willing to take a chance that you might be right, Ali. You're scared, I know you are. You wouldn't have come to the precinct looking for me otherwise."

"Yeah, but I'm okay now, aren't I?"

"That's not the point, Ali."

She could tell he was trying to soften his words, but his fear was obvious.

"Listen, Sam." She waited until he stopped pacing and looked at her. "I understand what you're going through."

"Do you?" He turned away, rolling up the sleeves of his shirt and finally running a hand angrily through his hair.

Ali shook her head. How could he not know? How could he be so blind?

She swallowed hard, trying to suppress her own anger. "And just what the hell do you think I feel when you're two hours late?" she spat.

Sam stopped, speechless, as if she'd just slapped him on the face.

"It's no different, Sam. Your life is at risk every damned day of the year."

He shoved his hands into the pockets of his jeans and turned away.

"Believe me, Sam, I've lived this life before. I've had the frantic hours, the sleepless nights, constantly jumping whenever the phone rings or there's a knock at the door. You don't think I know what it's like? Living in fear that the man I love is going to end up shot by some punk in an alley, or by a maniac who's got nothing else to live for, or hell, maybe even by one of his own colleagues."

He took a step toward her. "Ali, I—"

"No, Sam. You have to hear this, because if you think you're the only one who's feeling and going through the fear you have right now, then you really aren't seeing the whole picture. I mean, it's only been a few weeks, and I'm already afraid when the phone rings. I'm already expecting to hear Matt's voice on the other end of the line, telling me you've been shot."

Sam lowered his gaze to the floor again.

"And you know something else, Sam? It really doesn't make it any easier when you give me promises." Ali blinked back the tears. "You can't keep them, Sam. No one can. Especially a cop."

He turned away, the muscle in his jaw flexing as he pondered Ali's words. And when he finally faced her again, she saw defeat in his eyes.

"Are you suggesting I quit the force?"

"No!" Ali blurted. "Sam, don't be crazy. I'd never dream of suggesting something like that. Being a cop is what you *do*. That's like asking me never to pick up a pencil again. You couldn't just give it up. And even if you did, you know it wouldn't last. Besides, I'm not going to spend the rest of my life having you resent me for ending something you love."

"What am I supposed to do, then? Sit back and wait for this guy to come after you?"

"No." She shook her head and smiled softly, both at his helplessness and at the fact that it was his feelings for her that made him feel so utterly powerless. "No, Sam. You don't just sit back and wait. We do something. Whatever is necessary. But in the meantime, trust me, you've got to loosen up a bit. Now come here," she told him, beckoning him over to where she was perched.

He stopped in front of her and placed his hands on her knees. "I don't know what to say, Ali. I just...I don't want anything to happen to you."

"And nothing will." She smiled, knowing it would take more than her smile to ease Sam's apprehension. "So loosen up, will you?" She reached out to grasp the top of his jeans and tug him toward her. When he stepped between her legs, Ali lifted a hand to stroke his cheek.

"Don't worry so much, Sam. And don't let this guy eat away at you, okay? We'll get him."

He nodded and Ali trailed her fingers along the back of his neck and drew him closer. Eagerly he accepted her kiss as if needing it to reassure himself she was all right.

She felt the warm strength of his body moving against hers, pinning her as she wrapped her legs around his hips. She slid her fingers through his hair, arching toward his desperate kisses, and Ali's breath caught in her throat when Sam's hands moved to the top of her shirt.

Anxiously he unfastened the buttons. His kisses burned along her neck and shoulder, igniting shudders of longing as he worked his way toward the lace of her bra.

Impatiently she unbuttoned Sam's shirt, needing to feel his body against hers. And when she brushed his shirt open and felt the fiery tingle of his skin against hers, she let out a soft moan.

Sam's breath came in short gasps. His mouth moved back to hers, answering her hunger with his own. As he unzipped her jeans, Ali wrapped her legs more tightly around him and pulled herself to the very edge of the counter, drowning in the desperation of their need to be together tonight.

Breathlessly she fumbled with the buckle of Sam's belt until she was finally able to slide her hand under the restrictive denim and embrace the swell of desire she'd anticipated. She heard Sam groan as she trailed a finger just under the waistband of his shorts and felt his body tremble with longing. She felt his breath hot on her neck and then heard his whisper brush across her ear.

"I can't lose you, Ali," he said quietly as his hands moved up her back and cradled her face. "I really couldn't stand losing you."

"You're not going to lose me, Sam."

"Ali—" he brushed her cheek with his thumb, searching the silvery depths of her eyes for her understanding "—I love you, Ali."

And when she answered his kiss this time, Sam felt an urgency greater than anything he'd ever experienced. He kissed her as if it might be their last kiss. He carried her upstairs to his bed and made love to her as though it was their last night together. Even later, as Ali lay asleep in his arms, Sam still felt the fear. And in the silence of the early morning, as he watched Ali sleep and felt her life pulsing beneath his hand, Sam swallowed his fear.

He swallowed his fear and turned it into a dark and silent anger.

CHAPTER THIRTEEN

ALI AWOKE GRADUALLY. She grew aware of the slow, steady rhythm of Sam's breathing, warm against her neck. Then she felt the comforting weight of his arm around her waist and the reassurance of his body folded against the curves of her own. And finally, as she opened her eyes, she saw his hand on hers, strong fingers covering hers.

Ali stared at his hand for a long time, remembering the way it had caressed her body last night. Sam's loving touch, at first possessing the patient tenderness she'd come to expect of him, had grown to an almost desperate fervor as he'd pulled her to him with an urgency that stemmed from the fears of both of them.

She knew what Sam had been feeling last night. She understood the panic and alarm that had darkened his face when he'd barged into the lounge at the precinct. And then later, she'd felt his desperation in their love-making.

Careful not to wake him, Ali slipped out of his slumbering embrace and sat up next to him. His breathing did not falter. The sheet had slipped down to his waist and Ali's gaze was drawn to the ragged scar that marred the perfection of his chest.

Tentatively, Ali reached out to touch it. Her fingers whispered over the gnarled ridge of skin, feeling the slow rhythm of his heart just beneath it.

Why had she fallen for Sam? A man who faced the same dangers Duncan had? Was it something in her that drew her to men like Duncan and Sam? Was it the danger that attracted her to them?

No, Ali thought, covering Sam's scar with her palm, it had nothing to do with his being a cop. It was how Sam made her feel. After eleven months of emptiness, it was Sam who had made her understand that she could, once more, hope for a future. He made her feel alive again. And in spite of the short time she'd known him, Ali could not imagine life without him.

As much as she yearned for the strength to turn away from this relationship, to end it before her feelings grew any deeper, Ali knew she could not. Sam meant too much to her now. He filled that part of her heart that had been empty for too long, and it was his presence that made her feel whole again.

Sam's confessions of love last night were not empty words. She knew he loved her. But even more than that, Ali recognized the love for Sam in her own heart. She would, once again, learn to live with the risks.

Lifting her hand from Sam's chest, Ali reached over to gently brush back his hair. It was then that she noticed her wedding ring, and she withdrew her hand.

She twirled the ring around on her finger, rubbing the thin gold band, remembering the vows she'd spoken as if it were yesterday—"till death us do part."

Now there was Sam. As she looked down at his face, calm in sleep, Ali did not feel the pang of guilt she had when she'd first kissed him. Even though she could still hear Duncan's voice, even though she would cherish his memory forever, it was Sam who lived in her heart now.

Without hesitation, Ali slipped the ring from her finger. She reached for her jeans on the floor beside the bed and tucked the ring into a pocket.

When she looked back to Sam, he stirred in his sleep, his hand instinctively searching for her. She felt the tingle of his warmth along her skin as he drew her closer. His eyes were still closed as an easy smile graced his lips.

"So," she murmured, teasing him awake with her kisses, "how does spending another day in bed sound?"

Sam rolled beneath her, easily guiding her so that her body covered his. He lifted his hands to hold back her hair and looked at her with an expression close to wonder. "Sounds delicious."

Ali reached back for the top of the sheet and drew it up over their heads in one motion, blocking out the rest of the world. "We could just stay here all day and pretend the world doesn't exist."

"Mmm," Sam mumbled between kisses, "you know I'd love to…but unfortunately…the world is out there and so is… Harrington." He held her back long enough to look at her again, and Ali saw yesterday's fear shadow his expression. "We have to go in and talk to the chief this morning."

Ali stared down at him, about to protest. But she knew they couldn't ignore what had happened last night. In the light of day, everything always looked different. With the morning sun peeking through the blinds, she couldn't allow herself to forget her previous fright and the risk she faced. She should be grateful for any protection the Danby Police Department could offer her.

"Come on, Ali. We'd better get going." Sam tugged free of the sheet. "What time is it, anyway?"

"Eight-fifteen."

Sam rolled her aside, sat bolt upright and looked at the clock himself. "Shit, Ali. We'll be lucky to catch him even if we hurry."

Ali watched Sam spring from the bed and pull on his jeans. "Come on. You have to come with me," he prompted, picking up her jeans and tossing them to her. "If you're in Harrington's office beside me, he can't say no."

But Ali only lounged back on the bed, marveling at Sam's toned body as he zipped up his jeans and combed his fingers hurriedly through his hair. He threw on a fresh shirt and was about to button it, when he saw Ali and stopped.

Perhaps it was seeing her in his bed, or perhaps it was the affectionate smile on her lips, but suddenly he abandoned the buttons of his shirt and crossed the room toward her. In one fluid movement, he was on the bed, straddling her, lowering his mouth to hers and surrendering to her kisses.

A groan of frustration escaped from his throat as Ali swept her hands down his back and to his waist.

"You're a real tease, Ali Van Horn," he whispered raggedly in her ear. "And I love you."

He kissed her again and this time Ali wanted nothing else but to feel him inside her again. She *did* want to ignore the rest of the world. But even as she was about to tell him how much she loved him, Sam started to pull back.

"But I'm serious," he told her. "We have to get going. We have to talk to Harrington and get some protection assigned to you."

"I don't need protection," she said, wrapping her hands around his belt so he couldn't escape. "I have you, Detective Tremaine."

His lips curled into a smile as he stroked her hair. "Well, as much as I'd like to, I can't be with you twenty-four hours a day, Ali. Now, you're coming with me, even if I have to carry you all the way to Harrington's office."

ED HARRINGTON'S OFFICE was similar to the one occupied by the chief of police at the twenty-first precinct. It had the same torn vinyl-cushioned chairs, the same stale odor of moldy vents marginally masked by some diluted pine scent, and the same stack of paperwork.

Ali had sat in one of the chairs across from Ed Harrington's desk for close to fifteen minutes now. She'd added only brief comments whenever necessary as Sam had explained everything to the chief. He outlined all the details surrounding the case—Ali's reading from the pillows, the discovery of the bracelet and even their jealous-lover theory. Then Sam told the chief about the incident last night. Through the half-drawn blinds, Ali felt the eyes of the other detectives in the wing on her. Even though the closed door blocked out any sound, Ali imagined she could hear them murmuring to one another.

But Sam's colleagues were not the only ones who cast nervous glances at the woman they now recognized as the psychic on the Munroe case. Ed Harrington himself was noticeably uneasy about Ali's presence. He fidgeted behind his desk, leaned back in his chair and crossed his arms across his chest, acting as if maintaining a safe distance would somehow decrease the likelihood of Ali reading his mind.

Even when he'd extended his hand in greeting, the chief had hesitated and then made the handshake as brief as possible. His actions reminded Ali of the first time she'd met Sam.

Now the chief paced the floor of the office like a caged animal.

"So, let me get this straight," he said. "You're telling me you saw Jacqueline Munroe's killer at your back door last night?"

Ali quickly glanced at Sam before she faced Harrington again. In that brief gaze, Sam recognized her impatience.

"No." Ali shook her head. "I didn't actually see him. Look, I don't mean any disrespect, Chief Harrington, but I don't think you quite understand the situation here."

"Well, forgive me," he said, his voice holding an edge of condescension. "Perhaps you should explain exactly what you *did* see last night."

Sam watched Ali's back go rigid, and he wanted to put a hand on her shoulder to ease her tension.

"Look, Chief Harrington, I realize this is the first time your department has ever worked with a psychic, so I don't really expect you to understand how these things work. But as with most of the cases I've worked on in the past, I think I'm gradually linking with the perpetrator. What I saw last night was the hand of the man who killed Jacqueline Munroe. I didn't see his face, I couldn't pick him out of a lineup for you, and no, I can't give you his name. I truly wish it was that simple."

Harrington looked long and hard at Ali, and Sam was beginning to doubt his decision to bring her here today. He hadn't wanted to tell anyone about Ali's theory concerning Jacquie's lover or, more importantly, about the bracelet. He'd wanted to be certain first. He'd wanted a name—the name of the person who'd purchased the bracelet for Jacquie.

But he'd had to tell Harrington everything. It was the only way to convince the chief that what Ali had seen last night was real and that, as their only link to the killer, she needed protection.

"Okay," the chief said finally, "so you saw the guy's hand reaching for your door. But you didn't hear anything?"

"I thought I saw the doorknob move when I was going through the door to the garage."

"But you can't be sure?"

Ali shook her head.

"So, you're 'linking' with this guy. All right. How do you know it was happening at that moment?"

"You mean in real time?"

"Yeah. How do you know this guy hadn't been to your house before and what you were seeing was from the past? Or maybe, he hasn't even been there at all and what you say you saw last night was some kind of fortune-telling or something?"

"Come on, Chief, that's just the point." Sam stood in front of Harrington's desk and tried his best to stare the big man down. "Don't you see that it doesn't matter? Whether the guy was there before or after? Or, hell, maybe he's not even going to show up until tonight or tomorrow! The point is, we need to get some security over there for when he does show up."

Sam could see that Harrington was about to shake his head.

"Ali needs round-the-clock protection."

"We can't provide twenty-four-hour surveillance, Sam. You know that."

"I'll fill in when we don't have the manpower."

The chief pondered this proposal for a long moment. As much as Sam had hated dragging Ali into the precinct again, he knew that if he hadn't Harrington would have given him a flat no, and that would have been the end of the discussion.

Finally Harrington nodded and looked back at Ali. "All right, then. But it's going to be limited at best, Ms. Van Horn. And since Detective Tremaine here will be filling in when we need him, you'd better get used to his mug. And, Tremaine—" he turned his gaze to Sam "—we'll have to set up a schedule. One man on four-hour shifts in a black-and-white out front. We'll send Barratt home with her for now."

"Thank you, Chief Harrington." Ali extended her hand, and Sam noticed that he accepted the handshake with great apprehension.

Ali only half listened as Harrington thanked her for her efforts on the case and promised her they would do their best to ensure her safety. She saw the quick glance exchanged between Sam and Harrington just before she turned to the door—a look that revealed very clearly that the chief was not entirely pleased with Sam's tactic of bringing her in to the precinct. Ali wondered what kind of flak Sam would have to take once Harrington had him alone.

Sam was silent as they walked back along the corridor to the front counter. He remained so as he followed her out the wide doors of the precinct.

"Sam, it's going to be all right," Ali said. "I hardly think Jacquie's killer is going to try anything if there's a squad car parked right out front."

"No, you're probably right." A gust of wind tugged at his hair, and he lifted a hand to straighten it. "I just wish I could be there, instead of sending some rookie."

"You'll be there later," she reminded him, and discreetly slipped her hand into his when they reached the Cherokee. He gave it a gentle squeeze, reminding her of the night they'd spent together.

"Hey, guys!"

They both turned as Matt backed the Skylark into the parking spot next to them and got out. Ali returned his glowing smile.

"Are you guys just heading out? Don't tell me Harrington's given us the day off."

"In your dreams, partner," Sam answered.

"So, what's up? Did I miss something?"

"We were just in talking to Harrington," Sam told him, giving Ali's hand one more squeeze before letting it go.

"About what happened last night?"

Ali nodded.

"We're arranging for some security."

"It really spooked you, then," Matt said, crossing his arms and leaning back against the car. When a sudden gust of wind lifted the lapel of his jacket, revealing his holster, he reached down to straighten it.

Ali shrugged, sharing a quick glance with Sam. "I'm not even sure it was anything."

"Well, better safe than sorry," Matt told her. "You don't want to take any chances. So Harrington's giving you some surveillance?"

"Only minimal," Sam answered. "You know how he grumbles about the lack of manpower."

"Well, listen, you just let me know if there's anything I can do. I think I'm going to be free for the next few nights if you need me to cover for a few hours here and there."

"Thanks, Matt. I appreciate that." Ali gave him a smile she hoped conveyed her gratitude.

"In the meantime, what are you two doing on Saturday night?"

Sam shrugged and looked at Ali. "No concrete plans. Why?"

"Well, I was thinking we should get together for a barbecue."

Sam tilted his head, squinting at Matt. "Wait a minute. This sounds more like you're inviting yourself to dinner at my place."

"Hey, you're the one with the backyard, Sammy." He pushed off from the car and started to leave. "Look, I'll bring the steaks if it'll make you feel better."

"Sounds great," Ali said, giving Sam a nudge.

"Good. I'll see you both Saturday night. And listen, Ali, trust me, you're in good hands with Sammy. But if there's anything at all, you just let me know, all right?"

"I will, Matt. And thanks."

"I'll see you inside, Sammy," Matt said, giving him a jab in the shoulder before jogging up the precinct steps.

"You've got quite a friend in your partner," Ali noted as she watched Matt pull open the front doors and disappear into the station.

"Yeah, well, I'm going to have to talk to him about being a little more scarce now that..."

Ali smiled and slipped a finger through one of Sam's belt loops to pull him around in front of her. "Now that what?"

Sam returned her smile and, after taking a cautionary glance around the parking lot, gave her a kiss. "Now that I figure you're going to be around more often."

"Well, you figured right, Detective Tremaine," she whispered.

"You'd better get going."

Ali heard the reluctance in his voice and kissed him one more time before getting into the Cherokee with Tash. As she rolled down the driver's-side window, she saw Sam wave to a uniformed officer who'd just come out of the station.

"That's Ray Barratt," he told her as he leaned in through the window. "He'll follow you wherever you have to go."

"I'm familiar with the routine, Sam."

"All right. Well, I'll see you later. Probably around six. And I'll call this afternoon to see how you're doing."

SAM DID CALL—twice. He called at two to check that Ray Barratt's relief had arrived. And then he'd called at four to tell her he loved her.

When the phone rang again at five-fifteen, Ali left her drawing table and crossed the living room with a smile on her lips, anticipating Sam's voice on the other end of the line.

But it hadn't been Sam, and now Ali lounged back on the couch with the phone tucked under her chin as she listened to Jamie tell her about the mail that had been piling up in her apartment.

"I've forwarded a few things, but most of it's junk. I'll let you decide before I throw anything out. You should be back in a week or so, then, hmm?"

Ali cringed at the inevitable question.

Her hesitation was the only answer Jamie needed. "I take it, then, that this thing with your detective is, shall we say, developing?"

"Yes," Ali replied after a moment. "Yes, I suppose you could say that."

"So what are you going to do, Al? I mean, about the apartment and everything?"

She knew what she had to do. For the past week she'd thought about her life in New York. Even before she'd admitted her feelings for Sam to herself, she'd decided she couldn't go back. Not to the apartment she'd decorated and shared with Duncan. Not to the memories that still lingered there. She couldn't look back anymore.

"I've been thinking I might let go of the place."

"Well, that's not a bad idea. I know you would never admit to it, but the rent was a bit steep for a single income, anyway. Did you want me to send out some feelers for something new?"

"No, Jamie," she said after a short pause. "I think I might stick it out here for a while. I'm not sure yet. Besides, your place is big—if I need a place to stay in New York, I can always crash with you, right?"

"Anytime, Al. You're always welcome. So it's pretty serious, then, between you and Sam, huh?"

Ali stood up from the couch and paced across the room, needing to stretch. "I'm still not sure, Jamie. I think it is. I don't have to make up my mind right now, do I?''

"No, I suppose not. So when will you know? Should I call you in the morning?''

Ali laughed. "I'll know when I know, Jamie. Look, I have to go. The dog wants out. I'll call you this weekend, okay?''

"Okay. Okay. I'll talk to you then, Al. And take care of yourself, you hear?''

By the time Ali hung up the phone and made it to the back door, Tash was frantic. Ali let the dog out and stood in the open doorway for a moment. The sky to the west was darkening at a furious rate, and even the wind had the thick, dank smell of a storm. Ali shivered once against the damp chill and closed the door.

She headed back to the living room. Through the front bay window, she could see the black-and-white patrol car parked across the road. The young officer behind the wheel must have seen her standing at the window, because he gave her a wave before taking another bite of his sandwich. It was certainly a lot more lax than what she'd experienced in the past, Ali thought as she turned from the window.

She remembered the last time she'd needed protection. After a homicide suspect that Gary and Duncan had arrested made bail Ali had had several officers practically living right in her apartment for close to three weeks. Whenever Duncan couldn't be with her, they were there—going out shopping with her, sharing her dinner and even once helping her wash the apartment windows.

At least now she had Duncan's gun as backup.

As soon as she'd gotten home from the station, Ali had gone upstairs and unzipped her suitcase. Still in its leather holster, the Beretta had seemed out of place in the travel bag alongside her makeup and an unread issue of a fashion magazine. And it looked even more out of place buried in the bottom of her purse.

She'd taken it out, felt the cool metal in her hands and remembered the first day Duncan had coaxed her to the firing range. Then, as she'd become more comfortable with the gun, she'd started going on her own. There had been such a reassuring sense of power once she'd learned to fire the compact semiautomatic. And it was with that same sense of reassurance that Ali had checked the rounds in the magazine and tucked it into her purse beside her wallet.

She was on her way to the kitchen for a bottle of water when the doorbell rang. She opened the front door to the paperboy, who seemed intrigued by the patrol car out on the street.

"Yeah, hi," he said, when he finally turned to look at her. "I'm collecting for the paper. You owe five dollars."

"Okay." Ali nodded, looking past him to the officer across the street. He nodded to her once again through the open window. "I'll just get my wallet."

The boy stuck his foot out to hold the screen door open and glanced back to the street again as Ali fished through her purse.

"And have you got a pen, too? Mrs. MacGregor next door kept mine, and I need you to sign this sheet sayin' you paid."

"No problem." Ali handed him a five and rummaged through her purse again for a pen. Her hand brushed against the cool metal of the Beretta as she pulled out a ballpoint. "Where do I sign?"

The boy moved his finger to the bottom of a wrinkled form and Ali scrawled her initials.

"Thanks a lot, ma'am," he said, shoving the five in his pocket and pulling his foot from the door. "Have a good day."

Ali was still holding the pen when she closed the front door. As the latch slid into place, she felt the first rush of pain. An intense, thick pain. It pulsed behind her eyes, spreading to her forehead with such unexpected force she had to reach out a hand to the wall to catch herself.

How could she be having a vision now? What could possibly—

Another wave of pain. Ali bit her lip. As she brought her hand to the bridge of her nose, she realized she was still gripping the pen.

When the pain cleared for one blessed moment, Ali looked at the ballpoint. Its smooth shaft was the same white as her knuckles, and its end was notched by a pattern of faint toothmarks. She didn't recognize the pen—at least not immediately. It was only after the second nauseating surge of pain that Ali remembered where she'd picked up the pen. Then she almost dropped it.

With her heart racing and her knees weakening, she leaned back against the door, preparing herself for the headlong rush of images she knew was inevitable now. As she took a deep breath, they came.

In quick, obscure flashes that seemed meaningless at first, the images flickered before Ali's inner eye. She struggled to hang on to even one of them, and when she did, she gasped.

She saw the house—her house. From the backyard, at night, she saw herself at the kitchen counter, putting away dishes. In another series of flashes, she saw herself calling for Tash at the back door, moving through the house, turning off lights. She saw herself pulling the blinds in the bedroom. And then there was a blinding light before she saw the gloved hand again, its fingers wrapped around a steering wheel.

It was the distant rattle of the pen hitting the hardwood floor that snapped Ali from the dark images. She closed her eyes, feeling an iciness tremble through her even as beads of sweat broke out on her forehead and trickled down the back of her neck. The pen rolled along the floor, stopping when it reached the edge of the hall mat.

She took another deep breath and stared at it. It was the ballpoint she'd taken from Sam's desk last night when she'd needed to write him a note.

With her heart pounding in her ears, Ali reached for the pen. She had to be sure. She had to know if this was Sam's pen—if these were his memories she was reading so vividly now.

She was able to control the pain better the second time, expecting it and pushing it aside. Even so, her breath came in short gasps as she watched the images again, clearer this time. The gloved hand again, this time reaching for the latch on the gate to the backyard. It was night. She was walking through the yard, along the fence, and then she saw the hands again, this time reaching up to the top of the fence.

She didn't need to see more. Ali tossed Sam's pen back into her purse. Almost mechanically now, she checked the Beretta. She released the clip and let the magazine fall into her trembling hand. Fifteen rounds. She slid the magazine home.

When the phone rang this time, Ali didn't jump. Coldly she tucked the semiautomatic back into her purse and reached for the receiver.

"Hi, Ali. How are you doing?"

"Sam." She tried to check the waver in her voice.

"Ali? What's the matter?"

"Nothing, Sam. I was...I was just drawing. The phone startled me."

"Well, listen, I've got some news. Are you busy right now?"

"No. No, I'm just finishing up."

"All right. I'll come right over. Norm will be glad for the break. I'm sure he's getting hungry out there. I'll see you in a few minutes, all right?"

"Fine, Sam. I'll see you then."

"And, Ali?"

"Yes?"

"I love you," he whispered before he hung up the phone.

Ali wasn't sure how long she'd stood there, staring down at the phone before she headed for the backyard. Her mind was reeling by the time she stepped out into the cool afternoon and felt the wind tug at her clothes and hair.

What was she to believe now? Everything Sam had told her about Jacquie... Had he been telling the truth all along? And what about the bracelet? Why had he still not found out who had purchased it? Unless...unless *he* was the one who had bought it for her. Unless *he* had been her lover.

And, where had he gone last night when he was two hours late? Where was he when she'd seen the gloved hand reaching for her door?

Ali petted Tash as she followed her across the lawn. Then there was the dream. She had shot Sam. Had the dream been a premonition, after all? Was she about to discover that Sam was the man responsible for Jacqueline Munroe's death? Was she going to end up shooting him in self-defense?

She'd been so sure. Last night, when Sam had told her he loved her, she'd actually believed she'd found happiness again. With a staggering conviction, she'd known she loved Sam. Yet now, as doubt churned in her stomach, a dark and heavy fear took seed, clouding the certainty Ali had known just this morning.

She didn't want to believe it.

At the back of the yard, where the tall, wooden fence butted up against the row of maples that bordered the long yard, Ali stopped. Imprinted in the soft earth she could make out a partial shoe print, probably from a sneaker of some sort. On top of the fence, she found traces of mud where someone had used the fence to climb into the tree. And then, as she pulled herself up, scraping her arm on the rough bark, Ali found the wide crotch in the tree where he'd sat. Even through the thick canopy of leaves, she could see the windows of her bedroom.

"Ali?"

It was Sam. He was in the house, looking for her.

"Ali! Where are you?"

She thought she heard panic in his voice, but she couldn't be certain as the mounting wind rustled the leaves around her.

"Ali!"

She could see him standing in the open door now, looking out into the yard.

"Ali?"

"I'm here, Sam," she called, and watched him sprint to the end of the lawn.

"Shit, Ali. You scared the hell out of me. I didn't know where you were."

Above her, clouds black with rain lumbered across the sky. When she glanced down at Sam, the wind whipped at his dark hair, and he pushed it back with one hand as he squinted up at her.

"Ali, what are you doing up there?"

"You don't know, Sam?" She heard her own voice now above the wind. A voice with an edge so cold it sent a shiver even through her. "You don't know?" she asked again, and waited for his reply.

CHAPTER FOURTEEN

ALI SAW SAM'S EYES narrow as he looked up at her.

"Ali, I haven't the faintest idea why you're up there. Have you decided to build a tree house?"

She shook her head. His humor held genuine confusion. Maybe she was wrong. Maybe there was some other explanation behind the visions she'd just experienced.

Carefully Ali lowered herself to the top of the fence, accepting Sam's assistance. When she slipped her hand into his, she expected to feel something. Something that would have confirmed her doubts, something cold and dangerous.

But there was only his familiar warmth.

"Is there something I should know about, Ali?" he asked once she was finally standing next to him.

She stared at him, trying to see past his bewildered smile to catch a glimpse of something darker, something she should fear. But it wasn't there. Or at least, if it was, it was so well hidden even she could not recognize it.

She looked away. Jamie's words of advice whispered through her mind. Maybe he was right. Maybe she had to trust her instincts, instead of the disjointed images that haunted her. In her heart she didn't believe Sam was capable of killing Jacquie. And in her heart Ali didn't believe he could harm her. How could she fear something she had no true sense of?

All she knew was that Sam had always been there for her. She'd trusted him before. She had to trust him again.

"Ali?" He put his hands on her shoulders, tilting his head so he could see her face. "What is it? Talk to me."

She nodded up to the crotch in the tree where she'd been perched only seconds ago. "That's where he sits and watches me."

"Who sits and watches you, Ali?"

When she looked at him again, Sam thought he saw accusation shadow her gray eyes. "Jacqueline's killer," she said, and twisted from his grasp. She turned, gazing skyward as she crossed her arms over her chest.

"Wait a minute, Ali. Wait a minute." Sam reached out to pull her around and felt her flinch. "What are you saying? That he's been watching you? Here, from your backyard?"

She nodded, still not meeting his gaze, but he could see the anger in her eyes, along with the fear.

"How do you know this Ali?"

She looked at him but didn't answer. When she took a step toward him, he thought he saw a tear glisten in the corner of one eye.

"Hold me, Sam," she whispered so softly that, if she hadn't reached out for him, he might not have known what she'd asked.

She trembled once when he took her into his arms. He rocked her, stroking her hair, as the wind spiraled around them, tearing at their clothes.

But it wasn't just a sense of security Ali seemed to be seeking now from his embrace, Sam realized. He detected her doubts. He wasn't entirely certain where they came from, but he'd seen them in her face when she'd looked down at him from the tree. And he felt them now as she clung to him, as if there was something she needed to draw from him that would convince her of his innocence.

He wasn't sure how long they stood entwined in the backyard, but when the first drops of rain pelted down, Sam stepped back and held her arms. Ali winced.

"You're bleeding." He pointed to the blood congealing on her arm where she'd scraped herself on the tree. "Come on, Ali. We'd better get inside and clean this up."

Once in the house, Ali fetched the first-aid kit while Sam put the kettle on for tea. Now, with the tea brewing and Ali seated on the corner of the kitchen table, Sam cleaned the abrasion.

She told him everything—about the pen from his desk and the visions she'd received while holding it. Even when she obliged him and showed him the unassuming white ballpoint, even after he assured her it was a standard-issue pen that everyone at the precinct used, Sam knew that a part of her suspected him. Sneaking glances at her while he cleaned her arm, Sam knew there was nothing he could say to ease the doubt he saw in her eyes.

"I'm going to give you my gun, Ali," he said, reaching for a bandage.

She didn't say anything. Her gaze out the window at the rising storm remained unbroken.

He admired Ali's strength. With everything that had gone on, with what she'd seen and been through, she seemed more determined than ever to prevent this man from getting the better of her. Coupled with her experiences in her long string of cases with the NYPD and then the violent manner in which Duncan had been taken away from her, Sam could only begin to imagine the seemingly infinite strength that shielded Ali's heart. He'd never met another person like her. He'd never known someone to possess the spirit and resolve, the inner drive and stamina, that he'd come to recognize as a part of Ali.

"Ali?"

She turned to him.

"I said I'm going to give you my personal gun. I've got it in the car, under my seat—"

"I don't need it, Sam." She lifted her arm, inspecting his nursing skills.

"Ali, you're not going to argue with me on this. This guy is obviously after you, and I want you to have some additional protection. You need—"

"Sam, I don't need it. I've already got one."

He stared at her, hoping his shock was not apparent. Why shouldn't she have a gun? After working with the NYPD all those years, she would've needed some sort of protection. Still, he hadn't expected it.

Ali shook her head. "It's a long story. Duncan bought it for me. We were working on a case. Things got pretty sticky...." She dropped down from the table, took a couple of mugs from the cupboard and started to pour the tea. When she turned, Sam's mouth hung open. What had he expected?

"Listen, Sam, I've worked on some pretty violent cases with the NYPD, and believe it or not, I've been threatened before. Why do you think I'm so reluctant to become involved with cases now?"

Ali smiled in response to Sam's speechlessness. "Sam, it's not the end of the world, all right? So I pack a gun. Does that change anything?"

At last he nodded. "Well, yeah, Ali, it does. I mean, you shouldn't have to carry a weapon."

"Then what did I just hear you suggest a few seconds ago?"

He let out a long breath and sat down at the table. Ali handed him a cup of tea and pushed aside the first-aid kit as she sat down next to him. For some reason she felt compelled to put her hand on his arm. He'd been so concerned for her. From the moment he'd raced out into the backyard, she'd seen his panic. Then he'd patched up her arm with such gentle affection that her doubts had begun to dissipate. What few remained, Ali ignored as she lifted a hand to stroke his cheek.

"Sam?"

"So I take it you know how to fire one?"

"Seventy-five percent accuracy," she said, remembering the last time she'd gone to the firing range with Duncan, how he'd congratulated her and swept her into his arms.

Sam gave a low whistle and reached for her hand. He was silent again and Ali studied his face. Only a few weeks ago, when he'd first held her hand, Ali had sensed something between them. And when they'd kissed for the first time, she'd wanted more, in spite of the fact she'd hardly known him. When she'd laid her hand over his scar, allowing herself to be drawn into his embrace, she'd wanted to feel his body next to hers.

Now, again, as Sam stroked the back of her hand with his thumb, Ali wanted to feel his body moving with hers. She needed to be with him tonight. She needed to know it wasn't Sam she should fear.

"You said you had some news," she said eventually, and waited for his gaze to meet hers. "On the phone, you said you had some news?"

He nodded. "Yeah, about the bracelet."

Outside, the storm was still mounting. They could hear rolls of thunder in the distance, as rain pelted the windows.

"What did you find out?"

"I might have finally found the original retailer. He thinks he remembers having sold the bracelet several months ago. I'd questioned all the local jewelers with no luck, and I figured I'd have to start looking out of town. Anyway, the other day, I was at the precinct and needed a phone number. Someone had taken our directory, so the only one around was an old one Matt and I use to prop open the window by our desks."

He paused to take a sip of tea. "So there I was with last year's phone book on my lap, and I realized I hadn't taken into account any kind of time factor. You even suggested that Jacquie might have been having an affair before the separation. And there it was—a quarter-page ad for Wilson's Jewelers. It was a family business for over seventy years."

"And you hadn't checked them out before?"

"That's just it," he explained. "They've been out of business for the last seven months. Apparently Wilson's kid had no interest in the business and the old man was getting tired of running the place, so they sold the shop. It's a toy store or something now."

"He recognized the bracelet?"

"He recognized it, but he had no idea who actually bought it. He thinks his wife might have sold it during their going-out-of-business sale."

"And they're searching their records?"

Sam nodded, taking another sip of tea. "He did warn me, though, that because of the volume of their sales during those last few weeks, it could take him some time to find it. But he's going to call me the second he finds out."

Sam looked straight at her now, and Ali was surprised at the unflinching determination in his eyes. "We're going to get this guy, Ali. I promise you, we're going to get him."

IT MUST HAVE BEEN the thunder that woke Sam. He didn't start out of his sleep, but rather, woke up gradually as the rumbles grew closer and louder.

Ali lay asleep in his arms. In the dying flame of a candle on the dresser, he saw her eyes flutter once, but she did not awake. They hadn't been asleep for very long, Sam thought as he watched the candle flicker, sending shadows swaying along the bedroom walls. After discussing what little development there'd been on the case, he'd recognized Ali's need to be with him—because he had needed to be with her.

Carefully he eased his arm out from under her and propped himself up on one elbow so he could watch her. With her body tucked into the curves of his, Sam felt her slow, steady breathing. He could only guess at the energy her visions had sapped from her this afternoon. He'd been surprised by the exhaustion in her face when he'd found her in the backyard.

That exhaustion, however, had not been apparent later when they'd made love. She'd answered Sam's desires with a passion and longing greater than any he'd ever experienced. And afterward, when Ali had laid her head on his chest and he'd stroked her hair, Sam hadn't wondered any longer if Ali doubted him.

It was because of Ali's newfound trust in him that Sam was coldly determined to find the man who threatened her life. Not just for Ali, he realized, but for himself.

Sam knew he could never forgive himself if anything happened to Ali. And now, as he watched her sleep, the dancing light of the candle shimmering softly along her skin, Sam knew he couldn't live without her.

After Jacquie, there had been other women. Women who'd either been forthright enough to ask him out, or those he'd eventually approached after much prodding from Matt. But he hadn't taken any of them seriously. They'd all been transient relationships leading nowhere.

Not since Jacquie had Sam ever considered the possibility of sharing his life with someone. Even his preoccupation with his house had been a needling question in the back of his mind. He'd never really understood what had possessed him to buy it in the first place. What was he fixing it up for, anyway? It was too big for one person.

And then Ali had walked into his life. When she'd opened that front door and cast her gentle gaze on him, the pieces started to make sense. Slowly he'd come to realize why he'd bought the house, why he'd fixed it up and most importantly, why there hadn't been anyone in his life until now—not even Jacquie, not really.

Ali was much more than any of the women he'd ever known. Behind her calm and gentle smile lay a person of such strength, such determination and vitality, that every time Sam looked at her, he was both amazed and moved. And every moment he spent with her only served to prove he could not be without her.

Ali moaned softly and Sam watched her, wondering what dream had found its way into her sleep.

There had to be something they were overlooking. Ali admitted she was gradually linking with Jacquie's killer, seeing places he'd been, seeing what he'd seen. They were getting closer—that couldn't be denied. And yet the answer was so elusive. Patience was what he needed now. He'd have to wait for Howard Wilson's call. But sitting around and waiting was not easy for Sam—especially when Ali's life was at stake.

Something had been overlooked. He thought of the pen again—the pen that had fed Ali the latest barrage of visions. There had to be something behind it. Maybe something at the precinct.

Carefully he slipped out of the bed, drawing the sheet over Ali's shoulder, and reached for his jeans. He'd put on his shirt and was tying the laces of his sneakers when Ali stirred.

"Sam?" Her voice was thick with sleep. "Sam, where are you going?"

"It's okay, Ali. Go back to sleep. I'll be back soon."

"Sam." She sat up in bed and reached for her robe.

"Ali, listen, I just want to check on a couple of things at the precinct. I'll be back before you know it."

"Well, would you at least tell me what this is all about? It's—" she shot a glance to the clock on the nightstand "—ten o'clock."

Sam pulled back one blind on the window. Sheets of rain washed the dark pavement. Glistening in the light of a street lamp, the patrol car sat across from the house. Ali came up behind him.

"Can't it wait till morning, Sam?" She wrapped her arms around his waist and rested her head against his back.

"I won't be long, Ali. I promise."

"What is it?"

"Just a long shot."

He turned to kiss her.

"Call me from the precinct?"

Sam nodded, kissing her again as she buttoned his shirt. "I will. Now, why don't you go back to bed? The patrol car's out front, and I'll lock up behind me."

But Ali followed Sam to the front door, anyway. She pulled her robe around her more tightly as she watched him shove his arms into his leather jacket. And when he opened the front door to the driving rain, a flash of lightning ripped open the sky.

"Be careful driving," Ali told him.

"I will," he promised as he turned to her one last time. He lifted his hands to her face and drew her mouth to his, devouring her uncertainty with a kiss.

Ali watched him run through the rain, his jacket pulled over his head as he climbed into the Bronco. She watched him back out of the drive, stop to speak to the officer in the patrol car, and then he was gone.

Ali closed the door. And as the silence of the house closed in around her, she reached into her purse and felt for the polished walnut grip of the Beretta.

WHEN SAM CAME THROUGH the front doors of the precinct, he wasn't surprised at the ringing phones and the distraught look the night dispatcher, Clarice, threw him from beyond the front counter. Storms as violent as the one raging now were known to set off every alarm in the city. No doubt, all available units were out responding to one false alarm after another.

He gave Clarice a sympathetic wave and headed down the corridor to his desk. As he took off the dripping jacket and tossed it over the back of his chair, Sam wasn't entirely sure what he was looking for.

He was working on a hunch, nothing more. Yet, during the drive, the closer he'd gotten to the precinct, the more certain he was his hunch was right. In his mind's eye he'd worked with the few pieces he had, constructing a puzzle that would give him the answer. And it was the pen, he realized, that was one of the missing pieces.

He passed a glance over both his desk and Matt's, buried in case files and reports. And when his eye caught Matt's copy of the Munroe file, he slid it out from under the others.

Inside, as he'd seen before, were his partner's meticulous reports. Sam sat down and quickly fingered through the pages of notes, hoping to find something he may have missed before, something to prove his suspicions were terribly wrong.

"Detective Tremaine?"

Sam looked up from the open file in his lap. Clarice, her headset dangling from one ear, stood in the doorway.

"We've got a break-and-enter on Dawson Avenue. All of our available units are already out. Are you on call tonight?"

Sam didn't need this. Not when he seemed so close. And especially not with Ali home alone. "Yeah, yeah, I'm on call," he admitted, tucking the file back into the pile on Matt's desk. "Print me up the call. I'm on my way."

The door swung shut behind Clarice and Sam grabbed his jacket. A B&E wouldn't take long. Probably just another false alarm triggered by the storm, he thought, turning to the door.

But he hadn't gone two steps when his phone rang, its shrill tone echoing through the empty wing. Panic coursed through him as he thought of Ali. He snatched up the receiver.

"Detective Tremaine."

"Oh, yes, Detective. Howard Wilson here. Wilson Jewelers? Sorry to be calling you so late, but you said if I found that receipt you were looking for I should—"

"You found it?"

"Well, I think so. You know, my wife and I have been searching through our paperwork for hours, and I thought you'd probably want to know as soon as—"

"Do you have a name, Mr. Wilson?"

"Yes, I have a copy of the receipt right in front of me here. The bracelet you showed me was bought back at the beginning of December. I suppose it must have been a Christmas gift, by the looks of it. The bill indicates that the gentleman had wished it to be wrapped and—"

"The name, Mr. Wilson. Please."

"Yes. Yes, of course, Detective Tremaine. We have the name here of Dobson—a Mr. Matthew Dobson."

CHAPTER FIFTEEN

WHEN SAM TURNED onto Dawson Avenue, the break-and-enter he was speeding toward was the last thing on his mind. From the moment Clarice had tossed him the keys to the Skylark, Sam had been on automatic pilot. Thoughts of Matt—killing Jacquie, stalking Ali—made his mind reel and his stomach churn. Even after hearing Howard Wilson read the name over the phone, Sam still didn't want to believe it. Not Matt. There had to be some explanation.

He'd take this call and then head straight to Ali's. He'd convince her to come home with him. She'd be safer there. And then he would call Harrington and explain everything.

Sam banged his fist against the steering wheel as he struggled to see through the blur of rain on the windshield. He shouldn't be out here in this storm, responding to some call that any one of the night officers could handle.

Minutes after he'd left the station, Sam had heard a unit from the other side of the city respond via radio to the Dawson break-and-enter, and for a moment, Sam had hoped to hand off the call. But when he'd reached for the mike, he heard Clarice give the officers Sam's car number, informing them the call was covered. In the very same breath, she'd given the unit another call at the west end of the city, closer to their current location. Then Sam had heard Clarice radio for the first available backup to the Dawson Storage warehouse, and Sam had lowered the volume on the radio.

He'd have to handle this himself. He could be waiting a half hour before another unit was available. He needed to get back to Ali before then.

Sam slowed at the corner of Dawson and Claremont and pulled into the graveled lot. Through curtains of rain, he saw the Dawson Storage sign over the locked main doors. The only details Clarice had been able to give him were that the call had originated from a car phone and that the caller had claimed to be driving in the area when he saw some guy jimmying a side door to the warehouse.

Except for a couple of rusted station wagons and the skeletal outline of a boat trailer, the lot was empty. Sam steered the Skylark to the side of the warehouse and saw the open side door. But no vehicle. If someone had broken in, surely they'd intend to steal something, and most certainly they'd have a car or van.

The side door flapped a couple of times in the wind, but other than that, all was quiet. Whoever the caller had seen breaking open the door was probably long gone.

Sam jammed the Skylark into Park and reached for the radio.

"Dispatch, this is car sixty-two. I'm at the Dawson Storage warehouse on Dawson and Claremont. Everything looks quiet here. I'm going in to take a look around. Over." He tossed the mike onto the seat.

There was a short hiss and crackle over the radio and finally he heard Clarice's voice. "I copy, sixty-two." Then there was only the pounding rain and the side door banging in the wind.

ALI LIFTED the pencil from the sketchbook in her lap and went over to the window, scanning the night sky as lightning shattered the darkness.

After Sam had raced out into the storm, Ali hadn't bothered going back to bed. She knew she'd only lie there tossing and turning, worrying about him until he called from the precinct. So she'd put on jeans and a T-shirt and come downstairs to try to work.

She moved back to the couch and looked at the shaky sketch in front of her, then flipped to the next clean sheet. She was uptight. She considered calling the precinct just to hear Sam's voice. He'd been gone an hour.

She looked around the living room, feeling the unbearable silence press in on her. There was another roll of thunder.

She decided to call Sam. Surely he'd still be at the precinct. Ali tossed her sketchbook onto the coffee table and went to the phone. But as she reached for the receiver, she felt a wave of pain shudder through her—dull at first, then growing sharper. She braced herself against the back of the couch. A piercing dagger of pain stabbed behind her eyes.

She cried out. She pressed her hands to either side of her head, trying to find release from the burning spasm. It was stronger, sharper than what she'd experienced with other visions.

She'd felt this kind of pain only once before....

And then, in a blink, she saw Sam. It was nothing more than a quick flash in the midst of white, blinding pain, but she saw him in the Skylark.

She had to clear the pain and try to concentrate. She had to look beyond the shadows of her fear and focus on the vision.

Through the blur of the rain and her own agony, she saw Sam in the parked Skylark. In another flash, she saw the street signs—Claremont and Dawson. And then she saw the big sign over the door, dimly lit by the street lamps—Dawson Storage. Sam had already stepped out of the car. She watched the rain drench his hair as he walked to the side door and stepped inside.

Gasping for air, Ali dragged herself from the vision. The bitter taste of panic rose in her throat as she grabbed her purse and raced to the door.

This wasn't a dream. This wasn't a premonition she could shuffle to one side. This was real. She was linking with Sam for the same reason she'd linked with Duncan.

Only this time she prayed, she wouldn't be too late.

THE SIDE DOOR of the warehouse slammed behind him. It banged against its frame a few more times as the wind whistled through the opening, and then stopped. Sam peered into the murky cavern, giving his eyes time to adjust to the darkness before taking a wary step forward.

To his left were three banks of light switches. He reached for them. One after another, he clicked them uselessly. No doubt the owner had switched off the main breaker at nights to save himself the hassle of putting out every light in the building.

There was no sense in going back to the car for a flashlight. Even though Sam was certain the trespasser had long since fled the scene, he wasn't going to announce himself with the bright beacon of a flashlight. Besides, with the dim light of the street lamps outside filtering through the filthy windows, Sam's eyes were beginning to adjust to the dark—he was already able to distinguish vague outlines of the two main corridors of the warehouse. On either side, he could make out the rows of storage units, the steel railings and girders, and the network of stairs and catwalks reaching up into the shadows of the three levels.

His sneakers made no noise on the concrete floor as he stepped toward the main corridor and glanced around the corner. Nothing. The building was dead quiet—only the drumming of the rain against the tin roof could be heard.

As Sam moved away from the corner, his hand reached for his holster. Something deep within him, something he could only define as his cop's sixth sense, needed to feel the reassurance of the .38 at his side as he stepped into the wide corridor.

THE GLARE of headlights splintered across the rain-covered windshield of the Cherokee. Taillights fragmented into bloodred shards, then momentarily returned to distinct points of light as the wipers swept the windshield. Ali maneuvered another lane-change, passing slower traffic.

The car dragged sharply when it hit a deep puddle of water, and Ali struggled with the wheel. She checked her rearview mirror again, desperately hoping one of the sets of headlights behind her belonged to the patrol car that had been posted outside her house.

When she had backed the Jeep out of the garage, she'd considered asking the surveillance officer for help, but just as quickly decided against it. How would she have convinced him Sam was in danger? Tell him she'd seen Sam in a vision? No, she didn't have time to educate the man on her abilities. Now, she could only pray the patrol car was behind her.

She yanked the wheel to the right and the Cherokee swerved onto Dawson. The warehouse couldn't be far now, she guessed as she sped past one street after another. In the rearview mirror she could only see the dark, wet street behind her. No headlights, no patrol car. There was no one behind her. She was on her own. Beside her on the passenger seat, the Beretta gleamed.

She wouldn't let it happen again, she thought, gripping the wheel more tightly. She wouldn't be too late this time.

And then she could feel the familiar energy welling up within her. From the far reaches of that endless tunnel, the vision hurtled toward her in a rush of pain—hot and piercing with a force that trapped her breath in her throat—until it consumed her.

She saw Sam walk down the main corridor of the warehouse. He searched the shadows, his hair plastered flat from the rain and his face glistening. She saw him reach for his holster and draw out his gun. And when he looked up, Ali followed his gaze.

With a final surge of fear, Ali recognized the large circular vent high above him. The soft light that washed through it cast a long shimmering shaft to the warehouse floor. And as a chill seized Ali, she saw the four-bladed fan.

IT WAS THE PLACE Ali had described in her dream.

When Sam looked up and saw the old air vent, he stopped. The four blades cast the shadow of a cross in the pale circle of light on the concrete floor. And when he took a step closer to the shaft of light, Sam remembered how easily he'd dismissed Ali's warnings.

He'd told her that her dreams were nothing more than the culmination of her fears—past and present.

He'd promised her that there were no churches in Danby with round windows like the one she'd described. It hadn't occurred to him that it mightn't have been a church window at all.

Instinctively he cocked the .38 and released the safety with his thumb.

There was someone else in the warehouse with him. He sensed it. There was no movement, no sound, but Sam could almost feel the other person's eyes following him as he took another step down the corridor.

And then, even before he heard the voice, Sam looked up to the railing of the second level.

"Hello, Sammy," Matt said, stepping out of the shadows and onto the steel-grate walkway.

Sam brought his gun around, but he was too late. Matt's own gun was already trained on him. Beyond the gleam of its muzzle, Sam saw the hard lines of Matt's face, and in that moment, he didn't recognize his partner at all.

"You were pretty fast responding to the call. I'm impressed." Matt leaned his hip into the steel railing, steadying himself above Sam. "No doubt you wanted to get this call over with so you could rush back to sweet Ali's side, hmm?"

Sam swallowed hard. He had to keep Matt talking. Stalling was his only chance. "How did you know it would be me responding?"

"I knew you were on call tonight. It was only a matter of time until the calls stacked up enough and they asked you in. Besides, I've got an extra radio in my car." The dim light revealed his cold grin. "I heard you were on the way. All I had to do was wait."

"Then you also must have heard Clarice call for backup." Sam's hand tightened around the grip of his pistol.

"Yeah, but it's going to be a long time coming, what with the storm and all. You know that, Sammy. That's why you're stalling."

"So, what is it you want, Matt?"

"Why don't you start by giving up the piece, huh?"

Sam felt the curve of the trigger beneath his finger. Giving up his weapon was sure death.

"Listen, Matt, I know about you and Jacquie, all right? Why don't we just talk about this?"

"There's nothing to talk about, Sammy."

"I think there is, Matt. We're friends. You know you can talk to me. Haven't we always been able to talk?"

"Sure. But like I said, there's nothing to talk about."

Sam dared to take a step closer. Then he saw Matt's grip on the gun tighten, and he stopped. "So, killing me is the answer, Matt? You think I'm the only one who knows about you and Jacquie?"

"Oh, and who else knows, Sam? That little psychic of yours?" Matt's thin lips pulled together in a taunting grin. "Well, I doubt she'll be difficult to handle. And I really doubt you've told anyone else. You're too tight-lipped about your work, Sammy. You don't tell anyone anything until you're absolutely certain. And you really weren't a hundred percent certain, were you, Sam? Not until now, right?"

Matt raised his gun a little higher, his stance stiffening. "Now put down your piece, Sam, or so help me—"

"And how is this going to look, Matt?" Sam challenged him, his own weapon still positioned.

"This? This isn't going to look like anything, Sammy. This is just a routine B&E, except you didn't have the backup you'd requested. When they got here, they were too late. Hey, it happens. Even to the best of 'em."

"Matt, wait. This is Sam you're talking to. It's me, your partner, for God's sake. You can talk to me."

"You're stalling, Sammy. Pure police-psychology shit. It won't work here."

"I'm not stalling, Matt. I just don't want you to do something you're going to regret. I want you to talk to me. I want to help you. You loved her, didn't you, Matt? You loved Jacquie?"

"So what if I did?"

"Matt, listen to me. I know the anger and hurt you felt when she told you she was going back to Peter. I felt it, too, years ago, when she told me she was marrying him. When she told me she was pregnant. God, Matt, don't you see? I know what you went through. Maybe no one else does, but believe me, I do."

Sam watched the hardness of Matt's face lessen for a brief moment.

"I know you went over there to talk to Jacquie, Matt. I know you went over that night to tell her how much you loved her, to persuade her not to go back to Peter, to marry you, instead, like she'd promised, right? You tried to convince her you could offer her a better life than Peter could, that you loved her more than he did."

Sam didn't move. He didn't dare. As long as he was able to hold Matt where he was until the backup unit arrived, he might still stand a chance of talking Matt into giving himself up.

"But she wouldn't listen, would she, Matt? You got into an argument. You started fighting. You did what you thought you had to do, right? She was screaming and you had to keep her quiet. You never meant to harm her, did you, Matt? I know you never meant to harm her."

Matt's steel gaze wavered briefly, his stance easing a bit, and for a fleeting second, Sam thought he might have an opening. But just as quickly, it passed and Matt's expression hardened again. He raised his gun.

ALI SWERVED the Cherokee in alongside Sam's Skylark and killed the engine. Even the rain pelting against the roof of the Jeep could not drown out the panic that hammered in her head. She reached for the Beretta and opened the door.

She raced across the short distance to the warehouse side door and stepped into the gaping darkness. She brushed back her wet hair and peered down the corridor between the rows of storage units.

She heard the echo of voices off to the left. Cocking the Beretta, she followed the sound.

But even before she had reached the turn in the corridor, Ali felt the next vision about to sweep through her. It was so strong now, her link with Sam, so desperately vital and immediate.

She had to push the vision away. She had to concentrate on the voices. First there was Sam, then another voice. A familiar voice.

And then it all came together. The second Ali recognized Matt's voice, she thought about the pen from Sam's desk. It had been Matt's pen, not Sam's. It had been Matt who'd watched her, Matt who'd killed Jacquie, and Matt who now threatened the life of the man she loved.

The energy of the vision swelled through her, almost uncontrollable now. But Ali forced it aside, determined not to let it interfere.

It had been the visions that had prevented her from saving Duncan that night eleven months ago. It had been the visions that had taken over her, immobilized her for too long, so that she hadn't been able to reach him in time.

She couldn't let it happen again.

"COME ON, Matt, listen to me. Listen to reason. It can't work this way. You know that," Sam pleaded, hoping his voice didn't reveal his desperation. "We can talk about this, Matt. Just the two of us—but not here, not like this."

Initially he'd hoped to rattle Matt enough so that he would lower his gun a little, just enough so that he could get a clear shot. But as he watched him, Sam realized that, even if there was an opportunity for a clear shot, he might not be capable of taking it.

This was Matt—his friend and partner. This was the guy who walked freely in and out of his house with pizza and beer, and could find a ball game on television no matter what time of day.

"Matt, listen to me, please. It doesn't have to be like this."

"I'm afraid it does, Sammy," Matt said, his voice possessing a cruel intensity that warned Sam even before he heard the explosion of the bullet.

ALI HAD MADE IT to the second level of the warehouse and was within earshot of Sam and Matt when the gun's discharge ruptured the silence.

She felt the bullet's impact the second it ripped through Sam's flesh. She felt the searing pain of Sam's wound, as if she herself had been struck by the bullet. Tears welled up in her eyes from the familiar burning. She collapsed against the wall of a storage unit, biting her lip to stifle her cry.

From just around the corner, she heard Matt's voice again. Steadily she pulled herself together and followed its sound. Fueled now with the immediacy of Sam's injury, Ali left the shadows and edged along the walkway.

Then she saw Matt.

He had his back to her and was looking down to the first floor. Ali's fingers tightened around the Beretta. She raised the semiautomatic to shoulder height in front of her and looked down its sight at Matt.

"I really wish things could've worked out differently, Sammy," Matt was saying, his gun trained downward. "But you and that little psychic of yours were getting too close."

Ali took another step. Her hands ached from her iron grip on the gun. She strained to see past Matt to Sam, to see if he was all right. But all she saw was Sam's gun lying on the cement floor in the circle of light.

She focused again on Matt.

"So you see, Sammy, it does have to end this way."

"You're wrong, Matt." Ali heard a voice, fierce with determination, and was startled to realize it was her own. Her hands steadied. With the tip of her index finger, she felt the smooth curve of the trigger, still wet from the rain.

Matt spun around. His gun, still raised, came with him. And when Ali saw the deadly intent that burned in his eyes, she knew she'd have to fire first.

Something as cold as death gripped her in that split second. Something that had lived in her heart from the day she'd cradled Duncan in her arms and felt his life slip away. Something that would not allow her to watch Sam die the same way.

With all the certainty of her love for Sam, Ali squeezed the trigger. She neither looked away nor blinked when the bullet exploded from the gun. She felt the kick of the Beretta and quickly brought it back into position, lining Matt into its sight once again, ready for the second shot.

But it wasn't necessary. The first bullet had found its mark. Matt's gun let off one useless round before dropping from his hand and clattering onto the steel walkway. Ali watched him stagger back, the force of the bullet driving his body against the railing. He lingered there for a moment, one hand clasped to his chest. Then, slowly, his body pitched over the rail to the concrete floor below with nothing more than a gentle thud, which whispered through the tomblike warehouse.

Ali lowered her gun by degrees. Only then did her hands begin to shake and her knees weaken.

"Ali!?" Sam's voice echoed through the building.

With the gun still in one hand, Ali stepped to the railing. Sam was sitting on the floor, just outside of the light, clutching his right arm with his hand.

"Ali, are you all right?"

But she didn't answer him. She raced along the walkway and flew down the closest set of stairs. When she reached Sam's side, she could see the blood he'd already lost spreading in a dark, glistening pool.

Ali lay down the Beretta and knelt beside him.

"How bad is it?" she asked, lifting his hand from the wound. The sleeve of his leather jacket had been torn by the bullet, and Sam's blood warmed her hand as she pulled the jacket off his shoulder.

"Ali—" he reached out and took hold of her arm "—are you all right?"

She shouldn't have been surprised by the concern she saw in Sam's eyes. She'd seen it before, when he'd realized her life was in jeopardy, when he'd told her he couldn't lose her. And yet, when Ali met the intensity of his gaze now, she found herself swallowing back tears.

She wanted to cry—knowing Sam was alive, knowing she hadn't lost him. Instead, she nodded, her eyes never leaving his as a tentative smile struggled to her lips.

"I'm fine, Sam," she said eventually, and reached out to caress his cheek. "I'm fine," she repeated just before she leaned over to press a gentle kiss to his lips. "But how bad is your arm?" The sleeve of his shirt was stained crimson.

"I'm okay, Ali."

"Sure, and then you'll be telling me it's just a scratch," she said, yanking the belt from her jeans. Quickly she secured it around the top of his arm to stop the bleeding and moved around to his other side.

Accepting Ali's shoulder for support, Sam stood, then walked into the shaft of light and bent to pick up his gun. When Ali came to his side, she tucked her

Beretta into the back of her jeans and slid her arm around his waist.

Sam slung an arm over her shoulders, pulling Ali to him, needing to feel her closeness. He knew she looked at Matt's motionless body, too, as they stood in the silence of the warehouse.

"It's over now, Ali," he whispered, pulling her closer. "It's over."

She didn't say anything. She didn't need to.

As they listened to the distant wail of sirens, Sam wondered if Ali would ever be able to forget the memories of what had happened here tonight. And as the sirens drew nearer, Sam wondered how long her dreams would be plagued by images of what she'd had to do. But this time, he would be there for her, and that in itself reassured him as they walked down the corridor together.

EPILOGUE

SAM BALLED his hand into a fist and flexed it a few times. Thanks to the drugs, the pain was subsiding. He'd been lucky, the doctor had told him. The bullet had passed cleanly through the upper part of his arm with little damage to nerves or muscle tissue. Three or four inches over however, he'd explained, and Sam would have been past any doctor's help.

With his arm in a sling, Sam left the examination room and stepped through the swinging door. The odors of antiseptic and floor cleaner wafted down the hallway, and Sam kept his breathing shallow.

He stopped to make way for two medics who rushed down an intersecting corridor wheeling a stretcher at top speed. Sam thought of Matt. Unlike the man on the stretcher, clinging to life, Matt hadn't been rushed to Emergency.

No, Sam thought, the medics had tried their best, but Matt's body had been zipped into a black bag and carried to the ambulance with no sense of urgency. Even now, Sam couldn't quite grasp the reality of the night's events. It would take him a long time to accept the fact that his friend and partner was gone. Longer still to come to terms with the fact that the same man had been responsible for Jacquie's death—and very nearly his own.

At the end of the hall, past the main desk, he saw Ali. She was pacing the waiting-room floor, her hands tucked into the pockets of her rain-soaked jeans. Behind her, sitting on the edge of one worn chair, Nancy chewed a fingernail.

When he passed the main desk and stepped into the waiting area, both Ali and Nancy looked up.

"How're ya doing, Sam?" Nancy asked, slinging her jacket over her shoulder.

He nodded and caught Ali's exhausted smile. "Not bad. The doctor said there isn't anything to worry about. I should be as good as new before you know it."

"I called Harrington. Told him about Matt. I also told him you were too drugged up to talk to him tonight. He wants to see you first thing in the morning."

"Thanks, Nance."

"You two going to be all right getting home?" she asked, looking at Ali. "I can give you a lift."

Sam watched Ali shake her head. "I think we'll be okay, but thank you."

Nancy nodded. "Well, listen, it was nice meeting you again, Ali. If you need anything, to talk, whatever, just call, okay?"

"Thanks, Nancy. I appreciate the offer."

"Listen, Sam," she said, turning to him, "I'm...I'm really sorry about Matt."

"I think we all are, Nance."

"Yeah, well, take care of yourself, Tremaine. I'll see you guys in the morning."

Only after Nancy had left the waiting room and disappeared down the corridor did Sam look at Ali. Her hair still hung in short wet curls, and under the jacket Nancy had lent her, Ali's white T-shirt was smeared with Sam's blood.

"Hey, you," he whispered to her softly, ignoring the bustle of people around them, "come here." He snaked his good arm around her waist and pulled her to him. He lifted his hand to her chin.

"How are you holding up?"

"I'm all right, Sam." She reached up to kiss him, needing to feel him now more than ever. His lips brushed hers, caressing them lightly as if to prove he really was here with her now. Beneath the hand she rested on his chest, Ali felt the steady beat of his heart.

Sam was alive. He was with her. She hadn't been too late this time.

Ali felt everything rush over her in one great wave of relief. She wrapped her arms around Sam, fighting back her tears. He must have felt her body shudder, because when he pulled back and looked down at her, Ali saw concern in his eyes.

"Ali? What is it?"

She shook her head. "Come on, I'll tell you outside. Let's get out of here."

She led him away from the noise and bustle of people, out through the automatic doors and into the wet night. The rain had eased off, and the wind had died down to a gentle breeze.

"What is it, Ali?" Sam asked again, once they reached the Cherokee. He leaned back against the side of the vehicle and Ali stepped between his long legs and pressed her body close to his.

She drew herself up so that she could kiss him again and Sam welcomed it hungrily. When their lips finally parted, Ali swayed in the rapture of his touch.

"I love you, Sam Tremaine," she whispered.

"Does this mean you'd say yes if I asked you to marry me?"

Ali put her hands on Sam's chest and pushed herself back so she could see his face in the soft glow of the street lamp. She loved this man, there was no more denying it. And even though she knew how close she'd come to losing him tonight, even though she knew she was destined to sleepless nights of worry, Ali also knew she couldn't be without him.

"That depends," she said at last, smiling. "*Are* you asking me?"

Sam gazed down at her soft lips, looked into the shimmer of those pale gray eyes and, for the first time, wished that Ali *could* read his thoughts. He wished she could reach into his mind and soul, seeing everything she meant to him.

"Yeah, I suppose I am. Will you marry me, Ali?"

There was no hesitation in her voice when her lips left his long enough to answer. "Yes, Sam," she murmured. "Yes, I will."

And as he drew her into his embrace, Sam knew this was where he belonged—with Ali. Without her, nothing made sense. Without her, he couldn't imagine living. Ali had become his world—a world of passion and contentment, of love and constant wonder.

HARLEQUIN®

Deceit, betrayal, murder

Join Harlequin's intrepid heroines, India Leigh and Mary Hadfield, as they ferret out the truth behind the mysterious goings-on in their neighborhood. These two women are no milk-and-water misses. In fact, they thrive on

Watch for their incredible adventures in this special two-book collection. Available in March, wherever Harlequin books are sold.

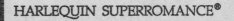

The Wrong Twin
by Rebecca Winters

Abby Clarke is unmarried, unemployed and pregnant—but she's not *really* on her own. Not while she's got her twin sister, Kellie.

Kellie insists that Abby go to her husband's ranch in Montana for a few weeks' rest—but she insists that Abby go *in Kellie's place.* Despite Abby's reluctance, Kellie manages to convince her.

Then Kellie disappears. And Abby is left trying to explain to Max Sutherland why he's come home to find the wrong twin in his bed—a woman who looks exactly like his estranged wife. A woman who's pregnant with another man's child...

Rebecca Winters is an award-winning romance author known for her dramatic and highly emotional stories. The Wrong Twin will be available in March, wherever Harlequin books are sold.

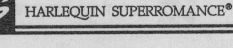

Reunited

ADAM THEN AND NOW
by
Vicki Lewis Thompson

It's been twenty years since Loren Montgomery last saw Adam Riordan, and a lot has happened since. For one thing, Adam now has an eighteen-year-old daughter named Daphne—the name Adam and she once dreamed would belong to *their* daughter. And Loren has a son, Joshua—the name they'd chosen for the son they'd hoped to have.

Is history about to repeat itself? There's no doubt that the kids are attracted to each other—a development Loren isn't entirely happy about. There's also no doubt that the chemistry between Adam and Loren is just as strong as it was when *they* were teens. All Adam has to do is convince Loren that sometimes dreams are simply put on hold....

REUNITED!
First Love...Last Love

Available in March, wherever Harlequin books are sold.

HARLEQUIN SUPERROMANCE®

WELCOME BACK TO ETERNITY!

For generations, couples have been coming to Eternity, Massachusetts, to exchange wedding vows. Legend has it that those married in Eternity's chapel are destined for a lifetime of happiness. And the townsfolk are more than willing to help keep the legend intact.

ETERNITY...*where dreams can come true.*

MARRY ME TONIGHT
by
Marisa Carroll

Everyone in Eternity is really excited. Weddings, Inc. bridal consultant Bronwyn Powell—after planning weddings for countless other people—is about to become a bride herself. The townsfolk have braced themselves for a wedding to end all weddings. The only thing Bronwyn and her fiancé, Ryan Mears, have to do is set the date—and stick to it. Nobody understands why they're finding that so hard....

Available in March, wherever Harlequin books are sold.